PURRFECTLY FRAMED

PURRFECTLY FRAMED

A Mobile Cat Groomer Mystery

Ruth J Hartman

To my husband Garry, who always cheers me on, and is a cat lover too!

Praise for the Mobile Cat Groomer Mysteries

"*Brushed Up On Murder* was a very entertaining read that I thoroughly enjoyed. I am looking forward to visiting Molly, Percival, Jasper, and the rest of these fine characters again soon in the next Mobile Cat Groomer Mystery."—Escape with Dollycas Into A Good Book

"The first in a new series, *Brushed Up On Murder* is an enjoyable cat-centric mystery. There's action, laughs, and intrigue along with several plausible suspects and two adorable cats."—Cozy Up With Kathy

"I look forward to spending more time with this fun cast of characters, and especially watching Molly's relationship with hunky vet Hank evolve!"—Melissa's Mochas, Mysteries, Meows

"*Brushed Up On Murder* by Ruth J. Hartman is an entertaining cozy mystery with likable characters (both human and feline) and an intriguing plot with several layers to unpack. 4 stars / loved it!"—Carrie, Reading is My Super Power

"If cozy mysteries and cats are some of your interests, *Brushed Up On Murder* will be a cute read for you. Clues are gathered, the crimes are discussed and evaluated, and there are cats, cats, and more cats and delightful small-town vibes."—JoAnne, Novels Alive Book Blog

"Full of twists and turns, *Brushed Up On Murder* kept me on the edge of my seat as I attempted to solve the murder with Molly. I look forward to the next book."—Sapphyria's Books

Chapter One

When a cancellation from a black and white tuxedo cat's mom gave me a break in my cat grooming schedule at Fabulous Felines, I took the opportunity to visit my friend, Evan, at his photography studio. He'd phoned earlier, saying he had proofs of kitty pictures he'd taken for some of my clients. I couldn't wait to check them out. And who better to take along with me than my own two felines?

A tug came from my fingers. One of my cats, Jasper, was pulling against his harness, ready to run. Percival, his adoptive brother, was finally becoming alert after his long nap. He yawned, licked his paw, then looked up at me as if to say, okay, let's do this. The short walk had us there in no time, even with both cats feeling the need to sniff, rub against, or paw at everything that was at their eye level. And that was a lot of things. Grass, pebbles, park benches, and cracks in the sidewalk—nothing was safe from wet kitty noses and twitchy whiskers.

When I opened the door to Evan Lakes' photography studio, I blinked, always forgetting how dim he kept his main room, with small spotlights positioned so that his work was beautifully on display and caught the admirer's attention.

When my vision adjusted to the low light, a movement caught my eye. It was Evan, who stood near an open doorway to his darkroom.

"Hi Evan." I waved.

He didn't answer. His usual wide grin had been replaced with a scrunched brow and glassy-looking eyes, as if he couldn't focus.

Something was wrong. I stepped closer. "Evan? Are you all right?"

He jerked. Had I startled him? Maybe he hadn't heard me come in, although that seemed odd considering the loud bell on the front door and the sound of my voice.

"Oh. Um, Molly?" he asked, like he wasn't quite sure who I might be.

Wow, he really was out of it. Concerned, I reached out and touched his arm. "Are you ill? Can I help you ?"

He shook his head slowly. "I..." His throat moved as he swallowed. "It's..."

Maybe he'd gotten some bad news. Or didn't feel well. "What happened? Do you—"

"In there," he whispered, his voice raspy.

"What is it?" Now I was really worried. What had I walked into?

Evan pointed toward the open doorway.

"Something is in there?" I asked. Had an animal gotten in overnight and destroyed his photos? Or maybe our recent rain caused a roof leak and ruined his beautiful work. What a terrible loss that would be.

"No. Some*one*," he said. He took in a quick gulp of air. Was he having trouble breathing? Maybe I should take him to see our local doctor.

"Evan, do you need to sit down?" I pointed to a grouping of chairs set against his front wall.

He shook his head, causing strands of his light-colored hair to brush against his forehead. "Somebody"—he shivered —"is in there."

So we were back to a person in his darkroom. But why weren't they coming out? "Um, is it a customer? Who—"

He grabbed my free hand, something he'd never done before, and towed me behind him into the room. I nearly stumbled as he tugged me harder. What was going on? I squinted against the bright lights, such a change from the dim front area. In here, the lights were ablaze, making the term darkroom seem inaccurate. Percival and Jasper's leashes bounced in my other hand as the cats trotted behind me, the shrill sound of their claws scraping against the wood floor planks making me shiver.

Evan dropped my hand, then pointed again, this time to his right and toward the floor.

What was going on? Was there an injured or ill customer back here? "Evan,

I don't under—"

"Right. There."

I edged closer and then I saw it. Or should I say, saw her. And gasped.

Agnes Temple, a woman in her early sixties, who was a high school teacher, lay in a crumpled heap beside a counter filled with bins of finished photographs. Her gray cotton pantsuit, normally without wrinkle or blemish, had a dark stain on the shoulder, and a tiny rip at the sleeve. A large bottle of something I couldn't identify lay near her head. Jasper strained against his harness, obviously wanting to get closer, but I gently tugged him back. Percival stared at the body, his whiskers twitching, but he stayed parked next to my feet.

My mouth went dry, and I swallowed. "What happened?"

Evan shook his head. "I don't know. I mean, she was here when I opened up a few minutes ago."

I glanced down to make sure the kitties were still sitting at my feet. This wouldn't be a good time for them to explore. Even though they were on leashes, they were sneaky enough to occasionally escape and go their merry way. "Okay…have you called the sheriff?"

"No, I guess it hadn't sunk in what I was seeing. I'd only just found her when you walked in. I don't understand. How… how did she get in here? And what…happened to her?" He rubbed his forehead.

Poor guy. He was obviously going into shock. I doubted his thoughts were making much sense right now. "Want me to call him for you?"

He nodded. "I…yes, if you don't mind. I don't seem to be able to… think clearly."

"Believe me, I understand." After having found one of my pet parents in a similar state a few months ago, I remembered the feeling of shock, like my mind and body were sluggish, refusing to work properly. It had taken a while for me to have coherent thoughts afterward.

I dialed 911. The sheriff's assistant, Betsy Jones, answered. "Sheriff's office. How may I help you?"

I kept a watchful eye on Evan as I spoke, hoping he wouldn't keel over right next to me. "Hey, Betsy, it's Molly Stewart."

I heard a smile in her voice when she said, "Hi Molly, how are you?"

"Well… There's been an incident at Evan Lake's studio and, long story short, Agnes Temple is dead."

Silence came from the other end of the line. Then, Betsy said, "Uh… um… Let me alert Sheriff King. He'll be there… as…as soon as he can."

"Thank you." I ended the call, frowning at the phone. Betsy was normally so efficient, so professional when doing her job for the sheriff. Maybe I'd caught her on a bad day, although she'd sounded cheery enough when I'd first called.

Had she been friends with the deceased? I didn't know of any connection between them, but in a small town it was hard to tell. So many citizens were related or had a past history and the details came out later on. Like when somebody turned up dead—that always shook skeletons out of closets.

"Is the sheriff on his way?" Evan asked, his face pale and hands shaking.

I placed my phone back inside the purse hanging from its strap on my shoulder. "Yes, Betsy said he'd be here as soon as he could."

Evan nodded, but his pupils were dilated, and a sheen of sweat showed on his face.

"Hey," I said, grabbing his hand as he'd done mine a few minutes earlier. "Why don't we go and wait outside? Maybe get some fresh air." He'd still be in the same situation, but at least he wouldn't have to look at Agnes in her current state for a little while. Although from what I'd gone through, that image would play again and again in his mind for quite some time.

Evan blinked. "Air. Yes. Air is good." He took a step, then faltered, grabbing onto my arm for support. Poor guy. It wasn't every day someone discovered a body in their workplace.

While I'd been speaking to Evan, the cats had sidled closer to Agnes. Though they couldn't touch her because of their leashes, both had their necks stretched out, nostrils flaring, as they tried to take in all the strange new smells. Jasper reached out his paw, but contacted only air. Percival didn't bother with trying to touch Agnes, instead he let out a long, loud hiss at the woman's body. Yeah, kitty, that'll show her.

Agnes hadn't been a nice woman. Even though Percival hadn't known her personally, he must have sensed she hadn't been a human he wouldn't have liked. Or maybe he hissed simply because she was no longer breathing, and it freaked him out. I never knew with cats.

Once Evan had found his sea legs and didn't seem as wobbly or confused, we headed toward the door. Percival came willingly, but Jasper needed convincing with a gentle tug on the leash. Finally, we all stepped outside.

"Good morning," came from behind us. I jumped and turned, relieved to see Jillian Wells, my best friend.

"Hey," I said. "We, uh, he…" I tilted my head toward Evan.

"What's going on?" Jillian frowned in concern, pushing her long hair over one shoulder. Then she placed both hands on her hips, giving her signature stern look she'd perfected after years of scolding wayward library patrons.

Waiting until two women passed by us on the sidewalk, I leaned closer to Jillian and whispered, "Evan just found a body in the—"

"A body!" she screeched.

"Not so loud," I whispered, not wanting anyone else passing by to know about the death before the sheriff got here.

"Sorry. Who…"

"Agnes Temple."

Jillian's mouth dropped open. "I just spoke to her yesterday. She came into the library to get some information on…" She eyed Evan, then clammed up.

"On what?" I asked.

She shook her head, causing her long gold earrings to dance. "I'll tell you later."

What did she want to tell me about Evan? I looked in his direction, but he wasn't paying attention, still appearing befuddled and lost. Would he even notice we were talking about him?

I tugged her to one side, a few feet away. "Tell me what's going on."

She glanced at Evan, seemed to make a decision, then whispered, "Agnes was in the library a couple of days ago. She asked for help using the internet on one of our computers."

"Okay," I said. "That doesn't sound too strange." Some of our senior townspeople often needed assistance with the newer technology at the library.

"What's strange was the subject matter she looked up. She typed in Evan's name."

I frowned. "Why would she do that? If they know each other, couldn't she just have asked him what she wanted to know?"

Jillian shrugged. "Not sure. I wondered that, too. But once she had what she needed, she told me in no uncertain terms to go away. I couldn't very well stand there and snoop." Her eyebrows lowered. "Well, I could have, but honestly, that woman scares me a little. And you know I don't scare easily."

"I guess she's not so scary anymore," I glanced over at Agnes's still form.

"No, I guess not." Jillian stared at Evan for a few seconds, then at me, shook her head, and let out a sigh.

Without warning, Evan let out a loud gasp, headed our direction, and collapsed right onto Jillian. She was quick enough to wrap her arms around him before he sunk to the sidewalk.

My eyes widened as I rushed to help her hold him up. The adrenaline after finding Agnes on his floor appeared to have left Evan feeling weak.

A siren wailed as it turned the corner and headed in our direction. Naturally, it got everyone's attention who was walking nearby, and also those who were working or doing business in surrounding buildings. Office and shop doors opened as people spilled out to see what the latest excitement was. In a small town, anything happening that was different was bound to add excitement to an otherwise quiet day.

Sheriff Lawrence King opened his car door and stepped out, giving a wave to his impromptu audience, as if he were some sort of celebrity. When I glanced at Jillian, I caught her in the middle of an eye roll. I hadn't given one, but I wanted to. The sheriff rubbed me the wrong way. But that might be due to his hounding me during a previous murder when he all but accused my uncle Russ of doing the deed. Thank goodness the real killer was apprehended, and my uncle was spared any of that awfulness.

Aside from that, Sheriff King liked to ridicule my profession—a mobile cat groomer— as if what I did for a living wasn't valuable or worthwhile. I had lots of kitties and their pet parents who would stand behind me and give their support. Some of them might even purr.

The sheriff adjusted his hat, hitched up his pants, and strolled over to us.

He eyed us one by one. "Evan, Jillian, Molly." When he glanced down, he let out a small gasp, taking two steps backward. One more step and he would have tipped off the sidewalk and ended up on the street in a tan polyester-covered lump. A tiny part of me wished…. *No, Molly, play nice.*

Besides, I knew the reason for his gasp and partial retreat. It was due to my little furry friends who were at the moment staring up at the sheriff. In the past, his actions made it clear he not only didn't like cats, but was afraid of them.

After gaining his composure, the sheriff, while avoiding glancing down again, said, "What's the emergency here? Betsy said something about a body?"

His voice was loud enough, it carried down the sidewalk and across the street. A collective gasp sounded before pointing and whispering took over from those watching the developing spectacle.

I shook my head. But what had I expected? Whitewater Valley likedspicy news, and it didn't get spicier than murder.

Wait. How did I know Agnes hadn't died accidentally?

Was it because her body was crumpled in such an unnatural position? And she'd bled from a wound on her head, but the way she was lying, it hadn't appeared she'd fallen against anything to cause her injury. But mainly, it was because, having previously discovered one of my pet parents murdered in his garden, I had the same strange vibe I had that day. Yep, I felt it in my bones. Agnes had been murdered.

Evan was in a sort of stupor at the moment, unable to communicate. Jillian watched him. Was she wondering if he'd fall on her again? Apparently, it was up to me to answer the sheriff.

"You heard right, Sheriff," I said. "There's a body. In the photography studio." I tilted my head toward the front door.

"Who is it?" he asked. "Betsy wouldn't say. She just turned red and refused to look at me. Strange girl." The sheriff had no right to call anyone else strange.

"Why don't we go inside?" I eyed the growing crowd. "It looks like we're attracting a lot of attention." I didn't add that his yelling out about a dead body was a partial catalyst for the gathering, and also his use of car sirens.

His frown told me he didn't like me making suggestions as to what he should do. But I didn't care. The sooner this was over, the better. I glanced at Evan, who was indeed leaning heavily on Jillian again. She had him held tight against her, her expression of concern focused on his face.

Sheriff King and I stepped inside, and I motioned for him to follow me to the dark room.

"She's in here," I said.

"She?" He adjusted his hat, which had gone askew.

"Yep." I pointed toward the body. "Agnes Temple."

His eyes bulged out. "Agnes?" He quickly regained his composure and bent over to see her better. Next he reached into his shirt pocket for a pair of gloves and put them on. He touched her neck, took in her immediate surroundings, clicked some pictures with his phone, then made a phone call. I could make out from his end of the conversation that he was speaking to Tyson Berry, our local funeral director, who doubled as our medical examiner.

"Tyson will be here soon," he said. "Until then, why don't you tell me what you know about all of this?" His expression was one of judgment. As if I had something to do with how Agnes ended up here, cold as a pant-suit-wearing mackerel.

"Hey," I said, "I didn't have anything to do with what happened to her."

"Seems like you're protesting awfully loud for someone who's not involved."

My free hand landed on my hip. "Let's not go down that road again."

"What road would that be?" His mouth formed into a smirk. He knew very well I referred to Whitewater Valley's previous murder.

"The one where you automatically assumed that I, or someone I'm close to, committed murder," I said.

"Close to?" He turned his head toward the doorway. "Yeah, You're really tight with that other girlie, the librarian, huh?"

Girlie? Honestly, the man was a prehistoric troll. "Jillian Wells is a close friend, yes."

"And the guy who runs this place." He pointed his thumb toward the entrance.

"You know his name is Evan Lakes."

He shrugged. "Doesn't matter what his name is. All I care about is finding who did this. I need to speak to both of them. Go invite them to join us, why don't you?"

I glanced toward the doorway to the main area. If I wanted to get to the bottom of Agnes's murder, what choice did I have? Might as well get the awfulness over with.

Chapter Two

Rolling my eyes, and not caring if the sheriff saw me, I speedwalked through the main room and to the sidewalk. Jillian and Evan sat on a wooden bench positioned outside, beneath an old-fashioned streetlight, which sported a gorgeous hanging red geranium from a side hook.

"Guys," I said. "The sheriff has requested our presence inside the shop."

Evan, who seemed to have regained some color in his face, gave a reluctant groan.

Jillian patted his arm. "I know. Doesn't sound fun, does it? But let's see what the troll, I mean sheriff, wants to say."

I bit my lip, trying not to laugh. Jillian's sense of humor was so dry that often, people didn't get it right away. But I always did. I held out my hand to take one of Evan's, tugging him so he could stand.

"Everybody ready?" I asked, trying to keep my voice upbeat. I doubted it had the desired effect.

Jillian nodded, and Evan gave me a bleary-eyed look that would have fit on a man who'd worked a sixteen-hour day without the benefit of any caffeine.

We shuffled in through the door and back to the scene of Agnes's final moment of life.

Sheriff King leaned against a nearby counter, close to Agnes. She, unfortunately for her, hadn't moved.

He tapped his foot against the floor. "What I'd like to know is, what's the large bottle that's lying a few inches from Agnes's head? Appears to have blood on it. I'll send it off to the lab for verification, of course, but I know blood when I see it."

Evan stared at the bottle as if he'd never seen one before. He jerked, seemed to focus, and finally gave his attention to the sheriff. "That's fixer."

"Is that something you normally keep around here?"

"Sure. It's essential for processing photos. There's a whole cabinet of it right behind you." Evan pointed to a spot over the sheriff's shoulder. "I use it all the time."

Sheriff King angled around and opened the door. "Yep, looks like the same thing to me."

Jillian and I raised our eyebrows at each other. Right, as if the sheriff knew anything about film developing. Probably less than I did, which wasn't all that much.

Sheriff King eyed Evan, making him squirm. "So, Mr. Lakes, any reason you can think of that Agnes might have ended up dead on your floor?"

"No. I have no idea." Evan glanced at Jillian, then me. Was he wanting confirmation of what he'd told the sheriff? I had to admit, when I was on the hotseat with the sheriff a few months earlier, all logic did tend to fly out of my head when feeling as if interrogated.

"Maybe you just need more time to think about it," said the sheriff. "I've found that a trip down to the local jail often loosens people's tongues. Makes them remember things they might have overlooked."

Evan's face paled. "You want to arrest me?" His voice squeaked at the word arrest.

He held up his hand. "Now, don't get yourself in an upheaval like some hysterical woman."

My mouth dropped open. Jillian's expression mirrored mine. Good thing my assistant, Veronica, wasn't here. She might have beaned the sheriff with a bottle of fixer just to make him stop saying asinine things.

I crossed my arms over my chest. "Sheriff, why can't Evan just answer your questions here?"

"You sure do know how to take the fun out of everything, Molly," replied the sheriff.

I shrugged. And I wasn't sorry.

"Now," he went on. "Why don't you explain to me what happened here?

"I can't explain…I mean, she was dead when I got here," said Evan.

The sheriff's eyebrows rose. "Can you prove that?"

Jillian stood up straighter next to me. "Can you prove he didn't, Sheriff King?"

The stink-eye the sheriff gave my friend would be enough to cause lesser people to shrink. But Jillian was a librarian. She dealt with all sorts of people in her line of work. She had developed a pretty good stink-eye of her own when it came to argumentative patrons. Or someone who didn't want to pay their library fines.

Sheriff King watched Jillian, shrugged as he seemed to decide her comment and facial expression either wasn't worth his time, or he was a little afraid of her, then focused again on Evan.

"Continuing on, Mr. Lakes," he said. "Did you know the deceased?"

If possible, Evan's face grew even paler. "I…. uh, yes. I knew her."

Jillian stood to her full height next to Evan. "Sheriff, be realistic. Whitewater Valley is a small town. Evan has lived here his whole life. So had Agnes. Doesn't it make sense they would have crossed paths somewhere along the line?"

He rubbed the back of his neck. "I suppose. But that doesn't get me any closer to why or how this woman here"—he pointed down as if there might be a second body in the room, and he wanted to clarify—"ended up splattered on the floor."

I winced at the word splattered. Did he had to be so macabre when describing the recently departed?

"All right," the sheriff said, "Did Agnes often come into your shop?"

Evan avoided looking directly at Sheriff King. "As far as I know, she never came in here."

"Never?" He widened his eyes in an exaggerated fashion, as if Evan's revelation was astonishing.

"Not once," insisted Evan, as he crossed his arms. Even though he'd had trouble giving his answers to the sheriff before, he seemed completely certain that Agnes had never darkened his door. But with everyone who came and went over the years, how could he know for sure?

"So how did you know Agnes, Mr. Lakes?" The sheriff glanced at Jillian, who opened her mouth to speak, but he held up his hand to silence her. When Evan didn't reply, the sheriff repeated his question.

With slumped shoulders, Evan finally said, "I knew her from high school. She was a teacher there."

The sheriff tilted his head, watching Evan as if he was some sort of prey to stalk. "Did you have a good relationship with her?"

He closed his eyes briefly, then said, "No."

"No?"

"That's what he said, Sheriff," piped in Jillian.

He pointed at her. "Now look here, Missy, I've had about enough of you."

The way he spoke to my friend got my dander up, too. "Hey," I said, "you can't talk to her like—"

Sheriff King whipped around toward me. "And you, Molly Stewart, need to zip it."

Zip it? I started to speak, but the front door opened. We all turned.

It was Tyson, the funeral director, coming to collect Agnes. Evan seemed glued to his spot on the floor. He needed to move so that Tyson could do his job. After a glance at Jillian, I took one of Evan's arms, and Jillian grabbed the other. We propelled him out to the main room.

Once Agnes was firmly affixed in her temporary enclosure, Sheriff King followed Tyson out the door. I hated the sight of the creepy black body bag and the person being closed inside. I'd witnessed it twice now. That was two times too many. Jillian, Evan, and I watched as Agnes left the building, not by her own choice.

Knowing the sheriff would want the last word, the three of us trudged outside.

The sheriff turned and pointed at Evan. "Remember. Don't leave town. You're a person of interest. Since you knew her, her body was discovered on your property, and you've known her for several years, I want to dig deeper into what might have happened between you. You can be sure, I'll be in touch." He gave the cats a wide berth, then hurried to his car.

As soon as the sheriff was gone, Evan sighed and ran his hand through his hair, leaving a small piece sticking up, but looking handsome all the same. Jillian must have noticed, too, because she discretely reached up and smoothed down his hair. Evan gave her a small smile, then his face suddenly reddened.

"Um, Jillian," he said, "I...um, before when I grabbed onto you and..."

She patted his shoulder. "It's okay. Honestly. You were in shock."

"I think I still must be, somewhat."

I nodded. "Totally understandable. It might take a few days, or even longer. At least it did for me when I went through this before."

"Thanks. Both of you," he said. The color receded from his face, and his shoulders slumped. He glanced behind him toward the building. "Guess I should clean up in there. Now that Agnes is..."

Jillian caught my eye and lifted her chin toward the sidewalk.

I touched Evan's arm. "Listen, We can help you with that later. For right now, how about we do something else for a bit."

Jillian smiled. "Sure, let's get some coffee. What do you say?"

He looked first at her, then at me. "Don't you both have to get to work? I don't want you to get in trouble because of me."

After checking her watch, Jillian, gave a slight frown, then took her phone from her pocket. Holding up her finger in a 'give me a second' sign, she texted someone, then put away her phone. "I just let Valene know I'd be a tad late."

Valene Day was Jillian's assistant at the library. She was super flighty and sometimes needed lots of direct supervision, but she and Jillian seemed to get along okay.

"So, I'm good for a bit," said Jillian. "Molly? How about you?"

I'd already checked the time. I had a good half hour before I had to be back. "I'm good too. Let's go."

Evan pointed to the cats, who were staring up at me expectantly. "What about them?" he asked. "Do you need to take them back to your shop?"

I bent slightly and gave each cat a chin scratch, causing a duet of rumbling purrs to emanate from the area surrounding my feet. "They'll be fine. Carrie never minds when I bring them into her coffee shop, as long as they're on leashes. Besides, Florence Makes and Lottie Campbell take their cats, Helga and Eleanor, in there daily."

Jillian laughed. "And those cats aren't on leashes. Plus, they get to drink cream from little bowls at the table." She cupped her hands together in a saucer shape.

Evan's eyebrows shot up. "How do the ladies get away with that?"

I took a step in the direction of the coffee shop, a signal to the cats that it was time to move. "The ladies think they have people convinced that Helga and Eleanor are emotional support cats. Everyone knows they aren't, but because of the ladies' ages and their..." I shrugged.

"Eccentricities?" asked Jillian.

"Yes," I said. "Perfect word. Leave it to a librarian."

Jillian winked. "Why, thank you very much."

"Anyway," I said, "suffice it to say, my cats probably won't be the only felines in Carrie's Coffees today."

When we entered the coffee shop, a few customers were scattered around the room. But we snagged an empty table near the back, hoping for a little privacy. Once Jasper and Percival were seated at my feet, munching on snacks I had in my purse, we ordered lattes from Carrie, who grinned when she saw my cats.

Carrie nodded. "I always love it when you bring your kitties in to see me, Molly. They're so well-behaved."

I laughed. "They may act that way in here, but at my house, it's a different story. At that point, they become feline wrestlers who yell at each other."

Jillian pointed toward the door. "Carrie, I see you have your regular felines coming in now."

We all angled around to view the front entrance. Florence, carrying Helga and Lottie with Eleanor, ambled in, taking in the small crowd. The cats were wearing identical lime green dresses. But that was a good idea since Sphinx cats were always cold and liked to be covered up.

Lottie said, "Ooooh, look, our favorite table is available."

Carrie shook her head and whispered to us, "Everyone who comes in here knows those ladies like to sit there and wouldn't dare take it away from them."

Evan's eyebrows rose. "Really?"

I nodded. "Carrie's right. That's where they are every time I come in. People stay away from it for their benefit."

Jillian giggled. "Evan, when the ladies and their fur-less babies sit down, keep an eye on them and how spoiled those two Sphinx cats are."

We all watched for several seconds as the women made sure their cats each had their own chair, then ordered bowls of cream when Carrie's assistant, Zelma, took their orders. Florence tied a bib on Helga, and at the same time, Lottie outfitted Eleanor. Like two infants ready for their meal in matching dark green bibs.

"Fascinating," said Evan. "Even though I often pop in here to grab something to go, I don't usually take the time to sit down. Seems to be an interesting place."

I was glad we'd brought Evan here. At least his mind could focus on something else for a little while.

When Carrie had stepped away to get our orders, Evan appeared to deflate, as if our conversation had been too taxing for him. Maybe this little venture wouldn't be as good as I'd hoped.

I tapped his arm. "Evan? Doing okay, there?"

"Yeah, well, sort of." He rubbed his forehead.

Jillian watched him, then said, "Would it help to talk about it?"

After a few seconds, he nodded. "Yes, I think it might."

Carrie delivered our coffees and stepped away. I replenished treats for Jasper and Percival, then we settled in to listen to Evan.

"Well," he said, "Sheriff King didn't ask me a lot of questions. I mean, he did ask about today, about Agnes. I kept waiting for him to grill me for much longer."

"There's more to the story?" I asked.

"A lot more. You see, I knew Agnes Temple better than I let on. Did you two know her?"

We both nodded. "Her cat Lulu was my client," I said.

Jillian shrugged. "Every so often, she'd pop into the library for this or that. I knew she was a teacher at school, but never had her."

"Same here," I said. "I actually got to know her later on."

"Unfortunately, she and I went way back," said Evan. "She was my art teacher."

"She's a little...crusty at times," I said. "How was she back then, as a teacher?"

"Crusty is a great word for her." He let out a long sigh. "A very difficult woman to get to know. And an especially hard teacher to get good grades from."

I shrugged. "Guess I'm glad I didn't have her then."

Jillian nodded her agreement.

"The thing is," said Evan, "she gave good grades to other students. But when it came to me, she didn't like me. Not one bit. At least, not once I became a senior."

"I don't get that," said Jillian. "You're such a nice guy."

"Thanks." His eyes brightened for the first time since I'd entered his shop and found him pointing toward his darkroom and the body it contained.

"Anyway," he said, "I'd always been heavy into art. Drawing and painting. Agnes loved doing those too. She treated me halfway decently until there was a county-wide art contest open to everyone, students, and adults, during my senior year."

"I don't remember the art contest," I said, taking a sip of my latte.

Jillian shook her head. "I don't either."

"You probably wouldn't if you weren't into art. It was a pretty closed community."

"So what happened?" asked Jillian.

With a shrug, he said, "I...won."

"The whole competition?" Jillian smiled wide.

"Yeah." He smiled back.

"That's awesome," I said.

"I thought so too," he said. "I couldn't believe it. Was on top of the world. My parents were ecstatic that I'd have a great chance to get into the college they wanted for me."

Jillian placed her chin in her hand and watched Evan. "I have a feeling there's more, though."

"There is. The following Monday after the competition, Agnes pulled me aside after class. She berated me for cheating."

Jillian tucked her long hair behind her ears. "How do you cheat on painting a picture or drawing?"

"You don't. I mean, I guess you could pay someone else to do it for you and claim it's yours, but I didn't do that. She just wouldn't leave it alone. There was an open house for all of the kids who'd entered the contest so parents and others could see our work. Apparently, Agnes overheard someone saying the student was better than the teacher, then mentioned my name."

I gasped, trying to imagine her reaction to that. Agnes had been so difficult to deal with when she used to bring in her cat, Lulu, for her grooming sessions.

"Agnes was livid," continued Evan. "It seemed the more contests I entered and won, the angrier she became. She'd enter those same contests and wasn't even an honorable mention. I tried to tell her that art was subjective. It all depended on the judges, and what they like or don't like. But she wouldn't listen."

"What happened next?" I asked.

"That woman...Agnes..." Evan swallowed hard. "She got me suspended from school."

"What?" Jillian and I said at the same time.

"She accused me of cheating. The very thing I'd mentioned before, of having someone else do my work for me. And when it came time to fill out my college application for art school, they required a letter from my instructors. You can imagine what kind of reference Agnes gave me." He shook his head and briefly closed his eyes, obviously distressed at the painful memories.

"That's terrible," I said. "You must have been so hurt."

"I was. Still am, I guess. Although enough time has passed that I rarely think about it. That is, until today, and finding her dead. On my property, killed with something I own."

Jillian sighed. "I'm so sorry you're going through this, Evan."

"Thank you," he said. "To both of you. It helps to confide in friends."

"Was there anything else that happened?" I asked.

Evan picked up his latte, but set it down again without taking a drink. "Well, yes. Indirectly. Because of what Agnes had done, making it so I wasn't able to get into the college my parents wanted, the girl I was seeing at the time dumped me."

I frowned. "Because you didn't go to a certain school?"

"That's right. Penelope Withers, that's who I was seeing at the time, she had her sights on someone who'd go to a prestigious school. She hoped she'd get to tag along. She was an artist too. At least she was a wannabe."

"I don't think I remember her." I lowered my eyebrows. "She wasn't a good artist?"

"I'm afraid not. Agnes, along with other art teachers along the way, tried to tell her that. To get her to focus on something else. She's a smart girl. With lots of talents. But she'd decided she was going to be a world-famous artist, and nothing would convince her otherwise."

"That's a pretty big ambition," said Jillian, tapping her long, manicured nails on the table.

"Very big. So, with Agnes being the main reason I didn't get into the right college, causing me so much grief and embarrassment from being suspended, and then having my girlfriend at the time dump me for not being supposedly good enough, I seem to have acquired a motive for murdering Agnes. The sheriff didn't ask me specifically about any of that, so I didn't volunteer it. But it's only a matter of time before he discovers my full history with Agnes and comes to question me some more."

Jillian cleared her throat, glanced at me, then finally at Evan. "Um, your ex-girlfriend…. are you…. over her?"

Since Jillian had previously told me she had a crush on Evan, I knew she was taking a risk asking him this. One, he might still be head over heels for the girl, and two, he might take offense to her asking such a personal question.

But Evan surprised me when he said, "Ha, yes. I'm over her. I don't miss her at all. She did me a favor by breaking up with me. It never would have worked out. If you met her, you'd know. Hopefully, you'll never have to."

With a small grin, Jillian said, "Well, I'm glad at least you're not still thinking about her."

"Not in a good way, at least," he said.

I wrapped my hands around my coffee cup. "But if she broke up with you, I assume you haven't seen her for a while."

"Right," he said. "And also because she moved out of the country with her parents for a long time. They went to Europe."

"Would the sheriff use any of that against you as a motive for murdering Agnes?" asked Jillian.

He shrugged. "I don't know."

"I do," I said. "After having dealt with the man in the previous murder, I have no qualms about saying that I don't trust his judgment, and I wouldn't put it past him to use whatever he could find to arrest the person he set his sights on." My eyes widened. "Sorry, Evan. That came out harsh. I didn't mean to imply that you—"

He held up his hand. "No, it's all right. I need to know what I'm up against. If the sheriff won't search for the real killer, then I'll have to do it myself."

"Wait right there," I said. "You have me and the cats to help you."

"Don't forget me," added Jillian.

"Thanks, you two," said Evan. "I appreciate it. So very much."

The next few seconds were filled with silence. Jillian's concerned expression probably matched my own. Evan leaned over and crossed his arms on the table, then rested his chin on his arm. When I glanced down, even Percival and Jasper were staring at Evan, their whiskers drooping in sympathy.

How were we going to save Evan from being arrested for a crime he didn't commit?

Chapter Three

Later that day, as I stood behind my counter at the shop, I waved goodbye to Darby Townsend, who took her cat, Kiwi's, paw and gave me a kitty wave in return. Darby used what she must have thought was a cute fake voice, acting like she was the cat talking. "See you next month, Molly. Meeeooow!" She giggled as she took Kiwi out the door.

Veronica joined me at the counter. "Strange bird, that Darby woman."

"Bird?"

"Figure of speech. Would you rather I'd said strange ostrich?" Veronica fluttered her eyelashes and flapped her arms.

"Probably not."

She laughed. "Right now you're thinking this lady who's your assistant is a strange ostrich, am I right?"

I smirked. "Well, at least a bird. A pretty one, though. Maybe a goldfinch."

Veronica's smile was wide as she reached up to fluff her hair. "I always did think it would be fun to have yellow hair." She pursed her lips together as if she had a beak.

I filled her in on what had happened to Agnes, as well as Evan's reaction and Jillian's help.

"You know," she said, "I hate what happened to Agnes, even though she wasn't a nice lady."

I nodded. "I totally agree."

"But Evan is lucky to have you on his side. You and the cats." She poked me in the shoulder, something I'd grown used to over the years, even though there seemed to be a small indentation there that I was sure hadn't appeared until Veronica came to work for me.

"Thanks," I said. "I'm happy to help him, just sorry there's a need for it."

The door opened again, and our postal carrier, Ricky Notts, headed in. On his way across the room, he stopped to say hello to a couple of cats who sat in their carriers, waiting for their mom or dad to pick them up after their day of beauty at our Fabulous Felines Salon.

After a short conversation in which one cat simply blinked at Ricky and a second cat flicked her ears at him, Ricky moved slowly across the room. When he reached us, he slung his postal bag on the counter with a thump, causing a stack of our salon fliers to flutter to the floor, scattering in a starburst pattern.

Veronica held up her hand toward Ricky. "Don't bother yourself. Allow me to pick them up for you."

Ricky, looking like he didn't have a clue what Veronica meant, gave a shrug. "Sure, okay."

I kept from saying something derogatory, but just barely. Ricky was a nice man, but exasperating. His dependability in delivering the mail was ludicrous. Still, he was all we had, and we did like him, even if we often made unflattering facial expressions when he wasn't around. I smiled at him. "Hi, Ricky. How's it going?"

"How's it going? Well, just let me tell you all about it."

Under her breath, Veronica said, "Oh boy…" She placed the fliers on the counter, reassembled them into a neat pile, and took her place next to me to listen to Ricky's latest tale. We knew that once he began a monologue, we might be here for a while. And it never mattered to Ricky whether we were in the middle of doing something else or not.

"Well," he said, leaning against the counter as he made himself comfortable. "For starters, here's your mail." He whipped the envelopes out from behind his back like an amateur magician at a children's birthday party. "See what I did there? I'd already taken them out of the bag."

"Oh yes," I said. "I see it quite well." I didn't dare make eye contact with Veronica, or I'd start laughing for sure. "Thanks for the mail."

"You're quite welcome." He pressed his hand to his chest. "It's my honor and privilege."

We heard that line at least twice a week. But I guess it was a nice sentiment. And he appeared to be very serious about his words. I just wished I didn't have to hear it so often.

Wanting to get his daily speech over with—no wonder our mail was always late if he did this with every single postal customer—I asked, "What did you want to tell us about?"

He grinned. "I'm so very glad you asked, Molly. See, I heard Agnes Temple was done for. You know, dead? As in no longer part of this earth?"

"Right." I knew that all too well, still picturing her crumpled form in Evan's darkroom.

"So I guess it's okay to talk about her postal habits now. I mean, she won't have anything to say about it anymore, right?" he said. "And you know I'd never tell anyone's business to someone else if the person hadn't recently been snuffed out of commission."

Aside from a rather indelicate description of a person dying, Ricky's argument also had a very big flaw. The man lived to tell people about his postal customers' business to anyone who would listen. And even to those who wouldn't. I didn't think it mattered if they were snuffed or un-snuffed.

Veronica moved her hand in a circle. "Hey, Ricky, think you could go ahead and tell us what you think you need to? Cats to groom, and all that."

He glanced behind him at the two cats in carriers, gave them a wave, then angled back toward us and nodded. "Yup. That I can do." Ricky didn't need to know that those two cats were finished with their appointments, not waiting on us to groom them. And the cats wouldn't tell. They'd both gone to sleep.

My quick glance at the wall clock showed that my next client was due in ten minutes. Ricky had been known to talk much longer than that, but we'd do what we could. There'd been more than a few times we'd gone ahead and groomed cats while he kept rattling on about whatever earthshattering tale was his latest obsession.

"So here's the deal," said Ricky. "That Agnes lady was a real character."

And Ricky wasn't? I settled my hip against the side of the counter, trying to get into a more comfortable position. Again, I avoided eye contact with Veronica. I already knew she was smirking. I could feel it.

"There were loads of magazines every single month," said Ricky. "I mean, with people reading online, who does that anymore? My back screams every time she gets an order of them. Usually it's the tenth of the month. Or is it the twelfth? Now let me think about that for a minute." He looked toward the ceiling and frowned.

"It doesn't matter," I said.

Ricky flipped his hand. "Right, no, probably not now. Since she's never going to read any more of them. What do you suppose will happen to all those magazines that are stacked in her apartment? Can you imagine what the guys who pick up the recycling will have to deal with? Glad I'm not them."

I sighed, couldn't help it.

"Anyway," he said, "Agnes got regular mail too, of course. You know, like other normal people do. Oops, probably shouldn't say that. People might choose to not receive regular mail and instead might pick it up at the post office from a PO box. They might have their reasons. I just can't think of what those might be right now. Don't they realize the more people who pick up their own mail, the less I have to deliver? And the less I have to deliver—"

"Okay, so anyway…" I said.

He jerked as if my words had startled him. "Yes, well, Agnes got something recently that really piqued my interest. Did you see what I did there? Used the word piqued. Isn't that a cool word?"

I forced myself to nod. "Way cool, Ricky. What did Agnes receive that, uh, piqued you?"

"Well, there was an official looking envelope that was addressed to her from the state photography association, but said, 'regarding Evan Lakes' and—"

I held out my hand. "Wait a second. It had Evan's name on the outside of the envelope? They why were you delivering it to Agnes?"

His face turned pink. "Well, no. Evan's name was on the top of the letter itself."

I finally dared a glance at Veronica, whose eyebrows had risen toward her hairline, then I focused again on our postman. "Uh, Ricky?" I asked. "How would you know what was *in* the letter? Isn't that kind of difficult when there's an envelope between the letter and your eyes?"

His face reddened a shade darker. "It wasn't my fault! The glue on the envelope must have been faulty. The flap was a little loose."

Veronica's hands landed on her hips. "Loose? But not open all the way?"

He shrugged.

"Are you saying you, possibly, I don't know, helped it to open the rest of the way?" she asked.

Ricky waved his arms. "Ladies, you need to understand. It was a windy day, I tell you. I had no control over what happened. It just… popped open."

Now that he'd mentioned Evan's name in conjunction with Agnes, I wanted to know more. Not just for nosiness sake, although, to be honest, I had my days where that might be the case, but since I was sure Evan had nothing to do with Agnes's murder, I wanted all the information I could get.

"All right," I said, "What was the letter about?" I pointed my finger at him. "Just the part that was exposed from the um, wind, of course."

He looked both ways to make sure we were still alone in the shop, then said, "Do the words discredit a photographer mean anything to you ladies?"

Veronica caught my eye. If she was thinking the same thing I was, Agnes might have been out to make trouble for Evan concerning his photography skills as well as for his art. Unfortunately, that might be used as another piece of Sheriff King's puzzle in favor of Evan being the killer since it would sound as if Evan had reason to quiet her for good.

"Well," I said, "thanks for telling us that, Ricky, I think—"

"But I'm not finished. If you request the whole story, then the whole story you shall have."

"Oh. Okay." Not sure I'd actually requested it, but he was on a roll. It would be easier to just let him go.

"See, that Agnes lady, she…" Ricky's jawline hardened as he gritted his teeth. "She wasn't out to get just Evan. She was out to get me, too."

Now, this was interesting. "Why do you say that?"

"Because of her always complaining about me." He jammed his thumb into his chest. "She accused me of not delivering her mail on time. And also of delivering her mail to her neighbor. Or the neighbor's to her. And that I talked too much. Me! Can you imagine?"

I could very well imagine, since we had the same experience, as I was sure, did most of Whitewater Valley's residents. However, he'd never see it that way, so it was useless to even try. "But Ricky," I said, "as a professional, I'm sure you sometimes get complaints from your customers, right? I mean"—I pointed to Veronica—"We certainly do every so often."

"That's right," agreed Veronica. "It happens."

He frowned. "But do any of your customers ever try to get you fired from your job?"

He had me there. I wouldn't bring up the fact that I was self-employed so a chance of that happening wasn't likely, but still, it did seem a bit harsh on Agnes's part. "Gosh, I'm sorry, Ricky. That's rough."

"Thank you." He reached to the back of his head and grabbed his long ponytail, something I'd seen him do before when he was upset. Was it comforting, like a little kid with his security blanket? Not an attractive quality in a grown man.

I preferred men who were a little more manly, like a certain handsome veterinarian, Hank Chenoweth. The door squeaked open, and Hank walked in. My eyes widened. Had he somehow known I was thinking about him?

Of course not. There was no way he could have…

Hank stopped and tilted his head, then gave me a slow, one-sided smile. Wow, I must have given off vibes or something, and he showed up.

Ricky glanced over his shoulder at Hank, seemed to realize he still held his own hair next to his face, then dropped his ponytail like hot charcoal. When Hank came toward the counter, Ricky stood up straight and forced his shoulders back. "Hello there, Hank," he said. "Glad to have another hombre here to talk with. Been filling the women folk in on my activities of late."

Women folk? Was he trying to sound like the sheriff now? Maybe somebody should clue Ricky in that it wouldn't be a good move.

"Uh, hi, Ricky." Hank's eyebrows rose just a little when he looked at me.

Ricky glanced behind Hank at a clock on our wall. He gasped. "Good golly, is that the right time?"

I'd never seen Ricky wear a watch or check his phone for the time. It was no surprise he didn't get his mail route completed when he was supposed to.

He grabbed his mailbag, slung it over his shoulder, narrowly missing Hank's head in the process, and then skittered across the floor and outside. Once on the sidewalk, he took off at a jog to the right, but just as quickly spun around and headed in the opposite direction.

Veronica shook her head. "Our government worker at his best."

Hank chuckled. "You're right. Nice guy, though."

Veronica and I both nodded. And sighed.

"Well," said Veronica, pointing toward the front door. "There's my next appointment. Good to see you, Hank." She waved Mary Nolan and her cat, Wispy, to follow her to a back room, leaving me alone with Hank.

"You busy right now?" he asked.

I followed Ricky's example and checked the clock. "You have two minutes, sir."

"Guess I better make it quick, huh?"

I smiled. "Better seeing you for a couple minutes than not at all."

"I totally agree." He moved close to me and wrapped me in a hug.

A hug on an ordinary Tuesday? "Um, love this, but what's the reason?"

He pulled away a little bit. "I heard something about you being there right after Evan found Agnes Temple on his darkroom floor."

"Oh, yeah, that."

"Yeah, that. I heard it from Zelma at Carrie's Coffee."

I had dropped the ball on that one. Why hadn't I called him right away, knowing he should hear it from me instead of another person? "Sorry, Hank. I would have told you, honest. It got crazy with the sheriff, then Evan was in shock, and Jillian and I were trying to help him and…"

A final squeeze of my shoulders preceded him taking one step back. "I know that. I was just concerned for you, is all. Especially after Whitewater Valley's previous murder."

"Freaky, right?" I said. "Two deaths like that in such a short time. Who knew our tiny town would produce not one but two murderers?"

"Right. Not information we want plastered on the billboard outside town. It must have been a shock. Are you all right?"

I nodded. "It was awful, but Evan had it the worst. Jillian showed up, too. Good thing, since it took both her and me to hold Evan up when the sheriff wanted to interrogate him."

The door opened. I expected it to be my next client, but it was Opal Hyatt, picking up her cat, Fern, who'd been finished for a while now.

"Sorry to be late," Opal said. "I got stuck at a hair appointment. Or rather, I got caught up in the gossip that was going on in there."

I smiled. "No problem, Opal."

"I was actually talking to Fern."

Her cat meowed at her and made biscuits with her paws on the floor of her carrier. Opal picked up the enclosure and left.

Hank pointed over his shoulder with his thumb. "She does the same thing to me when she brings Fern in for checkups. They have a running conversation. I might as well not even be in the room."

"That's cats for you. Always wanting the last word."

Percival and Jasper must have heard me say 'cats.' But when they ran in from a side room after having been asleep together on a spare blanket I kept in the corner, they didn't make a beeline for me.

They went straight to Hank.

He laughed when they both pawed at his legs. He scooped them both up, and they gave him nose kisses on his cheeks.

The scene before me was cute, but why were my cats involved in kisses with the handsome vet, and I was standing to the side with my arms crossed? I had gotten a hug from him, but still....

Hank played with them for a couple of minutes before they got bored and began to groom each other's whiskers. It was a good bet they both still had a bit of canned food from breakfast stuck there.

The door opened, and my next appointment, a cat named Werner, walked in on a leash, led by his dad, Franklin South.

Hank glanced in their direction then back at me. "Guess my two minutes are up."

"Guess so. Sorry."

"We'll make up for it later." He winked. "Just glad you're all right."

"I am. Thank you for checking."

With a wave, then a hello to the newcomers, Hank left. As I motioned Franklin and Werner to follow me, I kicked myself for not having called Hank right away when I'd been in the middle of Agnes's body being discovered. I would have wanted him to let me know if the situation had been reversed.

But I also wondered about what Ricky had said, that Agnes had tried to discredit Evan through that letter. And that she'd also tried to get Ricky fired. As far as I could tell, Ricky's job was really all he had. No family that I knew of, and although he knew everyone in town and talked them nearly to death, did he have anyone special to him? Had he hated Agnes enough to have killed her?

Chapter Four

The following morning, I was thinking about Ricky's remarks when I drove my mobile grooming van to the auto shop for its tune-up. Ricky had been so keyed up, he sounded as if he'd been mad enough at Agnes to have done her in himself. Not that I wanted to believe it of him, but a person could do things they never thought possible when provoked.

I drove up to the entrance of Ollie's Garage, honked, then waited. That was the protocol that Ollie Smith, the owner, liked and what was printed on the now barely readable old sign posted on the outside of the building.

Ollie came to the large open doorway and waved me in. Once I'd parked where he indicated, I got out and grabbed onto Percival and Jasper's leashes.

He eyed them. "Brought a feline presence with you again, I see."

"That's okay, isn't it? Since I brought them here before?"

"Yeah, suppose so." He scratched his head. " 'Course, last time you were here, you wore that one"—he pointed down to Percival—"as a cat hat."

Ah yes. I'd obviously never live down having Percival with me, so frightened by the strange noises, that he stayed on my head for the tow ride to the shop and all through the appointment. I guess I could be thankful that it was before I also took Jasper everywhere too. I don't think I could have had both as a hat. Maybe two large fluffy earmuffs?

I handed Ollie the van keys. "It's running okay, just needs a tune-up."

"As you wish." He gave me a head bob, pointed to the grimy chair positioned in the corner that I'd sat in last time, and ambled toward his office.

I sighed, knowing how sticky and uncomfortable the chair was. I'd stand as long as I could, but if the appointment grew too long, I might be forced to take advantage of Ollie's hospitality, as it were.

My decision to bring the cats with me was two-fold. First, they were a good distraction when having to wait while my van was serviced. And second, even though they liked spending their days either in my shop or riding along with me when I did mobile grooming visits, sometimes they wanted to see the sights of Whitewater Valley. I glanced around. To be honest, Ollie's service station wasn't much to look at, but from a cat's point of view, there were lots of new things to sniff.

No other customers were in the shop. Was it a slow day for Ollie? It was fairly quiet, considering the normal cacophony when the shop was full of vehicles and people. Today's sound level wasn't much more than Jillian got at the library.

Jasper nudged his head against my shin, and Percival pawed my shoe.

"What's up, guys? Bored already? We just got here."

Percival turned his head and lifted his nose, nostrils flaring.

"Oh, I get it. You don't want to be stuck in the corner. Well, neither do I. Come on." With their leashes in my grasp, we set off around the perimeter of the garage, with me tugging them gently away from grease and oil spots. Even though I was a cat groomer and shampooed cats for a living, the thought of having to get motor oil out of paw fur was enough to make me shudder.

Our trek was slow, as their little noses and paws checked out every square inch. At least the cats were occupied, and I didn't have to endure the icky chair for the moment.

I glanced at my van, which was sitting alone and unattended. I checked the time on my phone. Yes, I'd been on time for my appointment here. Actually a little early. With Ollie having no other visible customers, why wasn't he working on my van? If we didn't get the ball rolling soon, I'd be late for my next grooming appointment. Ollie was usually so prompt and dependable, I could easily schedule my groomings around him. Apparently, not today.

Jasper pawed at a row of spare tires, hissing when one of them moved slightly. Percival, not wanting to miss anything, crept closer, sniffed the rubber, then sat back on his haunches as he studied the new objects.

However, Jasper was ready to move on. His little body wiggled and flounced like a kid on a twister mat. He fidgeted with his harness, and like a purring Houdini, was soon free.

Oh no....

"Wait!" I ran after him, with Percival trotting along behind as I held onto his leash. Jasper's empty harness thumped behind us as we ran. I must not have gotten it properly secured. Panic rose as I tried to catch up with him. What if he got into something dangerous and I wasn't close enough to protect him? If something heavy tipped over on him, or he licked a toxic substance? "Jasper, come back here!"

He ran beneath a pile of metal pieces leaning against the wall, a space too small for me to follow. Percival tried to head in behind him, but couldn't go far because of his leash. A scuffling noise came from inside the makeshift enclosure, then Jasper shot out from the other end.

I jogged around to where he now sat, staring at me. His eyes were wide, and his whiskers twitched. Did he want me to chase him?

"Listen, Jasper, this is not the best place for kitties to get into trouble." Not that any place was, but home was better than a shop where giant vehicles and tools could do them harm.

His meow came out as a playful trill, and he took off again.

Percival pawed at the neck enclosure of his harness, protesting the unfairness of being subdued when his brother was roaming free.

"Not gonna happen, Percival. Chasing one cat through here is more than enough."

He averted his eyes, then washed his paw, a sure sign of hurt feelings.

With a sigh, I continued after my wild child, relieved when I heard his trill again. But where was he?

The sound seemed to come from above. But how was that possible? Beside me, Percival sat on his haunches, head tilted back as he surveyed the indoor sky. Following his lead, I peered above us, letting out a yelp when I spotted my cat.

On the top of a very high stack of old tires, which leaned precariously to one side, was Jasper. "Hey!" I yelled. "You get down here this instant."

He didn't budge. But he did protest with a loud yowl.

"I mean it," I said, "right this instant." I pointed to the floor.

Jasper did a little dance on the top of the tires, his paws moving up and down. What was he doing? Any disturbance looked to be enough to send the whole tower of tires crashing down. He peered down at me and howled again. Great. He was stuck. Just like any cat in a tree.

What should I do? There was no way I could climb up there. And allowing Percival to go get him would leave me with two cats stranded.

My hand brushed against my pocket. Of course. My ever-ready handy stash of treats might just entice my cat to leave his rubber treehouse.

I removed the plastic bag, making sure to rustle it when I scooped out some food. Immediately, Percival pawed at my shoe and meowed.

"Yes," I said, "you can have some, but we need to save some for doodlehead up there."

I pointed toward Jasper, as if Percival might not know who I meant. He was already miffed at me. No use having him think the verbal slight was about him.

I gave one to Percival, hoping Jasper would see what he was missing. But he only yelled louder. I shook the bag. He did another paws-up-and-down dance.

Shoot. Now what? And it would be just my luck that Ollie might choose now to come out of his office. Having worn a cat on my head at my last visit had been bad. I could just imagine the ribbing I'd get if my cat caused a huge stack of old, smelly tires to fall, bounce, and roll across the garage floor.

Again, Percival pawed at me, wanting more treats.

"All right, one for now. But we really need to get—"

A scratching noise came from the tires. Jasper had climbed halfway down. Then stopped.

"Come on, little guy," I called. "You can do it. See?" I held up the plastic bag. "These treats are yummy." I pointed to Percival, but he'd already consumed what I'd given him. I didn't want him to eat them all and have nothing for Jasper, so I took a treat out of the bag, opened my mouth, and mimed putting it in.

"Yum," I said as I fake-chewed. "I can't get enough of these"—I wrinkled my nose—"Salmon-flavored goodies."

That did it. Jasper leaped the rest of the way down, landing hard on his paws. The thud reverberated around the quiet room, making me cringe.

I bent down to see him better. "Are you okay? Did you hurt yourself?" I picked him up, quickly checking his legs and paw pads. They didn't appear to have been injured. I set him back on the floor. His fur was puffed out but otherwise he seemed intact.

Not wanting to renege on a promise, I poured out several on the floor for each cat, letting out a huge breath that they were both safe.

I returned the bag to my pocket, finally ready to face the sticky chair in the corner. As I reached down to grab Jasper and re-harness him, he slipped out of my hands and trotted along the wall across the garage.

"Oh, come on!" With Percival in tow, again, we followed Jasper. "Mama needs a rest."

I doubted it was my words that caused my cat to stop, but I was so glad he did. He paused outside Ollie's office, crouched down, licking his paw as if nothing untoward had happened and he hadn't escaped from his mom. Twice.

"Jasper," I said, as I reached him. "That wasn't a nice thing to do. Don't run away from me, okay?"

His green eyes were wide and guileless as he gave me a tiny mew. Either he thought giving me an adorable kitten noise would make me forget what he'd done, or he actually didn't believe he was at fault. It was probably the latter, considering he was a cat. Either way, I was relieved he'd stopped.

Once I had Jasper's harness back on, securely this time, I was ready to stand. But Ollie's loud voice from the other side of the wall stopped me. It was a one-sided conversation with harsh words. Was he on the phone? I curled down onto my knees, hoping he wouldn't be able to spot me through the grimy window between his office and the main area.

Both cats fidgeted as I tried to hold them still. When Ollie, obviously upset, mentioned Agnes Temple, my ears perked up. I wanted to stay and listen. Maybe he'd say something useful that would help Evan not be the sheriff's suspect any longer.

A sound—a fist pounding on a desk?—came from the other side of the wall. Ollie's voice was shrill as he said, "What Agnes did was terrible. She might as well have stolen money right from my cash register."

A silence followed.

Then Ollie yelled, "That woman ruined my life! Now, he might remove me from his will. My business will never recover, and it was all her fault!"

I gasped. How in the world could an art teacher create so many problems for a mechanic? As far as I knew, they didn't have a connection. But there must be something. I was determined to find out.

A scuffling noise came from behind me. It sounded like someone's shoe. That ruled out the cats from making the noise. So that meant…

"Need some help there, Molly?"

I gasped and angled around. When I gazed up, Ollie's assistant, Ernie, was staring down at me. I stood too quickly, causing my leg to spasm. As I rubbed my calf muscle with one hand, I grasped the cats' leashes tighter with the other. "Um, hi, Ernie."

He crossed his arms. "Thought maybe you'd lost something."

"What?"

He nodded toward the floor. "With you sitting down there and all."

"Nope. I didn't lose anything."

"Okay." He held out his hand as if to say, *so, what's the deal?*

"Um, well…"

Jasper pawed at my pant leg.

"Well, the cats," I said.

"Your cats lost something?" asked Ernie.

"No, I was taking them for a walk."

"In here? Not much too look at unless they have a thing for checking out broken down vehicles." he said.

"They needed to stretch their legs."

He looked at them. "Little legs like that wouldn't need long to stretch. Wouldn't they need to walk only a couple of yards before they'd be tired? Seems like a very quick walk."

"Um, well, they were also bored."

"Don't really blame them." He shrugged. "This place bores me too."

I bent down and picked up Percival. "But you work here, Ernie."

"That makes it worse, doesn't it?"

I glanced at my van, still sitting where I'd parked it. If they didn't get to it soon, I really would be late for my appointment, or I'd have to reschedule. Either option was irritating.

"Will you be the one working on my van today?" I asked. Did I want him to if he wasn't interested in the job? Would he even give it his best effort? I'd rather not leave here and have my steering wheel come loose in my hands while driving or the gas tank tumble out. My mobile grooming van was the mainstay of my business. It needed to be dependable and run well.

Ernie shook his head. "Nah, Ollie will do it. He'll be out in a minute. I'm taking my break. Besides, Ollie can barely afford to pay me now. Why should I work for next to nothing?" He grabbed a cigarette lighter from his shirt pocket right below his name stitched in red letters on his shirt, then ambled toward the main entrance.

I'd never had much interaction with Ernie. Had he always been so lackadaisical? So negative about his employer?Thankfully, Ollie was normally personable and friendly, even if he was a bit odd. But considering all the off-kilter people in town, did it really matter? However, hearing Ollie having yelled like that on the phone, and about Agnes, was concerning. I'd never even heard him raise his voice to anyone before.

The sound of a chair scraping on a hard floor came from inside the office. Was Ollie coming out? I hurried back to the ugly plastic chair and sat down, then tried to place Percival on the floor. But he was having none of that. He turned in a circle and snuggled on my lap. Just as his eyes closed, Jasper leaped on top of him while Percival was still on my lap.

I rolled my eyes. "There's really not room for everyone here at the same time, guys." Both cats blinked at me, seeming not to care what I thought about the matter.

Finally, Ollie came out of the office, frowned at me, and said, "Sorry for the holdup. I'll get right on your van now." His face was red, as if he was angry.

"Thank you," I replied. Maybe I could still make my appointment if this didn't take too long. And if he didn't take his anger out on my van and cause damage to it in his huffy mood.

I petted the sleepy cats, hoping my legs wouldn't fall asleep beneath their combined weight. After a few minutes, I wasn't sure I could hold them any longer. I needed a distraction. Wouldn't it be nice if someone happened to come by and—

"Hey, Molly."

I glanced up. It was Evan. "Hi there. My vehicle's being serviced. Are you here for the same thing?" I hadn't heard the main garage door open. Maybe Evan had left his car outside for now.

"No, actually, I needed to pick up some oil for my car," he said. "This seems to be the only place in town I can find it." He glanced at the cats. "Um, looks like you have your hands, I mean legs, full."

"I sure do. I don't suppose our friendly neighborhood photographer could help me out and maybe remove half the kitty weight for me?"

He grinned. "No problem." Evan reached out his hands as I picked up Jasper and made the handoff. The cats never even woke up.

His eyebrows rose. "Hey, while I have you here, I can show you some of the photos I took of your clients recently. I happened to see Lottie and Florence at the park with their cats. Thought the impromptu session turned out great."

"Oh. I'd love to see them." That was a distraction I would enjoy.

There was a second chair, but it was useless, having only three legs. Instead of making Evan lean over to show me the pictures, I stood while still holding Percival, who yawned and twitched his whiskers at being temporarily woken from his nap. It didn't last long, though. He closed his eyes again and went back to sleep.

"Let's see," said Evan as he thumbed through the photos one-handed. "Those are in the back of the pile." He handed the pictures to me.

With my empty hand, I tried to go through them, but needed another appendage to accomplish it.

"Here," said Evan, "let me hold both of the cats."

"Sure you don't mind?"

"Not at all," he said. "After you giving me support with what happened in my studio with Agnes, it's the least I can do." Once he had a cat on each shoulder, as they gave off snoring purrs, I could view his new photos.

The pictures, as expected, were adorable. Some pictures were of Helga and Eleanor by themselves, sitting on a painted park bench and dressed in matching blue tutus and green hats. Other photos had the cats being cuddled by their moms. I was just about to return the photos to Evan when something in the background of the last picture caught my eye.

"Hey," I said, "check this out."

He frowned. "Is something out of focus?"

"No, they're perfect. But in this one, see those people in the background, standing in the shade of the tree to the side?"

Evan leaned closer to the picture as I held it, focusing on the spot that I pointed to. "I hadn't noticed that before," he said. "Hadn't taken the time to study anything but my subjects. Guess I was in a hurry to show these to Florence and Lottie. I was going to take these to them right after I picked up my car oil. I would have, of course, done some editing on them, but the ladies asked to see them as soon as I had them developed."

I tapped his arm. "I'm not criticizing. These are amazing. Believe me, I know how talented you are with photos. I'm especially fond of the ones with feline subjects."

He grinned. "Thanks, Molly." Then, he eyed the last picture one more time. "You know..."

"What?"

"I can almost make out the two other people standing there, but not quite," he said.

"If you enlarged it, could you tell?"

"Maybe, but I doubt it." He shook his head. "They're far enough away and in the shade, but there is one thing that stands out to me."

I watched him and waited for more.

"I think one of them is holding a bottle of fixer," he added. "Just like the kind that was used to kill Agnes."

My mouth dropped open. "I don't want to involve the sheriff, but do you think we should show this to him?"

Evan hung his head. "I've been keeping a low profile, hoping he'd forget about me as a suspect and move on. But he doesn't seem to be looking elsewhere. So yeah, I think it's time he sees this." He raised his head and looked at me. "Maybe this will help him find the real killer and stop bothering me with false accusations."

I nodded. "Yes, I think you're right." Hopefully, showing the picture to Sheriff King would send him on the hunt for the true killer. And leave Evan alone.

Chapter Five

A chorus of meows came from my right as I opened the door to Fabulous Felines. Veronica had come in earlier with grooming appointments for Siamese triplets, Sugar, Cinnamon, and Nutmeg. Thankfully, the cats were well-behaved. Having three from one family to do all at once was a chore. If the fact that the kitties were in their carriers waiting by the door didn't tip me off that their appointments were completed, their fluffy, clean fur and new pink ribbons around their necks would have.

"Veronica?" I called.

"In the back, Molly. Be out in a second."

I stuck my fingers into the triplets' cages, giving the cats pets on their noses and foreheads, then walked across the room to stow my purse beneath the counter.

Jasper and Percival, still worn out and lethargic from their adventure at Ollie's Garage, were sacked out at home on my couch. Normally I would have brought them with me, but they looked so peaceful, Jasper on his back with all four paws in the air, and Percival in a ball and snoring, that I left them there. I'd probably get scolded by them later when I returned home, but I'd worry about that then.

A few seconds after I'd set down my purse, my phone rang from an outside pocket. Hopefully, it wasn't a client's pet parent calling to cancel. I reached down and grabbed the phone, frowning when the screen didn't show the caller, since all of my clients were in there. I pushed the button. "Hello?"

"Is this Molly?" The voice was gravelly, like the person had something in their mouth, or had trouble speaking properly.

"Yes, It's Molly. How can I help you?"

"You can help by leaving well enough alone."

"Um, excuse me?" Was it a disgruntled pet parent? I didn't recognize the voice.

"You heard me. Don't interfere in the murder investigation. Got it?" said the voice.

"But I—"

"If you check things out on your own, you'll be very sorry. So will those rotten cats of yours. And by the way, this goes for Evan Lakes too. And his stupid dogs."

The call ended.

I swallowed hard as I stared at the now blank screen. Who was it, and why were they threatening me and Evan. And our pets!

"Molly? You okay?"

I jumped at Veronica's voice. She stood just behind me. "Um, not sure," I answered.

She stepped closer, putting her arm around me for a quick squeeze. "What's up? Your face is so pale."

I held up the phone so she could see it.

She squinted at the blank screen. "Sorry, doll, I'm not sure what I'm supposed to get from that. Is there a problem with your phone?"

"Right. Sorry." I shoved the phone in my purse, not wanting to hold it any longer.

"Did something happen? You got a call?"

"Yes, something happened." I rubbed my hands down my arms, hoping to quell the chill that came over me.

Veronica's brow creased. "Tell me. You're starting to scare me."

I leaned back against the counter and crossed my arms. "Yes, I just got a call."

"From..." She moved her hand in a circle, obviously worried about me, wanting to know more.

"That's just it," I said. "I don't know. I think the caller ID was blocked or something. Not even the person's number registered."

Veronica shook her head. "That doesn't sound like something one of our clients would do."

"It definitely wasn't a client. At least, I don't think so. I actually have no clue who it was." I mentally went through my client list, as well as Veronica's, but no one stuck out as a possibility. Sure, we had grumpy clients, some even rude at times, but never to the point of making a hateful anonymous call.

"You didn't recognize their voice?"

"No, it was rough. Gravelly. Disguised, maybe?" I shrugged.

"Well, what did they say?" she asked.

"That I shouldn't check into the murder. Leave things alone or else..."

"Or else what?" Veronica's eyebrows rose slowly, and she grabbed my arm.

"The person said I'd be very sorry. So would Evan. And so would our pets."

With a gasp, she said, "Oh, Honey. How awful. Is there anything I can do? Should I call Sheriff—"

"No."

She jerked, probably surprised at my sharp answer. "I know neither of us particularly cares for him, but don't you think we should report this?"

"Somehow, I think that might make things worse. For one, Sheriff King warned me to keep out of things."

"That hasn't stopped you before," she pointed out.

"True. But also, this person is warning me away for a reason. I wouldn't be so worried if they just threatened me, I mean I would, but it's so much worse since they included Evan, his dogs, and Percival and Jasper."

She watched me closely. "You think they might be doing it because they're the one who killed Agnes?"

I didn't want to believe it, but the timing was too coincidental, too close to Agnes's body being discovered in Evan's dark room. No, it had to be connected. Why else would they bother to try to warn me away? "That's what I'm thinking, yes."

Then, I filled her in on Evan, his picture, and the bottle of fixer the photo showed. He needed to tell the sheriff about the picture to help his own case.

But if I told Sheriff King about my phone call, he would only nag me to keep away. It wouldn't do Evan any good, at least not yet.

The shop door opened. But it wasn't one of our clients. I was still a little shaky from the weird phone call, so was relieved to see Betsy Jones. I waved, "Hi, Betsy."

"Hey." She glanced behind her, as if wanting to make sure she hadn't been followed into the shop. First, she'd sounded odd when I'd called in the murder to the sheriff's station when she'd answered the phone, and now she was jumpy and twitchy. I knew for a fact that Agnes's murder wasn't the first in town. Why had my reporting the death thrown her for such a loop?

Betsy reached the counter and stopped. "I was wondering if I could ask you something, Molly." Her face was pale, and her hands shook. What was going on with her?

I glanced to Veronica, then back. "Of course. Ask away. What can I do for you?"

"It's…" She shrugged one shoulder. "See…I have this cat and…"

"You do?" I grinned. "That's awesome. Congratulations."

Veronica bobbed her head. "Yes, great news. We love cats, obviously." She laughed.

Betsy didn't crack a smile. "Yeah, so, anyway, this cat, Lulu—"

My eyebrows lowered. "Lulu?" It was an unusual name for a cat, at least around here.

"That's right," said Betsy. "I was told she already comes here. I mean, used to. Um, her person used to bring…"

Sudden guilt hit me. I hadn't yet given thought to what would happen to Lulu after Agnes died. And I should have. The poor kitty wouldn't know what to make of her mom not being around to love her anymore. "You mean Agnes? You have her cat, Lulu?"

"Yep." Betsy's gaze wandered everywhere but to Veronica and me, like she was scared or hiding something. But what?

Veronica edged closer. "Why do you have her cat, Betsy?"

Leave it to Veronica to get straight to the point. It's what I wanted to know but hadn't gotten the chance to ask. But I'd love to know the answer as well.

It wasn't as if the two women had been related, or close. At least not that I was aware of.

"I'd rather not say, um, right now. Okay?" Betsy hedged.

I watched her for a second. Why did it seem as if she was trying to hide something? "Yeah, sure. No problem. So, what was it you wanted to ask me?"

Betsy waved her hand to encompass the room. "Since Lulu already comes here, would you be able to still see her? I could take over with paying for her grooming." Suddenly, Betsy turned her head away and sneezed.

"Bless you," I said.

"Thanks." She frowned. "So, do you think that would work?"

"I don't see why not." I glanced at Veronica, a question in my eyes.

"Yes," said Veronica, "Lulu is used to coming here and loves Molly"—she poked my shoulder—"so no problem there."

"Great," said Betsy, but she didn't smile or look the least bit happy about it.

What was going on? I'd never known her to have a cat before, or any pet for that matter. I just assumed she didn't like animals. And now she seemed to have taken ownership of a cat whose pet parent had been recently killed. But when asked, Betsy wouldn't give any details. Was it because she worked for the sheriff and wasn't supposed to talk about it because Lulu was connected to a murder victim?

Veronica tugged on my sleeve. I didn't bother to look at her. I already knew what she wanted. To get the scoop on Betsy and why she now had Lulu. Veronica was even worse than I was when it came to wanting to know details and having to wait to find out. I thought that deep down, she and I were both as nosy as all the cats we took care of every day. At least we didn't meow or purr. Yet.

The door opened again. This time, it was Sheriff King. He adjusted his hat, which had gone askew, and made a beeline for Betsy. "There you are. I've been looking all over for you."

She glared at him. "Why? Is there an emergency?"

"Uh, well, no." His face reddened at her sharp tone.

Betsy placed her hand on her hip and faced him. "Then what's the matter now?"

I blinked. Wow, I'd never seen Betsy talk to her boss that way. Or anyone, for that matter. What was going on with her? If she was that moody, was it a good time for her to take on the responsibility of an orphaned cat? Lulu would need lots of extra love and attention, not only from the loss of Agnes, but while getting accustomed to a new home and human.

The sheriff looked at Betsy. He shrugged. "I…well…" A cat meowed from the back grooming area where Veronica had just finished working on him. Sheriff King tensed, holding perfectly still, like he was trying to hide from the cat. As if a man of his girth would be good at hiding anyway.

Betsy continued to watch her boss, "So why did you follow me in here, Sheriff?"

He rubbed his hand along his chin. "Well, for starters, why are you even in here?"

Veronica and I stared at each other, then at him. Why did he need to know what his employee was doing on what I assumed was her own time? Didn't he have enough to do trying to figure out who killed Agnes? I frowned. Oh wait, he already thought Evan was the most likely suspect. He might think his work was nearly done already.

Betsy huffed out a breath. "If you have to know, and it seems that you do…I'm here to discuss my… cat and her grooming needs."

"A-ha." He pointed toward her. "Now we're getting to it."

I leaned forward. "What do you mean, Sheriff?"

"What I mean is, Betsy here is acting plenty weird."

This coming from a man who previously ran away from tiny, cute, furry creatures who only wanted his lap to take a nap on.

"I'm not acting any way at all," insisted Betsy. "Why would you say that?"

"Look, I happen to have overheard, uh, I heard you were taking on that cat." He said the word 'cat' like it was toxic waste. "The one that had belonged to the recently deceased."

"Yeah, so what? Aren't I allowed to have a pet if I want?" Betsy's eyes narrowed. In the past, they'd seemed to have gotten along fairly well. At least as well as any human could with Sheriff King.

He spread his hands. "A pet, sure. But why a cat?"

"I…happen to like cats." She avoided looking at him.

"No, you don't." He sputtered out a harsh laugh.

"Yes, I do," she insisted.

He tapped his shoe on the floor. "Betsy Jones, I know good and well from the medical forms you filled out when my department employed you, that you're *allergic* to cats."

Veronica and I let out collective gasps. It was the most terrible allergy we'd ever come up against. Where would we be if being close to felines made us feel miserable? We were both thankful we didn't have to endure it.

"Betsy," I said, "is that true? You're allergic to cats?"

She gave a one-shouldered shrug. "Well, sort of." As if on cue she sneezed again, and her eyes watered. Veronica grabbed a box of tissues from the other end of the counter and pushed them toward the sniffling woman.

Betsy's face reddened, and she sneezed four times in rapid succession into the tissues in her hand.

"See?" The sheriff pointed to Betsy's face. "I told you. The crazy lunatic is allergic to those wicked felines and she's taking one home to live with her. What do you make of that?"

I didn't think crazy lunatic was very complimentary, when Betsy was doing something nice for a homeless cat. But I had to admit, there didn't seem to be a logical explanation. If she was taking on a cat from a close friend or relative, for instance, maybe for sentimental reasons, I could understand it better. But as far as I knew, she and Agnes Temple didn't have that sort of connection.

That was something I'd have to check into more. Because my antennae just went up. What reason would Betsy have to want Agnes Temple's pet?

Betsy glared at the sheriff, then looked back at me. "Molly, can I call you to set up a time for Lulu's grooming?"

"Sure. No problem."

"Thanks." She slid a sideways glance toward her boss. "Today doesn't seem conducive to discussing it." She whirled around and practically marched out, the anger palpable in her wake.

Sheriff King rubbed his hands together, as if getting in the middle of something juicy. "Now that she's gone, I wanted to tell you something, young lady." He pointed his finger toward me.

"Wait," Veronica said to me. "He called you young lady, which you are. But just because I'm old enough to be your, um, aunt, should he be discriminating against me by singling you out as young?"

Sheriff King sputtered something I couldn't understand.

Veronica waved her hand and laughed. "Just toying with you, Sheriff. I know you're as old as I am. Please, do go on with what you were saying."

With narrowed eyes for Veronica, then for me, he said, "Molly, this is an official warning to stay out of this Agnes Temple murder business. You've gotten in my way in the past, and I don't want to have to deal with the likes of you trying to do my job again. I won't have it. Do you hear?"

I folded my arms over my chest. "Let me remind you, Sheriff King, that I, along with my cats, Percival and Jasper, were instrumental in discovering the identity of a murderer not that long ago. While you were floundering around like a trout on a dry dock, my felines and I were on the case. To top it off, you then took total credit for bagging the killer, never even mentioning us once."

"That's right," agreed Veronica. "And add in the fact that you ran from our grooming shop like a frightened chipmunk when any of the cats came near you."

"I did no such thing," he said.

Veronica turned abruptly, marched to the grooming area, and came back holding a gorgeous black cat. Seeing what she was up to, I quickly went over and retrieved another cat, this one a Calico, from her carrier beside the front door.

"Now, Sheriff, let me ask you a question," I said. I cuddled the cat and ran my fingers through her fur. "Isn't she pretty? Would you like to hold her?"

"No. I…" He glanced at his watch, then, as he backed toward the door, said, "I'm late for…something and—"

He ran out the door.

As I put the Calico back in her cage, I shook my head. "If the sheriff actually did his job, I wouldn't mind staying out of the way. But I know in my bones that Evan didn't kill Agnes. I won't stand by and let my friend go to prison for something he didn't do."

"You're a good egg, Molly."

"So I've been told. By you."

Veronica grinned. "I have your back, sister."

"I know." I smiled. "I couldn't do any of this without you."

"So, what do you think is going on with Betsy? I mean, while it's great that she wants to care for a cat, have you ever known somebody to be so adamant about it when they were allergic?"

"No, I haven't. There's something going on there, and I'm determined to find out what it is."

Chapter Six

On a break from the grooming shop, I stopped by Paula's Pastries to get something for Veronica and me. My assistant had a weakness for Paula's blueberry croissants. Truth be told, so did I. It was just easier to justify getting some if I said it was for someone else.

The line for food pickup was four deep, so I took a seat at a nearby table.I hooked my purse strap over the back of the chair and waited. Either Paula or her assistant, Wanda, would come over soon. I looked around, appreciating not only the tantalizing aroma of baked delights, but the cute way Paula had decorated with pink and green checked tablecloths, matching café curtains, and fresh cut flowers on every table.

I loved the flower idea, but if I tried that in my grooming shop, I'd have to tie them to the ceiling. That was the only place the cats couldn't reach them to destroy them or, even worse, have them for lunch.

The front door squeaked open, and I heard footsteps. When I looked over my shoulder, Ernie was there. "I think you dropped something, Molly."

"I did?" I glanced down to where Ernie pointed. "Oh, thanks. I can't tell you how many times my phone has leaped out of the outside purse pocket." I reached down to retrieve it.

Ernie raised one eyebrow. "Leaped? Really?"

I shrugged and laughed. "Just my weird humor."

He grinned. "Maybe keep a closer eye on your wayward phone from here on in?"

"Yes, good idea."

Ernie gave a wave and headed to the order pickup line. At least he seemed in a better mood than when he'd discovered me crouched on the floor outside his boss's window. Maybe he'd just been having a bad day the other time.

As someone approached again, I glanced up, this time expecting to give my pastry order, but smiled when it turned out to be Evan.

"Hey," I said, "doing the same thing as I am? Buying pastries for yourself but saying it's for someone else? Veronica is my very willing scapegoat."

He laughed. "Definitely buying for me. People might not believe me if I said I was getting them for my co-worker when I work by myself."

"Good point. Hey, while I have you here, I wanted to run something by you." I pointed to a chair next to me.

He took a seat. "Okay."

I glanced behind me to make sure Paula or anyone else wasn't on their way over. Satisfied we could talk privately, I said, "I got a phone call."

He nodded, encouraging me to continue.

"It was from…well, I actually don't know who. But they mentioned me. And you."

"Me?" His eyes widened. "But you don't know who it was?"

I shook my head. "The voice was gravelly, disguised like the person didn't want me to know their identity."

With a frown, Evan said, "Are you all right? I don't like the sound of this." Evan was such a sweetheart, always concerned about everyone else. Even when he was the one under a microscope for the most recent murder.

"I didn't like the sound of that either. But I wanted you to know."

"What did they say about you and me?"

I checked behind me again, seeing the coast was still clear. "Whoever it was said I needed to keep out of the murder investigation for Agnes. Or else."

"Or else what?"

"That you, me and… our pets, would be very sorry."

His face paled. "What? That's…"

"A threat, yes."

"Are you taking it seriously?" he asked.

I shrugged. "Yes and no. First of all, I'll be extra cautious at work and home, keeping an eye out for anyone saying or doing anything suspicious."

"Good idea. What else?"

"And as for Percival and Jasper, most of the time, they'll be with me.

As was my habit, I glanced down at my feet where the cats normally sat when I brought them inside. "But, wouldn't you know, today is the one day in a long while that I left them at home."

"I think I'd better take your advice about your cats and maybe do the same. I'll keep my dogs in my photography studio when I'm there, even though they'll get bored and bark when the front door opens—yes, every single time, but if I don't have them with me, or know they're safe, I'll worry constantly about them."

"Evan, you're a good dog dad."

His face reddened, and he averted his gaze. "Thanks, Molly. That means a lot coming from an animal lover like you." As he took a deep breath and let it out slowly, the color on his face went back to normal. "All right. You'd said 'yes and no' to taking it seriously. How are you *not* doing that?"

"The person doesn't want me to interfere in the investigation."

"Then maybe you shouldn't. I don't want anything to happen to you or your cats. Or me and my dogs, either. Should we just listen to what the caller said and let sheriff—"

I lifted my hand from the table. "I don't trust Sheriff King. I mean, he's an alright guy, I guess, but honestly? When he was supposed to be finding the real killer for the murder that took place a while back, all he did was keep blaming my uncle, Russ. He didn't even bother to look much further."

"And, of course, your uncle was innocent. So, you went out looking to find the person yourself."

"That's right. I had help from others and from my cats, but I believe that if I hadn't taken the initiative, Russ might be sitting in prison right now instead of enjoying his life, doing what he wants."

"But I don't want you to get hurt in any way," said Evan, "checking out possible suspects on my behalf."

"I feel like I'm involved already, since I was there right after you discovered Agnes's body. Besides, I seem to have discovered that I have a knack for finding clues. And Jasper and Percival aren't too shabby as detectives either."

He gave a faint smile. "Do they wear tiny detective outfits?"

I smiled back. "No, the only things they allow me to put on them are their harnesses for when we go out. But yeah, wouldn't those outfits be cute?"

Taking my hand briefly, Evan said, "Thank you, Molly, for helping me out. You're a good friend."

"You're welcome. I'd say you could return the favor someday but I kind of hope you won't have to."

"Agreed." He shook his head slowly. "And as far as me showing the sheriff that picture of a person with a bottle of fixer?"

"Yeah?"

"I tried. He didn't give me the time of day. Said it was a lousy picture, and shouldn't an actual photographer like me do a better job of taking a photo."

"I'm sorry, Evan. I was afraid of something like that happening. Even though I don't trust him, I thought maybe that particular piece of evidence might spur him on in the investigation. Guess It didn't work."

"It's not your fault. Thanks for all you're doing. I guess it highlights the fact that we need to keep checking out things on our own."

Paula approached our table, her order pad in her hand. "Hey guys, sorry for the wait. What can I get you?"

"Four blueberry croissants, please, two to go," I said.

She nodded and turned to Evan. "And for you?"

"Blueberry croissants also. Two, please."

I elbowed him. "Way to rub it in that you're eating lighter than I am."

Paula laughed. "I hate to tell you this, but eating even one isn't considered light."

Evan raised his eyebrows at me. "But since you're also buying for Veronica, it's not as bad as it appears, right?"

"Good save," I said. "Now Paula won't think bad of me."

She grinned. "As if I ever could, Molly. Okay, these will be up in a few." She hurried back to the entrance to the kitchen, the door swinging behind her in her wake.

Footsteps came from behind me. Had Paula forgotten to ask us something?

But when I saw Evan's expression at whoever was walking toward us, I knew it must have been somebody else.

"Evan," I said, "are you all right?"

He dragged his gaze from whoever had claimed his attention and finally focused on me. "I don't believe it. I just don't."

Unable to stand not knowing, I angled around in my chair. Everyone I saw, I already knew. Familiar faces from our town. Why would that freak Evan out so much? But the line of people shifted. And there was one face I didn't recognize. A very pretty woman with long red hair and enough makeup to make a clown giddy. "Evan, that girl, do you know her?"

He swallowed hard and nodded. "Do I ever. There's a history there. Not one I like to discuss."

I looked across the room again, then back to Evan. "Sorry, but you just might have to. She's headed this way."

He slid down in his chair. Was he hoping she'd change her mind even though she'd already spotted him?

Her boots tapped in rapid succession as she rushed to our table. "Evan Lakes, as I live and breathe!"

Evan groaned. "Oh, she lives and breathes, all right," he muttered.

My eyes widened as the woman placed her arm proprietarily around Evan's shoulders. He stiffened, but the woman didn't seem to notice. Or not care.

"Why, Evan," she said, her voice syrupy, "how have you been, Pumpkin?"

Pumpkin?

With what could only be described as misery, Evan eyed me. "Molly Stewart, I'd like you to meet Penelope Withers."

My mouth dropped open at the mention of Evan's old girlfriend, but I snapped it closed. After a couple of seconds, I'd regained composure to say, "Hello."

"Aren't you just the sweetest thing, Miss Molly?"

I blinked. "Um, okay, sure."

Penelope's smile was wide, with straight, overly bleached teeth. She glanced at Evan, "Aren't you going to ask me to join you and your lovely friend, Evan?" Her eyebrows lowered. "Oh, dear. I haven't misspoken." She looked pointedly at me.

"About…"

"You two are friends, right? Not…more?"

"No," I said, just friends.

She let out a breath. "Well, that's a relief."

Evan, who hadn't spoken since introducing me to Penelope, shook his head slowly. Finally, he pointed to a chair across from him and said, "Please. Join us." But his invitation sounded as appealing as inviting a bear to a picnic. And his cheeks had reddened again.

"Ooooh," she squealed. "I'd be delighted!"

I waited as she took her seat, which was a big deal in itself, as she took her handbag from her shoulder, set it firmly on the table, then proceeded to remove a compact with a mirror, a comb, and a tube of lipstick.

Penelope slid me a sideways glance. "Bear with me, Honey. You know how long it takes to become presentable."

I smiled. But if she knew that my *presentable* meant making sure I'd showered and didn't have toothpaste stuck to my chin, she might reassess saying that to me.

Finally, she was finished primping, smoothing, and what nearly appeared to be pruning as she did something outrageous to her eyelashes. She gave her compact mirror reflection a wink, snapped it closed, then replaced the items. Once her purse was hung on the back of her chair, she smiled wide. "Now," she said, "I'm ready." She turned to Evan, "So, Pumpkin, what's been going on since I last saw you?"

He opened his mouth to speak, but she held up one finger. "Hold on," said Penelope, "I think Miss Molly here should know my side of things first. That okay?"

With a defeated shrug, Evan waved his hand, giving her the go-ahead. His exhaled breath sounded like compressed air from a tire going flat.

"Perfect," said Penelope. "Now, Molly, here's the scoop."

I wasn't sure I was ready for her to scoop anything, but I couldn't just leave and abandon Evan. After checking my watch, I confirmed that I had a little bit longer until I had to be back to Fabulous Felines, so I folded my forearms on the table and settled in.

"Well," she said, "For starters, did you go to Whitewater Valley High?"

I nodded. "Yes. I did."

"Me too!" Her eyes sparkled like we had a special bond now.

I looked at her, trying not to frown. I didn't remember her at all.

She held up her hand. "I know what you're thinking. You don't remember me, right?"

"Well…"

"It's okay. My family moved away after my junior year. Evan and I were in the same class."

So she was older than I was, since Evan had been ahead of me. I nodded for her to continue.

"And to be honest, I looked different then. I was a late bloomer. And I went by Penny, then. Plus, Withers is the last name I took on when my mom remarried. So you see, there's no reason you should remember me. Anyway, Evan and I had been an item, you might say."

I caught Evan rolling his eyes, but Penelope didn't seem to catch it. Maybe that was a good thing. Would she have scolded her Pumpkin if she'd noticed his reaction?

"Let me tell you, when my family moved away, I was inconsolable. And poor, poor Evan was heartbroken."

Evan's gaze found mine. He gave a slight shake of his head. I widened my eyes in return. Oh boy, this was more complicated than I'd realized.

"Our parents insisted we break up. It was devastating," she said.

I placed my hand on my chin, fascinated at Penelope's version, because Evan's facial expressions told a completely different tale.

Penelope's mouth formed a pout. "Before I was forced to leave my poor Evan, he had quite a bumpy ride at school. You see, Evan is the most amazing artist. Especially painting."

I smiled at Evan, who simply shrugged.

"He won award after award, but our evil old teacher, Miss Temple, made his life miserable. Every time he accomplished something, she struck him down."

Having been pulled into her tale, I asked, "Were you in Agnes Temple's class, too?"

"Oh yes. What a witch she was. Did you have her?"

"No, I had a different teacher."

"Lucky you." She waved her hand. "That woman was hateful and mean. Especially to my poor Evan."

Whatever Evan muttered didn't sound polite or appropriate for public hearing.

Penelope smoothed some of her flawless hair away from her face. "That Miss Temple changed the course of Evan's entire future. And mine."

"Yours?" I asked.

"That's right. Evan will tell you that I, in my own right, am an extremely talented artist as well."

He bit his lip, and his nostrils flared, as if words to the contrary longed to escape.

She patted Evan's arm. "He and I had a plan, you see. To go to the same college. Study abroad. Become world famous artists together. I've always had Evan's best interests at heart. He's such an amazing artist, that I was appalled when I discovered he'd opened a *photography* studio." Her face took on an expression of having tasted burnt seaweed.

"Oh," I said, "his studio is great. Have you seen it?"

She glanced away. "Um, why no. I haven't." She tugged at her shirt collar, as if uncomfortable. Or lying. If she'd been there, why wouldn't she want to admit it?

"Molly," she said, "in my humble opinion, Evan is wasting his life."

"What?" I asked. "Why?"

"Because taking pictures of people is beneath him, when he could be painting them, or beautiful landscapes instead." She tapped her toe on the floor in a staccato beat. The noise was annoying, and Evan closed his eyes briefly. Was that a habit she'd always had and which he'd grown to hate?

I averted my gaze, thinking about the recent cat pictures Evan had done, which, in *my* humble opinion, were the bees' knees. I frowned. Did bees really have knees?

"Oh," Penelope said, "I see the look on your face. You agree with me, don't you, that poor Evan should close down his wretched studio and start painting again."

I sat up straight. "What? No, of course not."

Her eyes widened. "How dare you!" She stood so suddenly her chair screeched against the floor. Several people in the shop turned to stare. Evan placed his hands over his face, like a kid thinking he's hiding because he can't see anyone else.

Penelope stomped her foot. "I'll be taking my leave now. And Evan? I'm staying at the Valley Inn in room nineteen. I'll be expecting you to stop by soon. And by that, I mean today."

As soon as she was gone, Evan let out a huge breath. "First of all, I am so sorry you had to endure that. And her. She's…."

"I'm fine. Evan. Is it true what she said, that you two were going to…"

"No. Well, in her mind, I guess. What is true is that we dated. Briefly. We were in the same art class. I always thought we were more friends than anything, but Penelope thought otherwise."

"Obviously."

"Yeah." He rubbed the back of his head.

"Evan," I said, "if she was in love with you—"

He shuddered.

"—and as she said, wanted the best for you, do you think she might have had something to do with Agnes's death? Could she have hated her so much that she might have murdered her?"

He gasped. "Wow, um… I'd have to say yes. It's possible. I mean, she hears about my photography studio, then happens to come back to town right when I find Agnes dead in my dark room. Maybe she thought if Agnes was out of the picture and not causing trouble anymore, I'd be free to pursue my 'art.'"

I glanced toward the entrance door, then back. "But you haven't seen her in all this time, right?"

"Right, but…even though I haven't seen her or communicated with her…."

I leaned forward. "What?"

"That woman has been sending me mushy letters, emails, and texts ever since she left town." This time, the redness in his face traveled south, creating colorful splotches on his neck.

"For years?" That seemed extreme.

"That's right. At least weekly. Sometimes more. You'd think since I never once answered, she'd get the hint."

"Then I guess Penelope was right about one thing," I said.

"What's that?"

I patted him on the hand. "You really are poor Evan."

Chapter Seven

The next afternoon, I pulled my grooming van into Florence's driveway. I had to be careful to always alternate between hers and Lottie's, her next-door neighbor. The ladies were standing on their respective front porches, each holding her fur baby. Their cats were, as usual, dressed alike. Today's outfits were pink and white polka-dotted dresses and lacy white socks.

Jasper and Percival, tails wagging, perched side by side at the passenger window of my van, ready for their duties as official supervisors of every move I'd make with my kitty clients.

I hopped out of the front seat, strolled to the back, and opened the doors to my auto-lowering steps. The ladies carried their girls to me. I reached out my arms somewhere in the vicinity of both of them, allowing them to decide who handed me their furless baby first. After glancing at each other and communicating in winks and nods, Lottie gave me Eleanor, then Florence handed over Helga.

The kitties, so used to being together, cuddled up in a single purring ball against my chest. I took a moment to love on them before carrying them into the van.

"Okay, girls," I said to the cats, "who wants to go first today?" I eyed the ladies who now stood at the foot of the steps. They conferred again without words, this time with shrugs and raised eyebrows. Finally, Lottie said, "Eleanor goes first today."

"Perfect," I said. I placed Helga on a nearby blanket to wait her turn. She curled in a ball and closed her eyes, not even flinching when Jasper and

Percival climbed over the front seat, made their way to the grooming area, and began sniffing her from ears to tail.

I held Eleanor under one arm and prepared her weekly bath. She let out a sigh, but otherwise hung limply at my side like a wrinkled hand towel with whiskers.

Florence and Lottie dragged their folding chairs out to the end of Florence's driveway. She pointed toward the house. Lottie nodded, then hurried inside her own house, returning with two glasses of what I knew to be adult beverages. This time, the liquid was a dark blue color. It varied from visit to visit. Last time, it was cotton candy pink. I could only imagine what their lips would look like after a few of today's drinks.

The ladies were always up on the latest news, although I had to temper what they told me with their tendency to make things up and exaggerate, all in an effort to make their story more enticing. The tales really got outlandish when they reached their second or third drink. Good thing they opted for mobile home visits instead of driving to Fabulous Felines in an inebriated state.

Once I started pouring warm water over Eleanor's back, I turned my head toward my audience. "So, ladies, hear anything juicy lately?" I wouldn't normally pose a question using the word juicy, but it seemed to work with these particular pet parents.

"Oh yes," said Florence, waving her hand. Thankfully it wasn't the one holding the nearly full glass, although so many drinks had been spilled on their driveways, it shimmered. "Lottie and I heard something interesting. I—"

Lottie gave her neighbor a narrowed eye glare. "Why do you get to tell it?"

"I thought it was my turn."

"Well, it isn't." Lottie waved the hand holding her glass, seeming not to notice a small line of blue trailing down her wrist.

"How do you know?" asked Florence.

"Because I remember. Last time you told our news."

"Okay, what news did I tell and to whom?"

Lottie frowned. "I don't remember."

"Ha. See?" Florence pointed at her. "So it's my turn."

"No, it's not." Lottie took a sip of her drink, making a loud slurping noise, earning glares from not only Florence, but Eleanor, and Helga as well.

Not wanting to embarrass her, I acted as if I hadn't heard her slurps. Instead I applied the special shampoo I kept for my Sphynx clients, lathering, then, gently rubbing it into Eleanor's skin. She blinked but didn't utter a meow. When I checked on Helga, she was fast asleep, but then so were Percival and Jasper. So much for their supervising duties.

"You ladies can take your time deciding who gets to tell me the latest news," I said, "but it sounds interesting. Maybe I could hear it before I leave today?"

"See what you've done, Florence?" said Lottie. "Molly wants to know. Why don't you just let me tell it."

Florence crossed her arms, tipping her glass enough to splash liquid on her lap. "Fine. Stop pouting and tell her then." She glanced down at her glass. "Hmmm. I really thought I had more in there. I'd better get a refill soon."

I held in my laugh, which wasn't easy, but having spent a lot of time with the women, I'd gotten better at it.

"I wasn't pouting," said Lottie through her downturned, protruding lips. She stared at her neighbor. But when Florence didn't answer, Lottie let out a contented sigh and angled in her chair in order to see me better. "Well," she said, "We'd been discussing one of the latest happenings."

Nothing followed those words. I waited while still giving Eleanor her bath. The cat glanced at me over her shoulder, but didn't let out a sound. She and her sister were certainly spoiled by their human moms, but I had to admit, they were tolerant of having frequent baths.

When the silence continued, Florence nudged Lottie, startling her. "Were you asleep just now?"

Lottie blinked several times. "Of…of course not."

"Then go on with your story."

"What story?" she asked, wiping some blue drool from her mouth.

I bit my lip, holding in another laugh.

"You know," said Florence, "about that young woman."

Lottie's eyebrows lowered. Then, her eyes opened wide. "Oh!" she shouted and raised her hand, holding her cup in the air. "I know who it is."

"You also have blue drops in your hair," pointed out Florence.

Lottie reached up and touched the top of her head. "How in the world did that get there?"

"Never mind. Just continue telling Molly about…um, you know."

"Wait," said Lottie. "You don't remember now either, do you?"

With a shrug, Florence refilled her drink from a nearby pitcher sitting between their chairs on the driveway.

"Now, who was it I was going to tell Molly about?" Lottie frowned.

"You'd mentioned a young woman?"

"Of course." Lottie tried to snap her fingers, but it was the hand holding the glass. "That Lorna Thompson."My eyebrows shot up. "Really? What about her?"

"Who?" asked Florence.

"You know," reminded Lottie. "That girl at The Sandwich Shack."

"You mean Lorna Thompson?"

Lottie nodded. "That's right. But I already said that. She's in a load of doo-doo."

Florence wagged her finger. "Don't say doo-doo."

"Why not? It's a word."

"It's rude," scolded Florence.

"Molly, is doo-doo rude?" asked Lottie.

How to answer? If I agreed, I upset one. Or if I disagreed I might annoy the other. Finally I hoped for the best when I said, "I guess each person has his or her own views on what words are rude or not, right?"

The ladies tilted their heads to the left in identical poses, eyeing me. Then they leaned close together, and the whispers and eye winks began again. After a few seconds, Lottie nodded. "Very well said, Molly."

"Thank you." I blew out a breath, relieved that no one seemed offended. It didn't take much to have them put out about any little thing. And with the way they liked to spread gossip, I didn't need any bad reviews of my grooming shop because of some slip I'd let pass through my lips.

"Anyway," said Florence. "We heard Lorna was a poisoner. And that she'd done it several times to lots of people. You know, over and over. What's that called?"

"What?" I frowned. "You mean a serial poisoner?"

The ladies glanced at each other and shook their heads. "Lottie thinks it granola, but I think it's more like frosty flakes," said Florence.

"I didn't mean cereal like… never mind," I said.

The cat, tired of her bath, shook her whole body, drenching my midsection in the process. That was one of the many reasons I wore a smock over my clothes when grooming and bathing kitties. They did have limited patience, after all, and didn't mind reminding me they were in charge. I gave her a final rinse, then dried her thoroughly with a towel. I redressed her and tied a pink bow around her neck to complement her outfit.

Once I'd placed Eleanor on the blanket nearby, I picked up Helga. During all this, Jasper and Percival still blissfully dozed, Jasper's paws twitching as he dreamed.

"So," said Florence, "since Lorna is possibly killing people with poisoned food and drink, Lottie and I decided it wouldn't be such a far stretch to hear of her murdering Agnes, even though it was with a different weapon. Once a killer, always a killer, right?"

Lottie leaned forward in her chair. "We took our cats there just last week for shrimp cocktail. Not anymore. At least unless another killer is found and Lorna gets off the hook. I hope it's not her. She's very nice. And it's the cats' favorite place to get their shrimp, since they don't get it at home."

"Now, wait a second," said Florence. "I know very well you sneak shrimp to Eleanor. I've smelled it on her breath when she comes over to play with Helga."

Watching the lazy way Helga and Eleanor appeared now, with bleary eyes and droopy whiskers, I took "play with" to mean an extended nap.

Lottie waved her hand. "That was only once. It was a special occasion. It was her birthday."

"Then it was Helga's birthday too."

Lottie frowned. "What are you talking about?"

"They're twins," said Florence.

With her eyebrows lowered in concentration, Lottie finally blinked. "Oh. Right."

I undressed Helga and placed her outfit and socks next to her sister. Laying them any closer to the bathing area might get them damp. And I'd rather not experience the ire of either the cats or the ladies if something was amiss during or after the appointment.

"Anyway, back to Lorna," remarked Florence. "Didn't we recently hear about Jemima Splinter having a tummy ache after eating something at Lorna's shop?"

Lottie placed her finger on her chin as she thought. "You're so right. Amelia Brustkern tried to tell me Jemima's tummy ache was because of drinking too much Tequila the previous night at their Gin Rummy game, but I said that was ridiculous." She leaned closer to her friend. "Florence, You and I both know Tequila doesn't do more than make you a little giggly." That set them off, chuckling and snorting, tipping their sloshing glasses together in frothy blue toasts to each other.

I'd done enough of these visits with the ladies and had witnessed them imbibe quite a lot during those visits. They were definitely more than giggly when they consumed Tequila or any of its alcoholic cousins. Not that I'd ever say that to them.

"You know," said Lottie, "I had something I'd meant to tell you, Florence."

Florence frowned. "What?"

"What do you mean, what?" asked Lottie.

"You wanted to tell me something."

"I did?"

Florence glanced at me and rolled her eyes. She gave Lottie an admonishing look as she said, "You need to eat more fruit."

"Why?"

"To improve your memory."

"My memory is fine." Lottie's finger tapped against her temple.

When Florence flipped her hand, thankfully, it wasn't the one holding her glass. "Anyhow, why don't you tell me what it is you… uh, wanted to tell me."

Lottie narrowed her eyes. "Now I think you're just being mean, saying I was going to tell you something when I wasn't." She angled around in her chair. "Molly? Was I really going to say something?"

I shrugged, not wanting to get in the middle of the two ladies, who often did have spats. But if what Lottie had been about to say might have to do with Agnes's murder, I wanted to know. "Well, I think you were about to tell Florence something and…you got distracted by…" I glanced at the blanket with the sleeping kitties. "By Eleanor. Doesn't she look clean and sparkly now?"

"You're right." Lottie's eyes widened. "Quite sparkly."

Florence nodded. "I must agree. I nearly need my sunglasses to gaze upon her."

I sighed, hoping Lottie might remember what had been so important a little while ago. I placed Helga into the sink, then sprayed her gently with warm water.

"Wait," said Lottie. "I remember now what I was going to say."

"But I thought your memory was just fine," said Florence sarcastically.

"It is. It's like Molly said before. The sparkliness of Eleanor was a distraction."

"All right," said Florence, "I'll give you that. So? What was it?"

"When we were in the sandwich shop, you know that last time before the serial poisoner might possibly have done a person in?"

"You mean with frosty flakes cereal?"

"Yes, or granola, of course."

"Of course," agreed Florence.

I inwardly sighed. This wasn't going well. I massaged shampoo onto the cat's pink skin.

Lottie said, "Well when you went to the…" She paused and looked around, then whispered, "the ladies room."

"Yes, I'd had too much brandy that morning."

My eyes widened. Morning? Wow, their normal appointments with me were late afternoon. I hadn't realized the party started so early for them.

"So anyway," said Lottie, "while you were, um, indisposed, Lorna came over to the table."

"Was she going to bring you something else to drink?" asked Florence.

"No, this was something way different. Quite disturbing, actually."

"Really?" Florence leaned closer to her. "What'd she want?"

"Lorna said she hoped the cats enjoyed the shrimp. Because it would be their last."

Their last? My hand halted in mid-action, causing Helga to glare at me. Why would Lorna have said that?

Florence gasped. "Had she meant that if our cats ate it, they would expire?"

"Expire!" Lottie let out a moan.

All four cats, awake and wide-eyed now, whipped their heads toward the ladies.

"Now, now," said Florence, "let's think about this for a minute. If there had been something wrong with the shrimp, we wouldn't have our babies with us now, right?"

Lottie sniffled against her sleeve. "Yes. I suppose you're right." She angled to the side in her chair, peering inside the van. She gave a tiny wave to Eleanor.

"See, what I'm thinking is," said Florence, "since Lorna likes cats, and we know this because she's always glad to see us with them in the shop, she would never do anything to harm them."

I nodded, hoping to encourage them in positive thoughts. "Right. Maybe it was nothing more than they would be starting to use a new brand of shrimp in the future." I smiled.

Lottie refilled her drink, took a sip, then said, "But I still think she might have done in Agnes Temple, since Agnes isn't a cat."

My smile fell. So much for my encouraging words.

Chapter Eight

I walked over to see Jillian at the town library where she worked. Having seen her in action as Head Librarian, I knew she sometimes had to oversee unpleasantness from her patrons. I'd personally witnessed at least one heated argument between two men who were getting ready to duke it out in the DIY section. Thankfully, they'd left before anything else occurred.

Jillian equated some of her moody patrons to a few of my feline clients, who snarled and spit if they didn't get their way. At least my grooming clients were smaller and could be given time out in their carriers if something went awry. Maybe time out for humans would be a jail cell. I shivered, thinking of Evan and the possibility of just that hanging over his head. There must be some way for Jillian and me to help him out and discover who'd really done in the former art teacher.

I placed a sack from Paula's Pastries on Jillian's desk. She was nose-deep in a book, imagine that, but her sense of smell told her what was going on before she even knew I was there.

"Hey...what's..." She whipped around. "Molly? Bless you. How did you know I was hungry?"

"I heard your tummy growling from my shop."

She laughed. "Wouldn't be surprised. And being in a library where at least most of the time it's quiet, a growly tummy sounds like a sonic boom." She opened the sack. "You brought blueberry croissants. I love blueberry croissants. How did you know?"

I held up my hand. "Who is your best friend in the whole world?"

"Molly Stewart."

"I rest my case."

She grinned, offered me a croissant, then grabbed one for herself and took a huge bite. She let out a loud groan. "Oh *wow*, that's almost as *good* as…"

An older woman walking by halted, narrowed her eyes at Jillian, and shook her finger.

Jillian grimaced as her face reddened.

I covered my mouth, hoping my laugh wouldn't reverberate around the large main room. "You know why you said that, don't you?"

Her eyebrows lowered. "Um…."

"For one thing, Lottie and Florence still like to talk about The Book."

"Yes," said Jillian, "the one with the bodice-ripper couple on the front cover and the descriptions that seem to drive the local women crazy. Those two get me into more trouble. Um, the ladies, not the couple. However, I should say that The Book does get me in trouble, too. When it first came out, we only had so many copies to go around and three times that many ladies wanting to read it. What ensued was an all-out catfight."

"Welcome to my world. The ladies tried to get me to read it, and I kept making excuses. They don't understand that I love mysteries better than romance books."

"Same here, as you know."

I smirked. "And another reason you might have said what you almost said, almost as good as…?"

"What?"

"Not what. Who. Evan."

"Ugh. Stop." She took another bite of blueberry delight. Was that so she wouldn't have to answer what I'd said?

"You know you like him." I lightly smacked her shoulder. "You've told me so. And since I have a good memory, you can't tell me you never said it."

"Fine. I like him. So there." She took another bite of her croissant, groaned, and said. "It's almost as…"

I pointed at her. "Don't go there again."

With a guilty glance around for the finger-shaking woman, Jillian nodded.

"Yes, right. Good advice."

I finished my croissant, then grabbed a couple of tissues from her desk to wipe off my fingers.

"Aren't you having another?" She peered inside the bag again. "There are still two left."

"Nope." I nudged the sack. "All for you."

Jillian smiled. "Wow, you must really love me."

"Of course I do. I—"

A loud thump, like a person stomping his or her foot, came from my left. Jillian placed her dessert on a tissue and stood, then rushed to the main counter, leaning partway over the top to try to see better. "Wait, isn't that the mailman, Ricky?"

I joined her at the counter, mirroring her pose as I, too, leaned forward. "Yep. That's him. He delivers mail here, too, right?"

"Yes, but I don't see his mailbag. And why is he waving his arms around like a deranged chicken?" Jillian glanced around. "Good, nobody else seems to need me at the moment. Let's go."

"Go where?"

She motioned her hand for me to follow her. When we reached the edge of a tall shelving of books, she turned to me and pressed her fingers to her lips.

"Really?" I whispered. "Like I wouldn't know not to…"

"Shhh!"

My eyes widened. My best friend was in proper librarian mode. I'd seen it a few times and knew she meant business. With a shrug, I followed her lead and knelt down, peering between the books to watch the show on the other side.

When I scrunched down even farther to get a better view, I saw Ricky. He'd moved from when we'd initially seen him and was now standing in the historical fiction section. But he was speaking to someone else. Someone I didn't recognize.

I leaned to my right. "Uh, Jillian?"

"Shhh."

"Hey, I'm keeping my voice down."

"Shhh."

"I just want to know who…"

"Shhh."

I let out a long breath. Jillian's shushing was nearly as bad as my clients when they hissed. If she was going to be so huffy, I'd just have to wait until her surveillance was over to find out who our mailman was with.

The guy standing opposite Ricky was much older. His appearance spoke of authority and being educated. In comparison to his spotless shirt, pressed khakis, and expensive looking watch, Ricky's wrinkled shirt, dusty shoes, and unkempt ponytail were definitely at odds.

They kept their voices low, so I still couldn't make out what they were saying. But Ricky, who'd previously given foot stomps and arm flails, now had his hand out in the other man's direction, with his fingers curled like claws. What in the world was going on?

Then, when Ricky bared his teeth like some demented forest creature, I was ready to jump up and ask what he was up to. Had he gone berserk? He was odd on the best of days, but this was beyond anything I'd seen him do.

If he was trying to attack the taller, larger man, he wasn't going about it in a very effective way. From the older man's stance—crossed arms, feet planted firmly, a frown on his face—he appeared as intimidated by Ricky's theatrics about as much as a lion to a grasshopper.

There had to be some connection between the men, and I was dying to know what it was. But every time I opened my mouth to ask, Jillian gave me the Librarian Scowl. At least it was better than being shushed. Sort of.

Finally, the older man frowned, shook his head, and stomped out of the aisle. Jillian grabbed my arm, yanked me to a standing position, then acted like she was looking at some books.

"Molly," she whispered, "look."

Maybe she was done shushing me now. "Look at what?"

"A book," she said.

"You've got to be kidding." There were fifty of them within my reach. "Which book?"

Jillian pointed toward the row of books. "It doesn't matter."

Since when would Jillian try to push something on me that might not be to my liking? "What if I don't find it interesting? You know I only read mysteries."

After briefly closing her eyes, she said, "Just pick up a book and act like you're reading it. Try to look like you weren't listening to them." She tilted her head toward the shelves, indicating Ricky, who was now humming an off-key tune.

"Oh. Right." Jillian was so wrapped up in her job and concerned about everything library and book related, I never knew when she was being facetious about something or her usual militant head librarian self. I reached up and grabbed the nearest title, *How to Make Your Honeymoon Sparkle*, and acted as if I was totally absorbed in reading it.

Steps sounded from where Ricky had been, and soon, he popped around the corner of the shelves. "Oh, hey, Jillian. And Molly." His eyebrows lowered when he saw what I was looking at. "Um, Molly?"

"Yeah?"

"I didn't know you'd gotten married."

"What?" I glanced at the book title again. "No, I didn't, this is—"

His eyes lit up. "Oh! Did you and Hank Chenoweth get hitched?"

"No, it's—"

"Hey, then maybe this time next year, you'll have a baby."

Baby? I gulped. "Uh, Ricky, listen..."

"Well, I'll be a chimp's cousin," he said. "What a surprise. Wait until I tell everybody!" He took off at a trot before I could catch him.

I stuffed the book back in the empty slot, sighing as Jillian removed it and replaced it. To my eye, she'd put the book exactly the way I'd had it. I was sure she had a different opinion entirely.

"Honestly, Molly, you should leave it up to the library professional, in effect, me, to properly rehome any and all reading material to its proper resting spot."

I tried so hard not to roll my eyes, but I doubt I was successful. But anything I said in rebuttal about her words would only get me further into her library world, with me on the losing end. Instead, I sighed. "Well, great," I said. "Now, because of the stupid book I was holding and crazy Ricky seeing it, the whole town will think I'm living in wedded bliss with Hank."

Jillian snickered and elbowed me. "Gee, I could think of much worse things to happen."

"I thought you liked Evan."

"I do," she said. "I meant things that would happen to you. And your baby." She gave a pointed glance toward my midsection.

The groan I let out was too loud, and I was the recipient of Jillian's shushing again. Unfortunately, there was nothing I could do about Ricky's enthusiastic reaction at the moment. When Jillian headed back to the main counter, I followed. She sat down in her desk chair and patted the seat next to it. I complied, but had so many questions. Why had Ricky been acting so strange? Who was the man he'd been speaking to? And exactly how did one make a honeymoon sparkle?

Jillian tented her fingers on her desk. "That whole thing was unexpected."

"I'll say. Who knew I'd end up getting married today? Too bad I don't remember it."

"Haha." She shook her head. "No, I mean Ricky and Dodge."

"Dodge?"

"Yeah, don't you remember him?"

I shook my head. "Um… no. I don't think so."

"It's been a while, of course, and he's changed a lot in the last few years, but that was Dodge Zaminski."

I shrugged.

She eyed me. "Our high school principal? You don't remember him? Where were you when I was diligently studying and attending classes?"

I frowned, then widened my eyes. "Oh, right. I'd forgotten he had such an unusual first name. Not that I ever would have called him by it back then. He looks different now. He's bald and thinner. And always used to wear a suit. How did you recognize him so fast?"

She waved her hand. "Dodge is a regular in the library. Practically lives and breathes anything historical."

"Oh, That's right. I remember now. Didn't he teach before he became principal?"

"Yes, he did."

"What do you suppose he and Ricky were talking about?" I asked.

"From the way Ricky flailed around, I wouldn't even call it talking. Our postal carrier is a tad dramatic."

"True," I agreed. "For a second there, I thought he'd fling his whole body at Dodge, um, Principal Zaminski, sorry I can't call him by his first name. It feels wrong somehow."

"I get that," she said. "It was hard for me, too, when he first started coming in here. He insisted I use his first name, but I kept wondering if I'd get called into his office and accused of talking too much in class or snapping my gum too loud." She laughed.

I rolled my eyes. "Please, stop talking about that. I'm having flashbacks."

"You were never called down to the principal's office. I would have remembered something like that."

"True, but I was always afraid I'd do something to anger him, and I'd get kicked out of school or…"

She patted my hand. "Don't worry. He can't hurt you now."

"Thank goodness. Even though I still have nightmares sometimes about being back in high school. Didn't you have those feelings? That you'd get in trouble when we were still in school?"

She thought for a minute. "Nope."

"Oh, sure. Because you got all A's to my B plusses."

Jillian shrugged. "Yes, I was fortunate that school came easy for me. Especially reading and literature, obviously." She indicated the room around us with her hand. "But every person is good at different things. For you, taking such great care of your feline clients is amazing."

"Really?"

"Sure." She smiled. "I could never do that. One loud hiss and I'd be in tears."

"Why? You're so good at keeping people in line here at the library." I wanted to mention the shushing but kept that part to myself.

"Because I'd think the cats didn't like me. I'd take it personally."

"Don't you mean purrsonally?"

"See?" She grinned. "This is why you're so good at what you do. You're so attuned to cats that you can figure out what they're feeling and thinking. And they love and trust you for it."

"I have to admit, I couldn't do your job either," I said. "Too many humans in one place all at the same time. At least when I see the people who come into the shop, they don't bring lots of other people with them, just their cats."

Jillian let out a happy sigh. "I can't imagine doing anything else. Getting to spend my time around books and people who love to read them is my dream job. And on my breaks, having a chance to do the online newspaper's daily crossword puzzle." She sighed dreamily.

"Let me guess. You do them in ink, right?"

"Doesn't everyone?"

"Frankly, no." I glanced toward the front entrance where Ricky had just gone. "For now, I'm going to work at my other job."

Her eyebrows lowered. "Other job? Which is what? Are you grooming unicorns now and forgot to tell me?"

I smiled. "No, I'm on duty now to find out who the heck killed Agnes Temple. And to see if what Ricky was just up to had anything to do with that."

"I'm right there with you. Finding out who did it will get Evan off the hook. And that's got to be a high priority for him and us right now."

Now might be the best time to fill Jillian in on Evan and what I'd witnessed at Paula's Pastries. Not that I wanted to, but she'd hear about it soon enough. "Listen, uh…"

"What's up?"

"When I was in Paula's Pastries, Evan was in there and…"

Jillian's eyebrows lowered. "Did something happen? Is he okay?"

"He was really ticked to see a certain person walk in there."

She turned in her seat to face me. "Who?"

"Penelope Withers."

"His ex?" Her eyes widened, then narrowed. "What did she want? To get back with him?"

"Hey," I gave her arm a light squeeze. "It's okay. He doesn't want anything to do with her."

"Oh. Well… okay then."

"That girl is a piece of work," I said. "Acted like she hadn't dumped him, just that they hadn't seen each other for a while. Kept talking about how his photography studio was a big mistake, a step down."

"Wait, she said that? He's such a talented photographer."

"I agree. But she was so intent on him being a true artist and her, too. But after she left, Evan said she was never any good, but she thought she was."

"Wow, sounds like I missed a lot," she said.

I wanted Jillian and Evan to get to know each other better, and my being in the middle wouldn't help. I stood suddenly.

"Hey, are you leaving? I wanted to know more."

I glanced at my watch, even though I actually had plenty of time. "I need to run. But, why don't you ask Evan about Penelope's unfortunate visit? I'm sure he'd tell you everything."

"You think so?"

I nodded. Now that I knew they liked each other, I wanted to help their fledgling romance along. "Yep. I have no doubt he'd love to talk to you."

Her cheeks reddened, and she smiled. "All right then. I'll do just that."

I turned and walked toward the door, hoping she hadn't noticed my wide grin.

Chapter Nine

My mobile appointment that afternoon was with my uncle Russ. Or rather, his two cats. Usually, my uncle and I met once every week or two for lunch, but our schedules had both been crazy, so we combined Marcus and Welby's groomings with our catch-up chat.

As I pulled into his driveway, Jasper and Percival stood on their tiptoes, looking out the side window of the passenger seat of my van. Jasper's tail wagged back and forth in anticipation, and Percival let out a tiny trilling meow.

"Yeah, you guys recognize this place, right? And you get to see Uncle Russ and your cousins at the same time." Percival glanced at me over his shoulder and twitched his whiskers while Jasper continued to press his nose against the window glass as he swished his tail back and forth.

I laughed when I parked and saw Marcus and Welby staring at us through Russ's front window. Maybe they were looking forward to seeing us too. Russ's front door opened, and he waved, then after a few seconds, he came out carrying the cats in his arms like plump, furry infants. Since Russ had never had children, they were his babies.

Believe me, I understood since I wasn't married either. The fact that Hank and I had recently started dating, gave me hope, but since our relationship was still in its fledgling stage, I wanted to take it slow and make sure it was right. We were already friends, so at least in my opinion, a good foundation.

I left my cats in the front of the van while I got out and walked to the back to open the rear doors and let down the steps.

When Russ and his cats reached me, I wrapped my arms around all of them for a hug. Russ smiled. Welby gave a tiny hiss that was so soft I nearly missed it. I laughed. "Oh well, guess I got a good response from one of you."

"You know not to take it personally from a cat. Some are sweet, some are lazy, and some," he jiggled his cats in his arms, "have very strong opinions. About everything."

"True." I climbed the steps to the back of the van, then reached out for Russ to hand his cats to me. I placed Marcus on a nearby blanket, then snuggled Welby for a minute, hoping to get past the hissiness. Finally he pressed his body against my chest, letting out a tiny purr.

"Russ," I said, "your cat is so quiet. Does he ever howl and screech?"

"Not really. He doesn't make a lot of noise. Even when he's moody."

"If you ever want him to have lessons in either of those loud noises, send him to my house. Jasper and Percival would be only too happy to share what they know."

"I'll keep that in mind." He smirked. "Now," he said, "feel like filling me in on things while you work?"

"I'm assuming you want info on what happened to Agnes Temple."

"Yep, since I heard you were there."

"Well, sort of." I grimaced. "And yes, of course I was going to tell you. But you know how it is. Cats to groom. Murders to solve."

"I'll take your word for it. Just glad you're okay," he said. "Anytime a person hears something about a family member in the same sentence with the word murder, it's rather jarring until you calm down enough to listen more closely."

"I'm so sorry you were worried. I should have called you right away, knowing how many people happened to be standing outside Evan's shop when the sheriff showed up, sirens blaring." I frowned. "Wait. How did you know I'd be checking into whoever might have killed Agnes? It's not exactly common knowledge what I'm doing."

He crossed his arms over his chest as one eyebrow rose. "Seriously? I know you very well, Molly Stewart. Even as a little kid, you always wanted to know what was going on, who was doing it, and how they'd accomplished it."

"Yeah, that does sound like me." I laughed.

"Plus the fact that you worked so hard to find the real killer in Whitewater Valley's previous murder so I wouldn't have to go to jail as an innocent man." He placed his hand on his chest. "For which I'm still quite grateful."

"You're welcome. Any time." Having realized what I said, I held up my hand. "Um, not that you'll be in that position again, or…"

He smiled. "It's all good. I'm just glad you were on my side to help. Now, fill me in on the latest with Agnes's murder."

As I waited for the water to warm up from the sprayer in my sink, I set Welby on the table next to me and ran my hand down his back, calming him before his bath.

Percival and Jasper had made their way from the front seat to the back area and took their places on their favorite vantage point, a wide shelf below a window where they could take their choice of looking outside or watching me groom their fellow felines.

Even though Percival had once run off from me while the back door of my van was open, I could usually trust them to stay close. And I had to give my cat credit, he had run off that time for a justifiable reason. When I caught up with him, it enabled me to hear, okay, eavesdrop, on a conversation that helped me find the real murderer.

When the bath water was the right temperature, I carefully placed Welby on a thick towel I had laid on the bottom of the sink and petted him a few more times. I turned to Russ, who was now sitting on the top step of my van, waiting for my response. "So," I said, "in the short time since Agnes died, there've been several interesting developments."

"Okay, I'm listening."

"Well, first of all, Sheriff King is being his cranky, unreliable self."

Russ frowned, having been treated to the sheriff's unpleasant character traits when the sheriff accused him of murder and hounded him while not wanting to check up on anyone else. "Yeah, I know about that all too well."

I nodded. Russ had been put through so much stress because the sheriff refused to see what was right in front of him and properly do his job of a complete investigation into all the people who had motive for the murder.

"Okay, let's see. So far, I've come across a few folks who've done what I thought to be suspicious things."

"Who's the first?" His eyes lit up. I had his attention. Even though the previous murder had been tossed in his lap and he had to defend himself, my uncle was always up for solving a new mystery.

"Evan's ex-girlfriend, Penelope Withers," I said. "She showed up in town right at the time Agnes's body was found. I had the unfortunate experience of meeting her when I was sitting with Evan in Paula's Pastries."

"What did she do or say to make you suspect her?"

As I ran a gentle stream of water over Welby's back, I said, "Apparently, she and Evan have a past. When they were in high school, they dated. She claimed he was still, to this day, the love of her life. Although, according to Evan, they'd barely dated for a short time. He doesn't even like her."

Russ nodded, encouraging me to continue.

"Evan was a terrific artist even in high school and Agnes had been his teacher."

"That's right," said Russ. "I'd nearly forgotten she'd taught art."

I got my bottle of shampoo and poured a small amount into my hand. Welby turned his head and sniffed at the shampoo, then meowed.

"I know, Kitty. But this will make you smell and look even better than you already do."

The cat returned his focus to the front, but he hunched down slightly onto the towel as if resigned to his fate of getting his fur wet.

After massaging shampoo into the cat's fur, including between his toes and down his tail, I began lightly spraying Welby on his back, then tummy and legs. I then took a minuscule amount of suds and rubbed them gently on Welby's face; then, with one hand covering his eyes, I rinsed his face with the other.

As I finished the rinsing, I went on. "Evan succeeded in art, surpassing Agnes in local contests, making her furious and taking it out on him. Her negative recommendation letter caused Evan to miss out on a top ranked college."

Russ turned so he could see me better. "So Penelope was upset because of that?"

"Yes, she had a vision of her and Evan riding off into the sunset toward that college together and both of them being amazing artists together."

"Is Penelope talented too?"

I shook my head. "Not according to Evan."

"Ah. So she was hoping for a riding on coattails sort of experience?"

I grabbed a fluffy towel and began drying Welby's fur. "Yes, that's my take on it. She acted as if her life was over because she didn't get her way. She was furious just telling me about what had happened back then. Evan was so embarrassed, he acted like he would have been anyplace else."

"Who else do you have your eye on?" asked Russ.

"Well, just yesterday, our resident ladies had their grooming appointments for their cats and told me they suspect Lorna Thompson of trying to poison people."

His eyebrows shot upward. "Poison? But what does that have to do with Agnes? I thought she was struck on the head when she died."

"She was, but the ladies are certain there's a connection. Those two are eccentric and don't always make a lot of sense, as you know, but they hear and see more than anyone else in town. I think it's worth checking out Lorna. I've always liked her, but I am keeping an open mind."

"Good plan," he said. "You never know. The person who turned out to have been the guilty one in the previous murder was a shock to me, and everyone else."

"Exactly. I was stunned when I discovered who'd done it." After I finished towel-drying Welby, I quickly checked his eyes, ears, teeth and gave a quick trim to the ends of his claws. I glanced over at Russ. "And then there's Betsy Jones."

"From the sheriff's office?"

"Yep. For some strange reason, she's adopted Agnes's cat."

"Sounds like a nice gesture to me." Russ shrugged. "Now the cat won't be homeless since her mom is gone."

"I thought so too, until I found out she's highly allergic to cats and doesn't even seem to care much about Lulu."

Russ crossed his arms over his chest. "I'd think it would be very difficult to take care of an animal you were allergic to. I mean, I'm sure there are medicines for the allergies, but still, more difficult than most. Had Betsy and Agnes had a close connection? If so, it would be news to me."

"As far as I can tell, there wasn't a connection at all, past what anyone else would have had with her."

"That's odd. But definitely something to consider."

I nodded and picked up my blow dryer. Welby closed his eyes until I turned it off. That didn't bother me, though. When I got my hair done and they pull out the hairdryer, I closed my eyes, too. "And then there's Ricky," I said.

He smirked. "Ah, yes, our ever-dependable mail delivery person."

"Yep." I snorted a laugh.

Once I'd put away the blow dryer, I began to brush Welby's fluffy, shiny fur. "Ricky said Agnes tried to get him fired by saying he wasn't doing his job right."

"Hmmm, I can say for sure I rarely get my mail on time and often get my neighbor's packages, and vice versa," said Russ.

"Unfortunately, we have the same deal in Fabulous Felines."

"Even worse when it's at your business," he said. "I'm sure you have more mail coming in than the average person in their household."

"Yes. Not to mention when someone mails in a payment. I hate getting those late, especially when it's the end of the month and I have to pay several bills myself. Even with that, I can't help but have a soft spot for Ricky. He's like a sweet pet who needs guidance and someone to take care of him."

"Yeah, he's goofy." Russ grinned. "But likable."

My hand holding the brush stopped in mid-air, earning me a side glance from Welby. "Something weird is going on with Ricky and Mr. Zaminski, my old principal, although Jillian had to remind me who he was when we, uh, saw him in the library."

"Saw, or spied on?"

I gave him a one-sided smile. "Well…"

"Go on." He motioned me with his hand.

I continued brushing the cat, careful to be extra gentle around his face, especially his eyes. "Anyway, Mr. Zaminski had changed so much I didn't recognize him. Had lost most of his hair and lost a lot of weight."

Russ nodded. "Yes, those two things can make a person look very different. And when you get to be my age, at least the hair part happens all too frequently." He patted the top of his head.

Russ had a full head of hair, but had the tiniest thin patch near his crown. He was still one of the most handsome men I knew, but I was slightly biased.

"I haven't seen Dodge for a long time," said Russ. "He and I must hang out at different places. You said you saw him at the library?"

I nodded.

"That's a place I should visit more, but don't, I'm afraid. Too busy working to read as much as I'd like."

I gave a mock scowl in defense of my friend. "If Jillian were here, she'd shake her librarian finger at you."

He smiled. "I do like that girl."

"Me too." Now that Welby was brushed, I tied a bright blue ribbon around his neck. "There," I said. "All finished."

"Thank you. Beautiful work, as always."

I shrugged. "When a cat is as handsome as your two, my job is easy." Welby's eyelids drooped. He was getting sleepy, which happened sometimes after cats had been in the warm water and were under the blow dryer. I placed him next to Percival and Jasper on a blanket to nap, then picked up Marcus, who yawned and barely opened his eyes.

"You know, Dodge and Agnes did have a past," said Russ.

My jaw dropped open. "What? You mean romantic?"

"Good grief, no. They worked together at the high school."

"Oh, right, of course. I didn't really pay much attention to Agnes since I never had her for class. So what happened in their past?" I placed Marcus beside the sink, drained out the water, wiped down the sink, then started the process over again, testing the water.

"They used to argue all the time about school rules and procedures. If you'll remember, I was on the school board for a while. But that was before you were attending there. Many times, our meetings took on more of a circus mentality than anything resembling a dignified meeting between adults."

"Why did they argue about it?" I asked.

"In a nutshell, Agnes thought she knew better how the school should be run. She wanted his job. But Dodge wasn't about to give it up without a fight. It had been his dream of a lifetime to be a school principal. His mother had told him that if he didn't get that job and keep it, he was worth nothing."

"His mother? At his age, he was still trying to please her that much?"

"From things Dodge said, it seemed he and his mother had an odd relationship," said Russ.

I scrunched my face. "You mean, odd, as in icky…"

He held up his hand. "No, nothing inappropriate. At least I never had that impression. Just that he wanted so badly for his mother to take notice of him, and approve, that he would have done nearly anything to be principal."

"Wow, so sad. But why was it so important to his mom that he become a school principal? Had she been one?"

"No, but her father and grandfather had been, and it was a family legacy, to govern the youth of their day. His mother even said if Dodge didn't get and keep the job, he would no longer be welcome in her home or life, since he let his entire family down."

"I can't even imagine that much pressure from a parent." I ran my hand down Marcus's back as I made sure the water temperature was still all right.

Russ rose from the step he'd been sitting on, stretched his arms, then placed his hands on his hips. "Believe it or not, Dodge was a former boxer, which humiliated his mother. She was proud when he went to college and became a teacher, then on to be a principal. He's an only child and had always been a momma's boy to the extent he never got married or even dated."

"A boxer? I'd think that's a pretty big divide job-wise to switch to being a school principal."

"Yes. Of course, he was a teacher, history and gym, for a few years before becoming principal."

"I guess boxing goes with gym class, so that part makes sense." I checked

Marcus's paws and tail, not finding any bumps or bare patches where he might have scratched away his fur from irritated skin. His large patches of white fur made him more susceptible to skin allergies and itchiness than his brother. "So what happened between him and Agnes to cause such a rift?"

"Agnes threatened to expose him for bribing a member of the school board to get votes for him to get the job if he didn't resign."

"Had Dodge actually done that? Bribed someone?" I asked.

"Not that I knew of. I suppose it's possible, but I never heard about it if it happened."

"Do you think the threat of Agnes accusing him of that was enough for Dodge to have done Agnes in?"

He studied me for a few seconds. "I'd say it's possible. At times, Dodge had a temper. It didn't happen often, but certain things seemed to set him off. His ability to box only made him more capable of harming someone, in my opinion."

I then filled Russ in on Ollie's odd behavior and what I'd overheard him say on the phone.

"I've never known Ollie to be anything but kind and gentle. What you heard concerns me," he said.

"I know. It was like he was someone I didn't even know. I'm hoping it was a one-time thing. I mean, anybody can get upset and yell in the right circumstances."

"Yeah, I know. I've done it."

"So have I."

He gasped. "You? My sweet niece? Say it's not so."

I gave him a mock scowl. "Since you know me so well, you also know my faults. I'm even-tempered, but can lash out if it's something or someone I care about."

"Yes, I know." He winked. "You stand up for what you're passionate about. And I love you for it."

I adored spending time with my uncle, and also seeing his cats. But in this case it was especially rewarding as I talked out my thoughts about Agnes's murder, to get Russ's invaluable input.

Chapter Ten

Since Veronica had a craving for one of the turkey clubs from The Sandwich Shack the next day, and I had a little time between appointments, I volunteered to make a food run on her behalf. I always took her food cravings seriously. More than once, I'd ignored them and was left with a hangry, spitfire of an assistant, who come to think of it, was a lot like some of our furry clients on a bad hair day.

As I stood in line to place her order, and yes, I would get one for myself as well, I watched Lorna Thompson as she rushed around, getting orders ready. It would have been better timewise if I'd shown up a half hour ago when the place wouldn't have been so busy, but Veronica's stomach clock hadn't yet gone off.

I thought about what Lottie and Florence had told me about Lorna and her being a serial, or as they put it, cereal killer. I shook my head. Where did they get some of their ideas? Did they really think Lorna force-fed her customers tainted granola?

The lady in question stepped out from a back door to the kitchen, immediately washing her hands and tying on an apron. She stood behind the counter, waving the next person in line forward.

When Lorna saw me, she leaned to the side to view me better. "Hi, Molly."

"Hi." I waved from my spot in line.

With Lorna and her assistant, Anna, working at a steady pace, it wasn't long before it was my turn to place my order. No one had come in behind me yet, so when I gave my order to Lorna, she took a deep breath and gave me a tired smile.

"Thanks for being patient," she said. She glanced around the nearly full dining area where customers sat with their delivered food and drinks. People at a couple of tables kept turning to look toward the counter. They had drinks on their table but hadn't yet received their food. Hopefully, they'd be patient a little while longer.

"No problem. You guys were swamped."

She wiped her brow with her sleeve. "Yeah, good for business, but…"

I nodded. "But hard on you at the time. Waiting on customers and trying to make them happy is hard sometimes. And tiring."

"Yes, it is. I'm sure you get that sometimes at work, too."

"You bet I do. Like when a pet parent comes in on the wrong day but insists their fur baby can't go a moment longer looking messy, even though there's not a single minute free in my day."

She spread her hands. "Then what do you do?"

I shrugged. "Try to see them, somehow. It's a crunch, but with Veronica's help, we can usually get it done. We don't want any of our clients to get upset and stop coming. That's hard on the bottom line of income coming in if we lose them. Of course, some days, it's just not possible to accommodate everyone. And then we apologize profusely and hope they'll be kind enough to return, even though it was their mistake in the first place. I couldn't do it without Veronica, that's for sure."

Lorna glanced behind her, where Anna was putting together my sandwiches. "Yes, totally agree that having a second pair of hands makes a huge difference." She peered over my shoulder. "Hey, got a couple of minutes? I'm going to take advantage of the lull in orders and rest my feet for a bit. Anna said she'd get the rest of the sandwich orders plated up for me."

"Sure," I said. "Be glad to." We took seats at a table right by the front window, one of the few places that wasn't currently occupied.

Lorna let out a long sigh, then smiled. "This feels good."

"Yes," I agreed, "it does. Standing at work all day can take a toll, right?"

"Definitely." Lorna drummed her fingers on the table, then after a quick check around us, said, "Listen, I've heard you're helping Evan Lakes clear his name in that Agnes Temple business."

Oh boy. When Sheriff King got wind of people talking about me diving into the investigation, he'd be livid. Again. "Um, yeah, I am. Evan is innocent and…"

She held up her hand. "I have no doubt about Evan. I'm so glad you're helping him out. He's a great guy."

"Yes, he is."

Her eyes darted to me, then down to her fidgety hands. Why did she suddenly look so nervous?

I leaned closer. "Lorna, was there something you wanted to ask me about Evan?"

"Actually, something I wanted to tell you."

"Okay."

"And it's not about Evan," said Lorna, "but about Agnes. See, recently, she had been making trouble for me."

I knew what I'd heard from the ladies about Lorna and their opinion of killers not changing their spots, but I wanted to hear Lorna's version. "How so?"

"A few weeks back, we were having a really busy late afternoon. It was a Friday, and the place was packed."

I nodded. Having been here on a weekend, I knew how crowded it could be. One time, Jillian and I had regretfully left to go someplace else, as it was obvious there wouldn't be seating available for a long time.

"Anyway," said Lorna, "Anna had an emergency dental appointment and wasn't back yet, so I was on my own."

"Oh no. You must have been going crazy."

"I was. And I made a mistake." She blew out a breath.

I held out my hand toward her. "Hey, it happens. I would think people would understand under the circumstances. You're only one person, after all."

"Sure, most people would. But not Agnes."

Lorna had a point. Agnes was a terror when she'd brought her cat Lulu into the shop for grooming. I'd always dreaded those days. "So what happened?"

"In my frenzy of getting everyone's orders out to them, I grabbed the wrong glass by mistake and delivered it to Agnes. It was supposed to have gone to a woman at the next table."

I shrugged. "I can't see how that would cause much trouble. But Agnes can be super picky about everything. What was it? The drink, I mean."

"A pineapple daiquiri."

"Ooooh, those are really good." I grinned. Even though I made fun of the ladies for their colorful drinks, I enjoyed them too. Just not as often. And not early in the day. And not while sitting at the end of my driveway.

"Thanks, I agree," said Lorna. "It's actually one of my signature drinks."

"But Agnes made a fuss, even though the order was a mistake? I would have been happy to take it off your hands."

Lorna gave a weak smile, but shrugged. "I wish she had only been mildly fussy. In that case, I could have calmly apologized and made the order right. Heck, I would have even given her the order for free that day. Instead, in a really loud voice, Agnes declared that I'd ruined her reputation."

I blinked. "How in the world could you have done that?"

"She said that since people had now witnessed her with an alcoholic beverage sitting in front of her, she'd be forever known as a lush."

"That's ridiculous." But then, that was Agnes, always going to the extreme in whatever situation she was in. Not caring who got hurt in the process, as long as she got what she wanted.

"I know," she said. "But you know, um, knew, Agnes. Her ideas were often over the top and downright crazy."

"Yeah, you're right. Agnes always had her own opinions about everything, and you could never change her mind." The woman was even more picky about how her cat was groomed. I knew very well how difficult she'd been to deal with. If I inadvertently brushed a few strands of Lulu's fur in the wrong direction, Agnes acted mad enough to spit nails.

"On top of her yelling at me in a crowded room of people that day, she also wrote several terrible reviews on social media about the shop." Lorna blinked hard, trying not to cry.

I patted her hand. "I'm so sorry you had to go through that. Just know that all the people who come here would never believe anything negative written about your shop."

"You think?"

"Didn't you just say it's been super busy? If that line was any indication when I walked in, you're doing great. You guys make the best sandwiches in town, bar none. Actually, I'm here because Veronica wanted sandwiches from your shop and no place else."

Her lips rose on one side in a half-smile. "Thank you. I needed to hear that."

"You're welcome. It's all true."

She sighed. "That Agnes…I really wish she hadn't done what she did. Didn't she know she might have put me out of business by telling people bad things and posting negative reviews about The Sandwich Shack?"

"Well, for better or worse, Agnes won't be able to cause you any more trouble from now on, right?"

Lorna narrowed her eyes. "You've got that right. She definitely got what she deserved."

I jerked, unused to hearing Lorna talk that way about somebody. I sided with her, of course, that Agnes could have caused quite a bit of damage with what she said. But even though I'd never cared for Agnes, I wouldn't say getting bludgeoned to death with a heavy bottle of photography fixer was deserved.

Lorna turned at the call of her name. "Oh," she said, "Your order is up. Let me go get it for you."

"Uh, great, thanks." I grabbed my purse and stood, ready to pay for my order and head back to Fabulous Felines. By now, Veronica might have edged past being hangry to severely desperately starving. If I didn't want her to screech like a startled cat, I'd better hustle.

A shuffling noise came from my left. I turned to see Ernie standing in line. He waved.

Since Lorna and I had been talking, a few more people had entered the café. Anna was at the counter taking orders and giving Lorna a frantic look, which meant she needed help, and needed it right now.

I waved back to Ernie.

"Hey," he said, "I didn't mean to intrude, but I heard your conversation with Lorna."

"Oh?" Maybe she and I should have gone to a different room where others weren't around. I'd thought it was noisy enough with all the people that we wouldn't be noticed. Guess I was wrong. I hadn't even realized Ernie had come in. How long had he been standing there?

He made a face. "Sorry, I don't want you to think I go around eavesdropping." He pointed toward the counter. "Since I was standing in line so close to where you were seated, I couldn't help but catch the end of it."

I smiled. "That's okay. I understand the need to wait in line for those delicious sandwiches. Totally worth it."

"You've got that right." He huffed out a breath. "Although with my tiny salary, I probably shouldn't be spending my funds on takeout food. It would be smarter to buy something cheap from the grocery, but I can't seem to resist the stuff they make here."

"A treat every now and then is always good."

He laughed. "I like the way you think. Besides, never mind what that awful Agnes Temple said to Lorna about the mixed-up order that day. As much as I love their food, I'd never stop coming in here. Even if someone was spreading bad things about them. I figure some folks have too much time on their hands and just want to cause trouble."

He'd been a little brusque when he'd found me with the cats sitting on the floor at the garage, but seemed in a better mood now. Maybe he, like me and Veronica, was happier when well fed. I inwardly smirked. Gee, sounded like a few cats I knew, too, who were more worried about their tummies than anything else.

Ernie glanced over his shoulder when Anna said his name and waved him forward. "Good, it's my turn." He stepped up to the counter and gave his order.

Lorna hurried out from the kitchen, holding a white sack with the restaurant logo on the side. Even though the bag was closed, I could smell the tantalizing aroma coming from within.

"Here you go," she said.

"Thanks. Looking forward to the wonderfulness contained in this bag."

"No, thank you. For listening." She smiled.

"Happy to do it. Oh, and you can stop worrying about any bad press from what happened with Agnes."

She tilted her head. "I like the sound of it, but why do you say that?"

"For at least one person, Ernie," I said, pointing to him as he still stood at the counter finishing his order with Anna. "He just gave you and your establishment a huge compliment."

"Really? That's great!" She clasped her hands together in front of her waist.

"Yes, and maybe he'll spread the good word about your restaurant." I held up the bag. "I know I will."

As I left the restaurant, I wondered about Lorna. I liked her and didn't think she was a poisoner. I eyed the bag, a momentary qualm coming over me at the thought of the food inside. No, I didn't think she'd done anything to poison our order. But the ladies seemed adamant there was something to be concerned about. Of course, their information wasn't always correct. Especially if I caught them during happy hour.

But was there something to Agnes's claim that she thought Lorna had tried to ruin her reputation by setting an alcoholic beverage on her table? Maybe Agnes had been afraid it would make becoming a school principal harder if people saw her as having an issue with drinking. Then, she said terrible things about Lorna, trying to destroy her reputation in return. Would that be enough for Lorna to have snuck into Evan's shop and killed Agnes? It didn't quite add up, but I'd hold onto the information for later. It did still bother me a little when Lorna had said Agnes had gotten what she'd deserved. Her expression had been downright venomous when she'd mentioned it.

For now, I needed to hustle Veronica's sandwich back to the shop. If I knew her, she'd be waiting by the door, with her hand out, waiting for me.

Chapter Eleven

I needed to see Hank at his vet's office. Okay, I just wanted to, but needed made me sound not quite so…needy. He never seemed to mind me stopping in. I guess that was good since we were officially, kind of, sort of dating. The way it came about was a little unorthodox, but it worked.

Hank and I had been on a stakeout a while back when checking out a suspect I had for a recent murder in Whitewater Valley. When the suspect—a guy I learned had wanted to ask me out himself—happened to leave his house, walk down the sidewalk, and discover us hiding in a car nearby, I couldn't very well tell him the real reason. Hank saved the day by announcing we were in the car together because we were on a date.

It wasn't the most romantic of ways to ask a girl out, but I wasn't picky. Especially since Hank had been the guy I'd had my eye on for a while anyway.

Either way, I was glad to be able to see him today. As I pulled into his parking area, an older car I recognized as the one Ollie drove around when he wasn't working, was pulling out onto the street. Why would he have been at the vet's office? I'd never heard him mention a pet, especially not a cat.

Considering what I did for a living and how many years I'd been taking my van to his garage I would have thought he'd mentioned having a fur baby. It might be good to find out what he was up to. But even if Hank was busy when I went inside, there was a person I could ask about Ollie, who'd give me the scoop on my questions.

Andrea Evers.

She was Hank's receptionist. A really nice woman who loved to gossip. Not that I thought gossip was a virtue; far from it. I felt bad when I did it too. However, when trying to discover the identity of any and all murder suspects, getting information on them, no matter the source, sure did come in handy.

I stepped inside. Andrea was on the phone, but smiled and waved me closer. As I waited, I glanced at the wall, browsing through the dog, cat, and rabbit pictures Hank had in his waiting area. I liked how he had his chairs arranged, in small groupings as opposed to a circle of chairs pushed up next to the walls, along with the amazing photos of the animals. Had Evan been the photographer? It gave the effect of being friendly and quaint.

Andrea set aside her phone and smiled. "Hey Molly, how are you?"

I stepped closer. "I'm good. You guys busy today?"

She laughed. "Always. But you know Hank doesn't mind when you drop by."

Even though I'd just had the same thought, hearing it from someone else caused my face to heat. "Oh, um, thanks." To get the focus off of what I assumed to be my now reddened face, I pointed behind me. "Was that Ollie Smith who just left?"

"Yep." She pushed her keyboard out of the way so she could lean closer to the reception window.

"Oh, I didn't realize he was a pet owner. I don't remember him ever mentioning it."

She nodded. "He brings in his collie, Hoover, for his checkups. Just came in for some medicine this time. He has arthritis. Hoover, not Ollie. Although with Ollie working with his hands all day on vehicles, maybe he does too?"

Wanting to steer the conversation to different matters concerning Ollie than why he'd visited here and his possible ailments, I said, "I actually saw him recently in his repair shop. Have you noticed him acting a little differently lately?"

Andrea frowned. "What do you mean?"

I wasn't going to go into what he'd actually said on the phone, or how he'd actually yelled at somebody on the other end of the line. Instead, I said, "Well, when I was in there, he seemed….irritable."

Andrea's eyebrows rose. "He did?"

"Yes, he was very upset when talking to another person. Not so much me, but I got a vibe from him that things weren't going his way."

"You know, now that you mention it, he did seem a little standoffish. Which isn't his normal way when he's here. Usually, he's friendly. Always ready to chat. Not today."

I frowned. If Ollie hadn't spoken as much to her as usual, would she feel slighted in some way? Yes, Andrea would notice if a client wasn't chatty, since she spent lots of time doing that herself. "As you might have heard from Hank, I've been helping out Evan Lakes," I said.

Her eyes widened. "Oh, you mean because he's a suspect in Agnes's murder?"

"That's right." Even though Andrea would tell everyone who came in about Evan, it wasn't a secret. By now, people would have spread the word, thanks to Sheriff King using his sirens and practically shouting about the dead body from the rooftops.

"Yes. He told me," she said. "I think it's awesome what you're doing."

"You do?" Maybe she could have a talk with the sheriff, and convince him how awesome I was being. No, maybe not.

"Sure, helping out a friend." She pointed at me. "You've done that for me before, and I appreciated it."

Although Andrea's situation had been different, and I'd only listened to her when she'd been upset about a family situation, it was nice to hear, nonetheless. "I was glad to do it, Andrea." I smiled. It had been during that conversation that I'd gotten to know her better and considered her a friend from then on.

She glanced behind me. Was she making sure we were alone? "Listen, since we're talking about Agnes, what's the latest you've heard? That is, if you don't mind me asking."

"I don't mind at all." Actually, I'd been hoping for that very thing. Maybe if I started the conversation, Andrea would have heard something and could add to it as well. "Some of the latest news actually has to do with Ollie. After overhearing his conversation and the weird way he was acting, I decided to keep an eye on him." I fiddled with my purse strap, as if I wasn't particularly interested, then said, "What do you know about Ollie? Anything about his background that might help me out?" I wanted to know, but didn't want to appear too nosy. No need for her to spread that attribute of mine around to everyone else she talked to.

Andrea sat up straighter in her chair, obviously pleased at having been asked. "Sometimes Ollie talks on his phone when he's in the waiting area to different people, about various subjects. He doesn't seem to notice me here. Maybe because there's a partial glass division between me and the clients, and they think I can't hear?" She shrugged. "I mean one time a lady left a message on her husband's phone that her pregnancy test was positive. So I knew before he did that he was going to be a dad!" She chuckled. "Anyway, I don't actively listen. I mean, that would be rude."

I nodded, knowing good and well her listening was intentional. But how could I judge when I'd crouched down outside Ollie's service window to hear him on the phone?

"What I've heard about Ollie was that Agnes was dating Ollie's uncle before she died," said Andrea.

"Wow, really?" Now, there was a new twist. That might explain the connection between them that I couldn't figure out before now.

She rolled her eyes. "Yeah, I know. Old people dating. Who knew? Anyway, Agnes didn't like Ollie and tried to get in between him and his uncle. Told the uncle that it was her or his weird family and that he needed to choose. That he should keep Ollie out of his will."

I crossed my arms over my chest. "That seems harsh. Do you know if Ollie and his uncle are close?"

"Not sure. But either way, Ollie was very upset."

"I can imagine." Having to choose between people you cared about would be one of the worst things to go through.

"See," she said. "Agnes felt that Ollie was substandard because he ran an auto repair shop."

"That's crazy. What's wrong with doing an honest day's work? Where would we be without someone with his knowledge to help take care of our vehicles?"

"Oh, I agree. But apparently, Ollie's business is in danger of going bankrupt due to his gambling habit."

I blinked. "Gambling?" I thought about Ernie's comments about hardly being paid anything at his job at Ollie's garage. If Ollie was gambling, had he lost too much money and couldn't even afford to keep his employee?

A door opened from the back area, followed by footsteps. Hank walked around the reception area. "Hey, Molly." He gave me a quick one-armed hug, which, of course, made my face hot again. It was only one-armed because his other arm was currently occupied with a squirmy puppy.

Before I had a chance to answer Hank, the door opened, and a woman entered. "There's my Honey Bunch!" she shouted.

The puppy, as well as me, Andrea, and Hank all jumped. I assumed Honey Bunch was the dog. Otherwise, it appeared I might have competition for Hank's affection from the puppy's pet parent. I eyed her. The lady was little. And skinny. I could probably win in a fight. I snorted out a laugh at the mental image of us squaring off for Hank as the prize while he and Andrea cheered for me from the sidelines.

"Molly?" said Hank from beside me.

I startled and turned to see both Hank and Andrea watching . No they weren't cheering for me, their expressions looked more like they thought I might be nuts. Truth be told, there were days I thought that about myself too.

I laughed nervously. "Um, never mind. Had a brain disconnect there for a second."

Andrea's eyebrows rose as Hank gave a slow grin. He was getting to know me well enough to assume it was a result of my weird imagination. Thankfully, he didn't comment on it in front of Andrea, but that wouldn't stop him from saying something later, just to tease me.

The puppy's mom hurried toward us, grabbed the dog, and held it close to her chest. "Oh, Honey Bunch. Are you all right?"

Mystery solved about the name. Although, I'd been reasonably sure I wouldn't really have to fight the lady for Hank's attention. Even though my thoughts had taken a wrong turn and had us in a wrestling match.

Hank reached out and ruffled the fur between the puppy's ears. "He's fine. Didn't find anything except the usual puppy squirminess."

The woman let out a long sigh. "I'm so relieved. When I couldn't locate my house key, I was positive he'd swallowed it. I'd checked every place in the house I could think of and panicked when it was still missing. Thank you so much for checking him out and for seeing us right away."

"No problem. You were right to bring him in. Puppies do tend to eat anything they can get their teeth on. Rubber bands. Bottle caps. The occasional handle of a toothbrush. Of course, if they'd use it like they're supposed to, their teeth would be spotless." Hank grinned.

I rolled my eyes at his weird humor, but laughed.

The puppy's mom tilted her head and stared at Hank, seeming not to have understood that he was kidding. She shrugged her shoulders. "Well, now that he's ready to go home, I'll pay his bill. Let me get my wallet." She opened her handbag and peered into its deep abyss.

Why did some women carry the equivalent of a suitcase for daily errands? I studied the purse, guessing it to weigh at least eight pounds. It was large enough, she could even cart around Honey Bunch in there if she wanted to. And if my guess was right, she probably did.

"Oh no..." said the puppy's mom, as she continued to dig in her bag.

"Mrs. Downing," said Andrea, "is something wrong? Did you forget your wallet?" Andrea stepped around the reception area to stand beside her.

Hank smiled. "If you can't pay today, it's all right. We can bill you. We know where you live."

"It's not that," said the woman. "I just..." She reached into her bag nearly up to her elbow, and came out holding a tarnished key.

Hank bit his lip. Was he trying not to laugh? "I assume that's the missing house key?"

"Yes. I'm afraid so." She closed her eyes briefly and shook her head. "Oh, well, it will teach me to do a better check for items before panicking and hauling poor Honey Bunch in here to see you."

Hank waved his hand. "No harm done. I always enjoy seeing baby animals coming in for a visit."

She checked in the enclosure again. "I think I spotted my wallet near the bottom."

It must have been down deep in the depths of her faux leather suitcase. We waited as she practically dove in to retrieve what she needed.

Mrs. Downing took out her wallet, handed her credit card to Andrea, and they both returned to the reception desk.

Hank tilted his head toward a grouping of chairs, and we claimed a couple of them. We sat side by side with our backs to the picture window.

I pointed to Mrs. Downing, who was juggling her puppy in one hand and reaching out for her sales receipt with the other. "Just another ho-hum day in your practice, right?" I asked Hank.

He grinned. "Yep. At least today has been absent of anyone taking a nip at my fingers. Well, so far, at least. The day's not over. So, what are you up to today? No cats to groom?"

"I have some, but not until a little later." I glanced at Mrs. Downing, who was still yakking away at Andrea. "I came in to tell you the latest on helping Evan."

He angled around in his seat to view me better. "Okay, anything interesting?"

I filled him in on Lorna's trouble with delivering the wrong drink to Agnes, her reaction to it, and also about Florence and Lottie's serial, or cereal, killer theory.

"Sounds like Lorna might have had a motive to do in Agnes," he said.

"Even with the ladies and their wild theories about granola and frosty flakes, I can't totally discount their suspicions about Lorna. Also, when I got here, I had a chance to talk to Andrea for a bit."

"Did she talk your ear off?" He grinned. "You know how much I like her, but some days, I wish I could wear earplugs when we're here together."

Even though Andrea normally had done just that, I had to give credit where credit was due. "When she and I talked, it wasn't as bad as she's getting from the puppy's mom right now." I pointed toward Andrea's desk.

Mrs. Downing shifted the now sleeping Honey Bunch over her shoulder as she continued to talk. She was speaking so loudly, I knew neither one of them would overhear us.

"What did Andrea tell you?" asked Hank.

"We talked about Ollie. She gave me a fascinating view into his connection with Agnes."

He shook his head. "I didn't realize there was one."

I moved to the side until I was partially facing him. That meant our knees were touching, but I wasn't bothered by that. And watching Hank's slow smile, it wasn't bothering him either. "I hadn't known about a connection between them either. But according to Andrea, Ollie's uncle and Agnes were an item. That is, before Agnes...well, you know."

"Very interesting," he said. "You'd think in a town this small, somebody would have known about that, and we'd have heard. Maybe they wanted to keep their relationship a secret. So what happened between them?"

"Agnes was trying to convince Ollie's uncle to cut ties with him. She didn't think Ollie's profession was noble enough."

"That's cold. How would we all get along if we didn't have Ollie and people like him to do what we can't do for ourselves?"

I patted his arm. "Yes, pretty much what I said. But the really interesting part is, Ollie apparently has a gambling problem."

Hank's eyes widened. "That's news to me."

"Me too. Ernie made a comment to me recently that Ollie barely has money to pay him. I'm not sure about the whole story with Ollie, but something tells me he's worth keeping an eye on."

Hank nodded. "Now, something he said a bit ago makes more sense."

"What's that?"

"When Ollie picked up his dog and had the medicine for him in his hand, then he told me he couldn't pay me."

"He couldn't pay for what?" I asked. "Checking out the dog? Or the medicine."

"Either."

"Wow. I had that happen to me a couple of times over the years when a pet parent had forgotten their wallet or needed a couple of extra days until payday to take care of their bill, but I always knew before their appointment that it was the case, and I'd approved them coming in anyway. But to allow you to do the work and then hand him the dog's medicine before saying anything, that seems underhanded."

"I was really surprised," said Hank. "I would have done the exam and all anyway and, like you, given him a little longer to pay me, but it seemed odd that he purposefully waited until he was ready to leave to announce it."

"Now, from what Andrea told me about a possible gambling problem, maybe that makes more sense."

"Yeah, it definitely does."

Chapter Twelve

I groaned when the shop door opened. Ricky entered the room and stalked straight to the counter. I was in between appointments but was expecting my next one any time. I never knew how long Ricky might loiter or what he might say.

He dropped his bag on the floor with a thud. "I guess I should tell you part two."

I lowered my eyebrows. What was he going on about this time? "Part two? Of what?"

He shrugged. "Of my story, of course."

"I'm not sure what—"

He held up his hand. "Agnes Temple."

"Oh. I thought you already told us your thoughts on the subject." At least, I'd hoped at the time that he was finished regaling us with his latest tale.

"That's why it's part two. Pay attention please." He snapped his fingers in front of me as if to wake me up.

My eyes widened. Veronica slipped up beside me from her grooming room. If he had snapped his fingers at her like that she might have growled at him. She glanced at me, then Ricky. "What's going on?" she asked.

I pointed at him. "Ricky, here, wants to tell us part two."

She eyed me. "Part two of…"

"Don't ask." I grabbed her arm. "Please."

Ricky grinned. "You ladies crack me up. Acting like you aren't on pins and a pincushion, wanting to know what I have to say. But I know better." He tapped his temple with his forefinger.

Veronica and I exchanged wide-eyed expressions, then both sighed. Aside from bodily tossing the man out onto the sidewalk and locking the shop door, there was no way around listening to him. The best thing was to let him get it out of his system so we could move on with the rest of our day.

"Okay," I said, trying, but failing to hold in a groan. "Tell us part two."

"Well, it's like this. See, I couldn't stand Agnes Temple."

Veronica waved her hand at Ricky to stop him. From next to her, I could practically feel her impatience seeping out. "I think maybe you made that clear in part one, so—"

"Hey, who's telling the story?" asked Ricky. "I believe that would be me." He flipped his ponytail over his shoulder.

"Uh, sure, sorry," said Veronica. She knew as well as I did that if Ricky was pushed too far, he might cry. Unfortunately, we'd been here to witness that very thing. And no, it wasn't something I wanted to ever see again.

"That's better." He gave a sharp nod. "Anyway, You know how I normally like everyone." He stared at us until we nodded in agreement. "So it's sort of unusual that I would have such negative feelings about a person."

I stole a glance at the clock on the wall behind Ricky. He needed to get whatever momentous words he had to say, out, and soon. My client, Melody Horn, was not known for her patience. And neither was her cat, Prissy. They were way worse than Veronica, and that was saying something.

Wanting to hear what Ricky had to say about Agnes, but also to hurry him along, I said, "Why was it so different with Agnes? Your negative feelings, I mean."

"Well, for one, my hair." He reached back and grabbed his ponytail, flopping it at us as if it were waving hello.

Veronica waved back.

"What are you doing?" I asked her.

"I thought… It seemed like it wanted to be friends."

"Yeah, I know." I shrugged. I couldn't really blame her on that one. Ricky was so attached to his ponytail, it wouldn't surprise me if he'd given it a name. "Go on, Ricky."

He pouted. "That woman, Agnes Temple, hated my hair."

"What do you mean, hated it?" I asked. "I mean, it's your hair, after all."

Veronica nodded. "Right. Even if you wore it in a beehive, she'd have no right to say anything."

Ricky's mouth dropped open. "A beehive? What do you think I am, some sort of fashionista?"

Biting my lip against a laugh, I shook my head. "Um, no, of course you're not. She only meant that you have a right to wear your hair any way you'd like."

He looked at Veronica who, to her credit, didn't crack a smile or laugh, only gave Ricky a solemn nod.

"Well, okay," he said. "So anyway, every time she saw me, she made a rude comment."

"Oh gosh," I said, trying to smooth things over with him. "That's not nice. A person should be able to wear their hair however they like."

"Thank you!" His voice came out so loud, Percival, who'd been asleep on a nearby shelf, let out a startled meow. Ricky didn't seem to notice, and plunged ahead. "I mean I could have retaliated all those times and said something about that silver helmet of plastered hair she always wore. But did I? *Did I?*"

"I'm guessing not," I said.

"That's correct." He patted his hair, as if it was a treasured friend. What did I know, maybe it was?

Another glance at the clock showed four minutes until my client was due. I wanted to make the *hurry up* gesture with my hand, but that would only annoy Ricky and he'd talk even longer.

He patted his chest. "Agnes tore a tiny piece of my existence away every time she ridiculed my hair. My poor heart just couldn't take much more."

I reached out and touched his hand. "I'm really sorry, Ricky, I—"

"Oh, but there's more!" His eyes flashed, and he placed his hands on his hips, as if ready to do battle.

"Okay," I said, drawing back my hand. In his current mood, it might be in my best interest to keep my appendages close beside me.

"The really terrible, truly awful part was about Hildegard." Ricky's chin dropped to his chest.

I tried to remember meeting someone by that name. Or had it been a pet? I wasn't coming up with anything. "I'm sorry, I don't remember…"

"And why would you?" Ricky pointed at me. "Agnes squelched any chance of me ever finding true happiness with Hildegard. The flame of my love was snuffed out before it could ignite."

At this point, I desperately hoped Hildegard was not a pet. Or his ponytail. Not wanting to ask, but knowing it was the timely thing to do, I said, "So what happened?"

As soon as the words were out of my mouth, the sharp point of Veronica's elbow connected with my ribs. I gasped, mouthed, "Sorry" to her, then waited for Ricky to continue.

He slumped against the counter, as if he might expire any second. "It was like this. The only girl I ever loved was chased away from my life by none other than Agnes. She told Hildegard that I had a hideous contagious disease. But I don't. Have a disease, I mean."

As much as I longed for Ricky to finish his tale, my heart went out to him. "That's terrible how you were treated. I'm so sorry."

Ricky tilted his head. "Why are you sorry? You weren't there."

"Well, I…" I glanced at Veronica, hoping for assistance.

"Ricky," she said, "it's just something people say when they feel bad for another person."

He frowned. "That doesn't make much sense. None, actually."

This wasn't getting us very far, and the clock was still ticking. "Okay, so…" This time, I did do the *hurry-up* hand motion.

Ricky's eyebrows drew together. "Molly, you certainly are an impatient soul, aren't you?"

With a sigh, I admitted, "Uh, yeah. Sometimes. But I have this client coming in and—"

The door opened and there they were. Melody, already frowning, and Prissy sitting on her fluffy pillow that her mom carried her everywhere on.

Ricky turned and bobbed his head to them. "Hello. Molly and Veronica will be with you momentarily. They're speaking to me at the moment. So you'll just need to wait your turn." He faced us again. "Now, where was I?"

Veronica's eyes widened, and her fingers clenched together in a knot. I knew that look. Veronica, my organized, keep everything on schedule friend, wanted to physically toss Ricky from the shop. But that wouldn't solve anything. Melody already appeared irritated, and Prissy let out a hiss. I shook my head. We might as well let Ricky finish, but that wouldn't stop me from trying to move things along, even if it made him even more upset.

"Ricky," I said, "I really do want to hear the rest of part two. But I do have someone waiting,"—I waved to Melody, who grumbled something not very nice—"So maybe you could tell us the short version?"

Ricky's sigh was so long and so loud, Percival snapped awake again, this time hopping down from the shelf and jumping on the counter. The cat's eyes were only half open when he faced Ricky, who chuckled. "See," said Ricky, "even your cat wants to hear the end."

When Veronica's fingernails began a furious tapping beat on the counter, I covered her hand with mine. "Go ahead, Ricky," I said, "I have a couple more minutes to listen to your story."

The harrumph from Melody reverberated around the room, but I acted as if I hadn't heard it. I knew from prior appointments that once she was miffed, nothing would change it.

"Well, back to Hildegard," Ricky continued. "She was a distant cousin of Agnes. And of course, a lot younger."

I was sure I'd never met Hildegard. I mean, how would I forget a moniker like that? Although it would be a pretty name for a cat.

Ricky crossed his arms over his chest. "So, Hilly, that's what I called her, Hilly and I were getting to be friends."

Veronica held up her hand. "Just for clarification, did uh, Hilly, live here in Whitewater Valley?"

"Oh no. I met her in Center Grove."

I frowned. "I thought you'd always lived here, Ricky."

"Yup." He placed his hands on his hips. "Born and bred."

"Then how—"

"If you'd let me finish, Molly, I'll tell you. Boy, you sure do want a lot of information for somebody who only has a 'couple minutes.'"

I gave a sideways glance to Veronica in a silent plea to join me in not opening our mouths again until Ricky had completed his spiel. We waited, silent partners in an attempt to hurry our postman along. All those poor customers of his would be waiting longer than usual for their mail today. Hopefully no one was counting on anything life altering. Like a paycheck. Or heart medication.

Ricky ran his hand down his ponytail, spinning it around his finger. "Uh, where was I?"

Another harrumph came from Melody, who had taken Prissy, still on her pillow, and was now sitting in one of my chairs by the window. I'd give her a half off deal today for having to wait. But I was sure she'd still be mad.

"Oh!" said Ricky. "Right. I told you I met Hilly in Center Grove."

Veronica and I bobbed our heads.

"That was at camp."

"Camp?" I blurted out. So much for keeping quiet.

"Yup," he said. "Summer camp."

"Um, were you a counselor or something?" I asked. Although, I couldn't imagine Ricky being organized enough to be in charge of anybody. The way he got people's mail mixed up, I could imagine him misplacing some of the kids he was in charge of. Poor things would either end up in a lake or hanging from a flagpole.

Ricky shook his head. "Nope. I was a camper. Old Wala-Wala camp. Such a great place for a young lad."

Veronica pressed both hands on the counter and leaned forward. "You mean to tell me that this Hildegard person, the love of your life, was someone you met as a kid?"

"That's right. She was a beauty. I wish you could have seen how lovely she was. As a matter of fact, her ponytail was even longer than mine!"

I could tell Veronica was at the end of her rope when she said, between clenched teeth, "Had you been in touch with her all these years?"

"No."

"So you met at camp, and Agnes put the kibosh to your…um, relationship when you were, what sixteen?"

"Ten."

"Ten?" Veronica's eyes bugged out.

I grabbed her arm to stop her tirade. "Ricky," I said, "I guess I can see what happened. You liked this girl, and Agnes stopped it from going any further and—"

"And broke my heart. I never recovered from the loss. Never found another girl to love. Then as an adult, Agnes wouldn't let up making fun of me, always making my life harder. Threatening to get me fired. How much is a guy supposed to take? I'm so glad she's finally dead!"

His last word hung in the air. Veronica, Melody, and I all stared at him, open mouthed. Prissy, from her pillow was wide eyed. Percival, who'd had his back to Ricky and had been washing his paw, Percival's, not Ricky's, whipped around and growled.

Ricky hadn't seemed to notice the rest of our reactions, but when Percival made his feelings known, Ricky's head jerked. "Gee, guess a fella can't voice his opinions without being judged unfairly. Even by a feline."

He bent down, reached into his mailbag, then deposited a stack of envelopes on the counter. "Here's your mail. Guess I better be moving on. It's a sad, sad day when a guy can't tell his woes to people who are supposedly good listeners." He slung the bag over his shoulder and trudged from the shop.

The minute the door closed behind him, I rushed over to Melody. "I'm so sorry you had to wait. Let me offer you a half-price deal for today's visit."

Melody, still frowning, looked down at her cat, who still sat curled up on her pillow. The cat, yawned, then gave a slow blink.

"Fine," said Melody. "I would have said no, that it wasn't good enough, but Prissy has given her permission to continue. I guess it's your lucky day, Molly."

Forcing a smile, I said, "Yes, so very, very lucky."

As I led the two miffed females to my grooming area, I gave Veronica an eye-roll on my way past. Ricky might have loads of sad tales to give us, but I still wondered if he could have possibly killed Agnes. He seemed awfully gleeful that she was no longer breathing. Putting aside his hair issues and her comments about it, a lost love, and the threat of losing his livelihood might just be a motive worth considering.

Chapter Thirteen

I was suffering from a common ailment the following morning, severe caffeine deprivation, and headed to Carrie's Coffee before my first client arrived. It was early, but already, most of the tables were filled. Florence and Lottie were sitting in their favorite seats, Helga and Eleanor lapping something white, cream, or milk, from dainty blue and white ceramic bowls. Did the ladies bring the bowls themselves, or was Carrie kind enough to keep them on hand?

I waved to the ladies, who giggled and waved back. When Lottie picked up her cat's paw for a wave, Florence frowned and did the same with hers. Those two ladies were so competitive. But they were indeed fun. And kept in the loop with whatever happened around town, so always good news for me.

There was only one person in line ahead of me. With his back turned, I couldn't identify him. But as he briefly glanced to his left, toward the front window, I saw it was Dodge Zaminski.

It had taken Jillian to point out who he was, but now that I knew, I remembered his large build, square jaw, and heavy eyebrows. He was wearing dress slacks and a shirt, but no suit jacket. Maybe that was part of why I didn't recognize him today or in the library. He'd always worn one while at the school. And of course, he'd been much younger then.

Besides, I always tried to steer clear of anyone at the school who was in charge of student discipline. Not that I was a bad kid or anything, but I'd figured better safe than sorry, in case I caused some sort of infraction without meaning to. So I hadn't spent a lot of time looking at our principal's appearance.

I checked my watch, hoping I could get my caffeine fix soon. There was still plenty of time before seeing my client and her human, back at my shop. Besides, the kitty might not want me giving her a bath if my caffeine deprived mind wasn't fully on my task. A wet cat was okay. A mad wet cat? Nobody wanted that. Especially the cat.

Dodge tapped his knuckle on the counter like he was impatient. I felt bad for Carrie. What a way to start the day, with a possible complainer.

Carrie stepped to the other side of the order counter and smiled. "Hi, sorry your latte took so long. We were having a little problem with our latte machine. But it's fixed now. Here you go." She placed the cup on the counter in front of him, but he didn't pick it up or speak.

Her smile fell. I couldn't see Dodge's expression. What was he doing? Then I noticed that the back of his neck had reddened, as well as the tops of his ears.

Taking a tiny step back, Carrie said, "Is there a problem, sir?"

"I have something to say to you, young lady." His words came out harsh, almost gravelly. Had he been the voice on the threatening phone call I got the other day? But why would he threaten me, Evan, and our pets?

"Okay. Um, was there a problem with your order?" said Carrie.

He held out his hands to his sides. "How could I possibly know that? I haven't even tried it yet."

Carrie's cheeks turned pink. "All right, well, how can I help—"

"I'm afraid I'll need you to apologize."

"Oh, I thought I had. Well, I'm very sorry you had to wait on your latte today."

"No, not for that," he said.

She shook her head in confusion. "Excuse me. I'm not sure why…"

"You tried to ruin my livelihood." With every word, he knocked his knuckle against the counter for emphasis.

With her lowered eyebrows and tilted head, Carrie looked puzzled, like she wasn't sure if she'd met him before or not. "Listen, Mr.…."

"You know perfectly well who I am."

"No, I really don't." She glanced back toward me, then said to him, "Perhaps we could discuss whatever it is that seems to be the problem someplace more private."

"No. We'll talk here. And now. Your customers need to hear what sort of person they're dealing with."

I jerked. What was going on with my old principal? And if that was the way he treated someone he was unhappy with, I was super glad I'd kept out of his way during school.

Carrie eyed the customers, and her face went pale. When I checked, every last person had stopped what they were doing and were staring at the altercation. Even the cats, Eleanor and Helga, had turned, their ears standing straight up, as if to catch every word.

Poor Carrie. What a nightmare for a business owner. To not only get berated by a customer, but to have him do it loudly and for the benefit of a crowded room.

"You lived next door to that witch," said Dodge.

She shook her head. "I don't know who you're talking about."

"Agnes Temple, that's who."

Carrie's eyes opened wide. "Oh, yes, I live, um, lived next door to Agnes." She studied him, then, something seemed to dawn on her as she said, "Oh, you're…"

"That's right. Dodge Zaminski. And you stood up for Agnes, when she tried to take my job as principal away from me."

Carrie crossed her arms over her chest. "I lived next door to Agnes for years. We became friends. She begged me to support her, and I did."

"Do you know how much trouble you caused me?"

Nobody in the dining area had taken a drink or said anything. They all stayed motionless. Were they afraid if they moved or made a sound, they'd miss an important word or action?

"But you kept your job," Carrie pointed out. "The fact that I was on Agnes's side did nothing negative to you. You ended up getting what you wanted in the end, Mr. Zaminski."

"Only because Agnes was murdered!"

A collective gasp sounded from around the room. Carrie's hand shook. "Listen, Mr. Zaminski, if it's an apology you want, then I'll say it, I'm sorry you were caused distress. I never intended to hurt you. And that I didn't recognize you when you came in." She glanced down at the cup still positioned between them. "Could I offer you your order for free today?"

He held up his hand. "I wouldn't accept that from you for anything in the world. If I'd known you were the one who owned this shop, I would have avoided it like that plague, which your customers might just contract if they drink your coffee. Just stay out of my business."

Dodge turned so fast, he nearly smacked into me, but he moved aside then rushed out the door, followed by everyone's gaze.

I hurried to the counter. "Carrie, are you all right?"

Her eyes were wide, unblinking. Then she gave herself a shake. "Wow, that was…"

"Harsh, yeah. Can I do anything for you?"

With a glance behind me, she nodded. "It looks like there's no one waiting behind you, and I don't see anybody holding up cups for refills. Would you sit with me for a minute?"

"Of course." I pointed to the cup Dodge had abandoned. "How about I take that one off your hands for you."

She sighed. "Sure. Thank you."

I dug inside my purse.

"No charge, Molly."

I shook my head and, after long practice, handed her the cost of the drink and a tip. "I insist."

She smiled. "Thank you." She stepped out from behind the counter and joined me in the main room. "How about there?"

We walked a few feet from the counter to a small table tucked in an alcove close to the front entrance.

"Perfect," I said. I placed my coffee and purse on the table, then sat down. Carrie slumped onto the seat, letting out a breath.

I started to open the coffee, then stopped. "Would you like some of this?"

She chuckled. "No thanks. I like coffee, but with as much as I'm around it,

I don't crave it like I used to."

"Understood."

"Please, you go ahead, though." Carrie waved her hand toward my cup.

"Okay." I took a drink and sighed. "Perfection."

She crossed her arms on the top of the table. "I'm glad someone is pleased with what I do here."

"Oh, Carrie, everyone loves you."

"Not that guy," She pointed her thumb toward the door.

"He wasn't upset about what you do or even about you. It was because of Agnes."

"I know that. It just stung what he said and that he did so in front of my regular customers."

I nodded. "I get it. I've gotten berated by customers before, too."

"That's hard to imagine. You're so nice and good to everyone."

"Thank you. And so are you. But you have to understand, cat owners are sometimes like their cats. Moody. Unpredictable. And sometimes they like to hiss."

Carrie gave a snort, then covered her mouth briefly. "Thanks for that. It helps to laugh."

"Glad to be of service." I winked, then took another drink. "Honestly, this is the best latte."

"Molly, I'm sorry you had to witness Dodge's tirade today, but I sure am glad you were here."

"I'm glad I was here too. Would it help to talk about it?" I placed the cup down, then prepared to listen to what she might say.

"Yeah, I think it might." Carrie brushed her bangs away from her eyes and settled back against her seat. "What happened, the thing Dodge was talking about, went like this. Agnes came to me and asked, actually begged me to give her support. She said she wanted to be principal of the high school more than anything."

With a quick glance at my watch, I saw I still had a little time before I needed to head to Fabulous Felines. I was glad, though, that Carrie had been checking over her shoulder to look at the counter, so she wouldn't think I was trying to ditch her.

Carrie angled back around. "I saw no reason why Agnes shouldn't be, and she'd always been a decent neighbor, so I agreed."

"What did she want you to do?" I asked.

"Easy things, really." Carrie shrugged. "I signed her petition to be principal when the position had a possible opening. Apparently, Dodge had gotten a bad review from the board, and there was a chance he might have lost his job. Agnes took that information and ran with it, making an all-out campaign to get the job for herself."

"Anything else?" I took another sip of my drink.

"Agnes had signs made up boasting of her qualifications as a teacher and wanting the job as principal. I agreed to put one in my front yard so people driving by would see it. I didn't mind. It seemed harmless enough."

"Until today, right?"

"Yeah." Carrie shook her head. "I hadn't realized what a hot-head he seems to be. I mean, I can see him coming in here, maybe surprised that I own the place, and being annoyed that I'd helped her. But to yell at me in front of customers? I hope no one will take what he said to heart. Can you believe what he said about the plague?"

"Nobody is going to believe any of that. Look around." I pointed behind me. "Don't you know nearly everyone here? That they're you're loyal, regular customers?"

She nodded. "I hope you're right. You know, I'm still shaking a little. Dodge came across as though he'd be angry enough to hit somebody. Glad it wasn't me."

As I took another sip of my latte, I thought about Russ's comment about Dodge's former profession as a boxer. I bet those guys could hit hard enough to kill someone. Especially if the person they were mad at had tried to steal an important piece of their life.

Chapter Fourteen

I n an effort to get Evan's mind off of being under the sheriff's thumb, Hank and I devised a plan. Hank talked Evan into joining him, Jillian, and me at the local bowling alley that evening. Not that bowling was my normal thing. Far from it. I was lucky to get the ball all the way down the lane. But Jillian's one claim to athleticism happened to be bowling. In high school, she used to drag me to this very place, insisting that the more I played the better I'd be. I proved her wrong.

Still, I went along with her, time after time, in an effort to try to improve my skills but mainly because she harangued me until I gave in. A girl did a lot for her best friend.

Tonight's effort, however, was all for Evan. It didn't really matter if he was a bowler or not, we just wanted him not to sit in his apartment and stew over his current circumstances.

Hank had volunteered to pick Evan up, and they were meeting Jillian and me here. I trudged to the alley's front counter, ready to tell the person in charge that I needed a size nine in a pair of bowling shoes. I wouldn't add that I thought it was revolting and disgusting, wearing the same shoes other people had their sweaty feet in. But I wanted to.

Jillian, who had her own shoes, naturally, was already at one of the lanes, taking her pink bowling ball out of its specially sized pink bowling bag, and placed it on the rack. She waved, gave me a thumbs-up, and reached for her shoes.

I liked her better when she was in librarian mode.

But being Miss Bowling Queen was part of her persona, and she was my best friend, so I resigned myself not to think about the shoes I was about to place on my feet.

I tapped the counter with my fingers. Where was the person who worked here? Maybe there was no one to help me, and I couldn't get shoes. Then, I wouldn't be able to bowl. And could sit and watch the others. That wouldn't be so bad.

A rustling sound came from below, on the other side of the counter. What was—

A head popped up right at counter level. I screamed.

"Sorry, Molly."

It was Ollie.

I clutched my hands to my chest. "Good grief, you scared me."

"I was hoping that was the reason you screamed. Didn't seem to be your normal reaction to things."

I took a deep breath as my heart slowed. "Nope, just wasn't expecting to see your head, um…wait, what are you doing here anyway? I thought working on vehicles was your thing."

"It is. I just…" He ran his hand through his sparse hair. "I kind of, well, needed the extra money."

"Oh gosh, I'm so sorry. I hadn't meant that to come out rude when I asked."

"It wasn't. Believe me, you're not the first person to question me while being here. I wouldn't be here myself if it wasn't necessary."

Things must really be bad for him financially if he had to moonlight at the bowling alley for extra cash. Not wanting to embarrass him further, I pointed toward the rows of shoes. "Well, how about a size nine shoe for me?"

Ollie stepped on his tiptoes, leaned over the counter, and peered down at my feet. "Yep, that's the size I would have chosen for you. Kinda big for a girl, aren't they?"

I blinked. Did he do that with everybody who requested shoes? Some people might take offense. For me, I knew my feet were larger than lots of other women, so I was okay with that. But some ladies might not take kindly to comments about their feet.

"One pair, size nine, coming right up," he said. "Any specific requests for the shoes?"

"What do you mean?" I wanted to say, without sweat or germs, please, but I knew that would get me nowhere. Or else, he'd tell me to buy my own pair.

"Some of the women like the ones with a reddish hue, while others prefer blue."

I waved my hand. "Surprise me."

He gave a single nod. "Will do."

I was glad to see that Ollie seemed to be in good humor today. Maybe his recent crummy mood was only temporary, and I was reading too much into it. At least, I hoped so.

He turned, grabbed a pair from a cubby hole, then clomped them down on the counter. "Too bad you don't have your hat. Might go with the shoes."

"Hat?"

"Your cat hat?"

I reached up, as if expecting to find Percival perched on my head, like he'd been the one time while we'd been in Ollie's shop. I really was never going to live that down. "Oh, my cats are at home. Didn't think them chasing bowling balls down the lane would be a good idea."

"Probably not." He glanced behind me, gave a nod to someone, then focused back on me. "Anything else I can do for you, Molly?"

I paid him for the shoe rental, then shook my head. "Nope, thanks."

"Have fun," he said.

I smiled, though the thought of bowling again did not fill me with glee. Still, the reminder of why I was here, to help out a friend, kept me focused. I joined Jillian, who was already wearing her shoes, bouncing on her feet in excitement. "Ready for some fun?"

"Wow," I said, "that's a lot of moving around for a librarian."

Jillian placed her hands on my shoulders and looked me right in the eye. "Listen, when you spend a lot of time on your bum during the day, it feels good to get some exercise. You stand a lot at work, Molly. Don't you want to move around some?"

"While it's true I stand a lot, I also spend time in weird positions, trying to groom, check, and clean spots on cats they'd rather not have anyone touch."

She laughed. "That sounds like what a pediatrician might say about working with little kids."

I shrugged, causing her hands to move up and down on my shoulders with the movement. "There are moments when I believe those two occupations might be interchangeable."

"I can see that."

I sat on one of the scuffed red benches and removed my sneakers. I grabbed the bowling shoes, stuffed my feet into them before I changed my mind, and laced them up.

"Ooooh, nice, you got the reddish hues ones. I like those."

Pointing to her feet, I said, "Then why are you wearing pink shoes?"

"I didn't say I like them better than mine." She held out one foot for me to inspect her shoe.

"Very nice."

"Why, thank you!" Her smile was wide.

I laughed. "You're a strange mix of seriousness and giddiness. You're a conundrum."

"Thank you again." She winked. "Gotta keep people guessing. Otherwise, what's the point?"

When Hank and Evan arrived, They made their way across carpet that was decorated in bowling ball pattern—how many rolls of that would a carpet store actually sell?—and reached us.

"Nice shoes," said Hank, glancing at my feet.

"Thanks." I rolled my eyes, trying not to think about whoever had worn them last.

Jillian flopped her arm over my shoulder. "My friend here doesn't like wearing recycled shoes."

"Well, who would?" I asked.

Evan, who'd been somber when they stepped up, actually smiled. "I see where you're coming from, Molly. I don't like them either. That's why I have my own." He produced a bowling bag I hadn't noticed from behind him.

My mouth dropped open. "You're one of them, too?"

"One of who?"

Hank shook his head. "Molly thinks bowlers are a different species. Like anyone living on earth would be crazy to want to wear used footwear and force a ball toward weird looking pins."

Jillian laughed. "Then I guess I'm an extraterrestrial, because I love it."

"Me too," said Evan.

Jillian's eyes widened as she watched Evan. She ran her hand down her long hair, then flipped it over her shoulder. Her smile, slow at first, grew wide. Her attraction of the guy probably just increased ten-fold. Was she mentally planning the tiny bowling outfits their children would someday wear?

"How about you, Hank?" said Evan. "What species are you?"

He shrugged. "I like bowling, but don't do it very often. That's why I'm going to rent some shoes. "Besides, I'm on Team Molly and will wear someone else's shoes as long as she has to. Nothing good could come of leaving her out there, alone, in sweaty bowling footwear." He caught my eye and winked.

I grinned at Hank. Leave it to him to be sweet and funny all at the same time.

He turned around, then pointed toward the counter. "Hey, isn't that Ollie?"

"Yep," I said. "He says he's moonlighting here for extra cash."

"Interesting," said Jillian. "He owns his own business, and he has to get a second job? Things must be rough."

Evan shook his head. "I wouldn't have thought so. When I take my truck in there, it's usually full of vehicles waiting to be serviced or repaired. Hard to imagine why he'd be so strapped for cash."

"Especially with his high prices," added Hank.

We all watched Ollie for a few seconds. "From what I've heard recently," I said, "Ollie has a bit of a gambling problem."

Evan's eyebrows rose. "Wow, I'd think an addiction like that would be really hard to kick. And would cause a ton of problems for him and those he deals with."

I glanced behind us to make sure Ollie was still across the way, behind the counter. "Also," I added, "his financial woes would have been worse if Agnes hadn't been killed."

"What did you hear?" asked Evan, moving closer.

"Apparently, Agnes, who had a romantic interest in Ollie's uncle, tried to convince the uncle to leave Ollie out of his will."

"But since Agnes is dead, that's no longer an issue," added Hank. "If Agnes hadn't convinced the uncle yet, then she was killed; problem solved, right?"

We all turned and watched Ollie for a minute. If the others were like me, they added another mark by his name as having yet another reason to have killed Agnes.

"Well," said Jillian, finally, "I don't know about you guys, but I'm ready to roll. Get it? Roll? Like a bowling ball."

I shook my head, and Hank groaned. But Evan's expression was more like enchantment.

Smiling at my friend, I said, "Yep, let's roll."

"While Evan is putting on his shoes," said Hank, "I'll go rent mine.". Then I can join the sweaty foot group with Molly."

I grimaced. "What a fun club. I think you'd all be clamoring to join."

Laughing, Hank walked to the counter to speak to Ollie.

As Jillian bounced on her toes and Evan rotated his shoulders, I eyed the lane. Would my luck be any better this time than all the others that Jillian coerced me into playing? While I viewed other bowlers hitting their pins in the lanes on our left and right, I sighed. *Don't count on it, Molly. Just do your best.* Hopefully my best would be enough that I wouldn't embarrass myself too much. But when had that ever worked out for me?

Hank returned with his shoes. Once he'd put them on, Jillian typed our names on our board. She put me last. Of course. But I didn't blame her. Why not allow the three better bowlers to go first and enjoy their success?

Jillian clapped her hands together once. "Okay, guys. Let's do this!" She grabbed her perfect pink ball and bowled a perfect strike. With a grin, she turned and faced us. I clapped because what else would a best friend do? Evan was next. With amazing precision, he let go of his ball, as it rocketed down the lane. Another strike.

Hank was third. He gave me a wink, then stepped up to the line. As he pulled back his arm to gain momentum, then let his ball go, I admired his broad shoulders and muscular arms.

He didn't get a strike, but did knock down nine pins. I'd take that any day! And then, I was up.

Blowing out a breath, I trudged to the ball rack and picked up the purple marbly colored ball I'd chosen. At least the ball was pretty.

"You can do it," said Jillian.

I gave her a smile. It was the exact same phrase she'd been giving me every time she took me bowling. As I stepped up to the line, I was hyper aware of noises around me. Evan coughed. Hank whispered, "You'll do great, Molly," while a group of little girls two rows down chattered and giggled.

"Go ahead, Molly," said Jillian, "You've got this."

Since she'd said something a second time, that must mean I'd been standing here too long. Wanting to get it over with, I pulled back my arm and flung the ball forward.

It landed in the lane to our right.

Jillian clapped. "Good effort!"

My face heated, but I forced myself to turn around. Evan was giving me a sympathetic look, and Hank's eyebrows had risen to his hairline.

Maybe I should have clued Hank into just how bad I was before we came here. Poor guy hadn't seen it coming. Although, he had to know that I was sometimes clumsy and definitely not athletic. Should he be that surprised at my lack of prowess at the noble sport of bowling while wearing icky shoes?

Maybe that was my problem. If I had clean shoes of my own, I might be able to concentrate on holding the ball, my form as I pulled back my arm and let the ball go, and…

No, it was no use. Even new footwear wouldn't help me out in that realm.

I shrugged, then walked back to one of our benches, sitting beside Hank. He placed his arm around me. "Don't worry, Molly. You'll do better next time."

"No, I won't."

"Yes, you…"

I stared at him. "Trust me."

"Uh, Okay." He gave me a squeeze, then removed his arm. Instead, he held my hand.

"Sorry," I said. "Bowling is not one of my gifts."

"Why are you sorry?" His dark eyes watched me, making me feel like he really longed to know.

"Because I looked like an imbecile."

He shook his head. "Nope. Couldn't happen. You could never be an imbecile. I think you're adorable."

My face heated again. Especially when I noticed Evan and Jillian both actively watching us. I turned around, hoping my skin would cool off, because for me, that normally meant I'd turned a not so pretty shade of red.

After several more embarrassing bowling attempts by me, I turned and glanced at the counter. Ollie was leaning close to a man. Their conversation appeared to be intense.

Needing a break from my terrible bowling performance, I motioned Jillian to follow me. "Hey," I said, "see that guy Ollie is talking to?"

She nodded.

"He looks shady. Let's check him out."

"Come on, Molly. You think he's shady because he's wearing a shiny polyester suit?"

I shrugged. "I've had worse reasons to suspect someone of something nefarious."

Jillian snorted. "You may be right. And extra points for using a great word like nefarious. You're making this library girl proud."

"Besides," I said, "with Ollie on my radar, I wouldn't mind checking out people he interacts with."

"Good point. Let's go."

We walked across the carpeted floor, my feet sweating, and Jillian practically bouncing in her pretty, only-worn-by-one-person shoes.

When we reached the counter, we stood side by side, watching Ollie and his acquaintance. They whispered, so I couldn't make out their words, but a large manila envelope changed hands. When Ollie received it, he let out what sounded like a relieved sigh.

Jillian waved to get Ollie's attention. "Hi there. Could I possibly buy some new laces for my shoes? They're getting thin. I'm afraid they might break."

Ollie blinked at her. "Uh, yeah. Just give me a second, okay?"

"Sure, no problem." She gave Ollie a toothy smile.

I had to give Jillian credit. I hadn't been sure what excuse I'd have given to be standing at the counter again. After I'd already paid for my rental shoes, I wouldn't have had much reason to come back.

I watched the interaction between the two men. It wasn't common to see a man in a suit these days, especially at a bowling alley. Maybe the guy was Ollie's lawyer? Possibly to help Ollie convince his uncle to keep him in his will if Agnes had convinced him to cut him out.

Ollie nodded at the man, who turned and left. Giving his attention to Jillian, Ollie said, "Need new laces, then?"

Jillian glanced down and faked a frown. "Gosh, how silly of me."

"What's silly?" he asked.

"I guess it must have been the lighting over there in our lane, but standing right here, I can see that my laces don't need to be replaced. They're just fine."

With a shrug, Ollie said. "Sure, whatever."

I grabbed Jillian's arm, tugging her back toward the guys. "Good job. Very convincing."

She smirked. "I have my moments."

I glanced back at Ollie, who was peering inside the mystery envelope. Even though he'd seemed hot and cold with his moods, I did really like him. But I'd still keep him on my radar.

Chapter Fifteen

I'd had grooming visits with Lulu, the cat, before, but this time felt off. Of course, she'd always been with her mom, Agnes, in the past, and now Betsy was the one I would visit. Although I was glad Lulu had a new mom since I'd also acquired my cat Jasper after his human died, I couldn't figure out the reason Betsy wanted her, or any cat for that matter.

My van shimmied a little when I made the turn into Betsy's driveway. Well, perfect. Shouldn't it work well since it was just looked at? Hopefully, I wouldn't have to take it back to Ollie's for a re-check. Aside from the extra time and expense it would cost me, I never knew how Ollie's personality would be now: his nice, normal self or angry.

I turned off the engine and opened the driver's side door. I'd left Percival and Jasper at the shop with Veronica. Normally I would have brought them, but today they were being lazy. Even lazier than any cat on any given day.

Plus, with Betsy's allergies, I didn't think it was wise to compound her misery by adding two additional cats to the mix. Lulu would be enough.

Betsy's front door opened, and she stepped out. She had Lulu with her, but wasn't holding her like most pet parents would, close to their chests or over their shoulders. Instead, Lulu was in her carrier. Did Betsy make the cat stay in there all the time?

I hoped not. That wasn't healthy for Lulu. And being in the situation wouldn't strengthen the cat-pet parent bond. Trying to stay upbeat, I waved. "Hi, Betsy. And Lulu."

The cat peered out at me with enormous green eyes. On top of her new environments, the poor kitty was grieving the loss of Agnes. Even though the woman hadn't been kind or sweet to people, she'd still been a good mom to her cat.

Betsy held the handle of the carrier so that it was away from her body as she walked down the steps. It looked uncomfortable and difficult to do. I waited until they were on the driveway, then I lowered the van steps and motioned Betsy closer.

She came to the steps and held up the carrier. Didn't she even want to come into the van? I took the carrier from her.

Many pet parents on their first visit, liked to be closer to their new baby when the first grooming took place. However, Betsy stood with her arms crossed and hardly glanced up at us. I noticed she was clutching a handful of tissues, and her nose was a light shade of pink.

I opened the carrier and gently removed Lulu. She immediately started purring as I held her close to my chest and stroked her back. "Hi, Lulu. You remember me, don't you?"

Her purr grew louder, and I smiled. After a minute or so, I placed her on a soft towel on the counter beside the sink. "Betsy, would you like to join us? There's plenty of room."

Betsy shrugged. "Um, I guess." She stuffed the tissues into her front pants pocket.

On top of Betsy's reticence about being close to Lulu, I was having a hard time reconciling her attitude with how she normally acted. Before, she'd always been friendly and approachable. But now, she was standoffish and a little rude. What had happened to change her? And why had she volunteered to take the cat?

Betsy climbed the steps and stood on the other side of the bathing area. She eyed the small sink. "You're going to actually get a cat wet?" At least she showed a little interest in what I was doing. It was something.

"Yep." I smiled. "Lulu allows it. We've done it lots of times before. Right, kitty?"

Lulu's expression was one of resignation, but I was used to that from cats. With the exception of the Sphynx cats, most didn't love it, but complied.

"I had no idea," said Betsy.

"If a cat is exposed to grooming and bathing early on, most do fine with it." I removed Lulu's collar and handed it to Betsy. At first, she didn't want to take it but finally sighed, then stuck it in her other pocket. She rubbed her palms on her jeans after touching it.

I thought of Sheriff King, finding Betsy in Fabulous Felines and pointing out that she'd put down a pet allergy on her medical form. "Betsy, after hearing what the sheriff said to you in my shop, I wanted to say that if you have allergies to cats, maybe a trip to your doctor would help. He or she could give you an injection to help with the symptoms."

As if on cue, Betsy covered her mouth as she sneezed. "Excuse me."

"No problem, and bless you."

"Thanks." She grabbed a couple of her tissues, then shrugged. "It's okay. The allergies. I can put up with them."

"You don't want to see if you can get relief from them? I know allergies can be miserable."

She shook her head. "No…I don't know. Not now. Maybe later."

"Okay." I gave my own shrug, but couldn't imagine why a person wouldn't want to have relief from cat allergies right after adopting a cat and that they'd want to get that relief as soon as possible. Was Betsy anti-doctor? Afraid of needles? It was possible. I knew her, but not well enough that we'd ever talked about any of that.

I tested the water, put Lulu in the sink, and gently sprayed her fur. Then, I covered her face with one hand as I lathered her with the other. Betsy watched us, but when she noticed me glancing up at her, she looked away.

As I bathed Lulu, I tried to keep an eye on Betsy, who didn't seem all that interested in what I was doing. Maybe she just needed a tiny shove. "Betsy? Since you're a new cat owner, do you have any questions for me? Sometimes, new pet parents want a little advice when starting out."

She blinked and tilted her head as she looked at me with a puzzled expression. "Um…. like what?"

Wow, this was so different than other new cat moms or dads I'd met. Usually, they were so excited to know everything about what their new baby might need, they asked so many questions I could barely get a word in at first. "Well," I said, "to start with the basics, what kind of cat food are you feeding Lulu?"

"Oh, um, I'd been giving her leftovers of whatever I was having. Hot dogs, chips." At my widened eyes, she said, "Not good?"

I gave her a smile, not wanting to scare her off with my concerns. "Probably not. Kitties have certain dietary needs that people food can't provide. And our food can sometimes be bad for them."

She lowered her eyebrows. "Oh." She clasped her hands together in front of her, fidgeting her fingers, as if she was nervous. For whatever reason Betsy took on Lulu, maybe all of this was too much for her to handle.

"I'm happy to help you out with anything you might need for Lulu," I said. "I can give you a list of good brands to try if you'd like."

Betsy nodded. "Yeah. Okay." She reached into her back pocket and took out her phone, checking something on the screen. Had she gotten a text, or was she getting bored with watching her new cat being groomed?

I rinsed the shampoo from Lulu. As the suds swirled around her paws, she meowed. "Almost done, Kitty," I said. I glanced up at Betsy, who at least had put her phone away and was watching what I was doing now. "So, as for Lulu's care, it's the same with cat litter. I'll give you some ideas of what kinds to use." Almost afraid to ask, I said, "What are you using now?"

She waved her hand. "Nothing. Well, I've been letting her outside, just to, you know, do it in the yard. Sometimes, she doesn't want to do it, but I leave her out for a while. When I let her back in, I assume she's finished."

Alarmed, I tried not to let it show on my face. "Um, Lulu has always been an inside cat. It might scare her to be outside unless she's on a leash with a harness. Also, it's much safer for cats to stay inside, that way they won't be threatened or attacked by people or other animals, as well as the danger from vehicles on the street."

Betsy blinked. "Huh, didn't know that."

This was getting weirder by the minute. Betsy seemed to have no inkling of what to do with a cat and not much desire to even have one. What could possibly be her reason for volunteering to take Lulu?

"She'll need a place in your house for her litter box," I said. "Someplace where she can have a little privacy."

"Privacy? For a cat? You've got to be kidding."

"Some of them can be a little skittish about where they do their business. Especially now that she's living in a new, unfamiliar place."

Betsy huffed out a breath. "All right. So I put her litter box in a place she might like. Is that it?"

"You'll need to clean the litter box, too."

Her face paled. "Clean it? How often?"

"Every day."

She grimaced. "Oh." She huffed out a breath, as if already tired of taking care of a pet.

"It's not hard. Just buy a plastic litter scoop. They sell them wherever you buy your litter. Just scoop out the refuse and dispose of it. I use recycled plastic bags from the grocery."

"Sounds like a lot of work."

"Not really. Make sure to clean it every day to avoid the bad smell factor."

She wrinkled her nose. "Ick."

I laughed. "Yeah, that's one of the few downsides to owning a cat."

"I can think of several," she said, almost under her breath.

"Betsy. Are you sure you want to keep Lulu? Don't get me wrong, I think it's great what you're doing, that you're taking her in after Agnes was killed."

Betsy flinched, as if I'd struck her.

"Are you all right?" I asked.

She closed her eyes for a second, then said, "Yeah, I'm okay. I'll be okay."

"Like I said, I admire you volunteering to take Lulu, but if it's not something you really want to do, maybe she'd be better off with someone who adores cats?"

"No!" Her word came out so loud, Lulu and I both jumped. "I...I need to do this."

She needed to? She made it sound as if it was a requirement to get something accomplished. A task to check off her list.

"Okay," I said. "But if you change your mind..."

With her arms crossed over her chest, she said, "I won't. I won't ever change my mind. I…can't."

I nodded, but didn't say anything else about it. Betsy obviously had her reasons, even though for the life of me, I couldn't imagine what they could be.

Instead, I finished Lulu's bath and set her on a thick towel, drying her fur with another one. As always, Lulu stood still and allowed me to finish, only giving me an occasional glance or sigh. I reached behind me and picked up my hair dryer, putting the setting on low, so the temperature and sound wouldn't upset the cat.

Betsy wasn't watching us, just checking out her pedicure and looking up something on her phone again.

Once I'd checked Lulu's eyes, ears, and teeth, I pulled her closer and gently trimmed the tiny ends of her claws. She squirmed a little, but allowed me to finish. A bright pink bow tied around her neck was the final touch.

"There," I said, "all done. Isn't Lulu gorgeous?"

Betsy put her phone away, but seemed reluctant. "Um, yeah, sure."

"Did you want to put her back in her carrier?" I asked.

Her eyes widened. "Um, no. You do it, okay?"

"Sure." I didn't mind putting Lulu back in, but wouldn't Betsy, at some point, have to touch her own cat?

Betsy sneezed and grabbed another tissue. She reached inside her other pocket where she'd stashed Lulu's collar and held it out to me, then wiped her hands on her jeans again. I didn't usually put the cats' collars back on right away since I always added a ribbon after their grooming, but complied and attached it just below the ribbon. I doubted Lulu would care either way.

The ribbon was for the benefit of the pet parent. Kind of like the cherry on top of a sundae, to make it more attractive. However, I could see that it hadn't made any difference at all to Betsy.

I placed Lulu back in her carrier. "Okay, Betsy," I said, "that's it for today. Would you like to get Lulu another appointment? She was used to being groomed every few weeks."

"If that's what needs to happen, then all right."

"Veronica handles our schedule," I said. "Would you like for her to call you later and set it up?"

She closed her eyes briefly, then nodded. "Yeah. Sure."

I held out the carrier, and she took it.

"Uh, thanks." She looked down at the cat, who was peering up at her, then said, "So, cat, guess it's just you and me. Let's get through this the best we can."

I shook my head as they left, and Betsy took the carrier back up to her house. What in the world was going on with her?

I pushed the button to raise the steps to the van, then shut the rear door. As I was walking around the side to climb into the driver's side, someone called my name. When I turned, I sighed. "Hey, Ricky."

"Imagine seeing you here. How've you been?"

He asked as if he didn't see me every day and spends loads of time in my shop. "I'm fine. And you?"

"Well, I'm busy delivering mail, as you can see," He patted his mailbag.

"Uh, huh."

"Were you just at Betsy's house?"

Considering I was in her driveway, it seemed an odd question, but I nodded. "Yep. Since she's taken over Lulu's care, I came here to groom her."

"Who's Lulu?" he asked.

How much should I tell him? It probably wouldn't hurt to say the basics. "Lulu is, was, Agnes Temple's cat."

His eyes widened. "I can't believe it."

"Can't believe what?"

He set his mailbag on the ground. "First off, that an evil person like Agnes would have had a pet. Is the cat evil like she was?"

"Of course not. Neither one is evil." Even though Agnes had been mean, I wasn't going to give her the awful title Ricky was using.

"I'm shocked," he went on. "You could knock me over with a feather duster just now."

I glanced at the house and back. "Hey, Ricky, always good to see you, but I have another appointment soon and—"

He held up his hand. "Far be it from me to keep anybody from doing their job, Molly."

I pressed my lips together, hoping not to laugh at the absurdity of his statement.

"But," he said, "before you go, I feel there's something I must say."

I blew out a breath. "Sure. What is it?"

He pointed toward Betsy's house. "That woman doesn't deserve a cat any more than Agnes did."

"Why is that?"

"Because I heard her tell someone once that she thinks cats are detestable, abhorrent creatures." He grabbed his bag from the ground. "Well, gotta go. Mail to deliver. Neither rain, not sleet….and something else." He turned and trotted up the sidewalk and went around the corner.

I was already seated in my van when I realized that when he left, he missed delivering mail to several houses on the block, including Betsy's. Oh well, I didn't have time to chase him down to tell him about it. Besides, knowing him, it might happen on a regular basis anyway.

As I started the van's engine, I thought about what he'd said. I couldn't imagine Betsy using those particular adjectives, but they did sound like what Ricky might use. Still, if Betsy had said anything close to that, it was a cause for concern. Would she take care of Lulu and at least be kind to her?

Chapter Sixteen

Russ called and asked me to meet him for supper that evening. We decided on Whitewater Valley's only Italian restaurant, Leaning Tower of Pizza. I was glad he called. We'd been so busy, and our uncle-niece's time had been sparse lately.

When I walked in, he was already there, waving and giving me a goofy grin, one that had made me laugh since I was little. I gave him a hug, then sat opposite him, smiling wide.

"What's up?" he asked. "You look happy."

"Yeah, happy to see you. Things have been too busy lately."

He nodded. "That seems to happen when a murder takes place."

"So true."

"Unfortunate that you know this from experience," said Russ.

"Same for you."

I updated Russ on what had happened since we'd last spoken. Once we'd ordered our food, we settled in for a nice chat. But the woman who now sat two booths away from ours had other ideas. She started talking on her phone, loudly. Other diners were staring. She was situated behind me, so I couldn't see her.

Russ's eyebrows lowered. "I consider that to be rude."

"So do I. Wouldn't it be nice if restaurants and other establishments had rules for silencing your phones?"

"Yes. And I wish we could silence some of the people, too."

I snickered. Then, I sobered as I listened to the woman's tirade, which was somehow familiar.

"What's wrong?" he asked.

"I think I recognize that voice." Wanting to check it out and see if I was right, but at the same time not simply turn and stare, I dropped my napkin on the floor.

Russ frowned. "What are you…"

I held up my finger to signal him to wait. As I leaned down to fetch my napkin, I turned my head. And let out a sigh. I sat back up. "Yep, I was right. Unfortunately."

"Who is it?" he whispered.

I leaned closer to him. Keeping my voice down, I said, "Penelope Withers."

He held his hands up in the 'I don't know' stance.

"When I was sitting with Evan at Paula's Pastries, Penelope came in. She's his ex-girlfriend from back in high school. And boy, did she give him an earful."

"Uh oh. Not a good ending back then?" he asked.

"Very bad. But even though they broke up, he told me she still sends him mushy messages daily."

"Wow, that seems over the top. Isn't Evan about your age?"

"A little older," I said.

"And she's been doing this for all those years?"

"That's right."

He shook his head. "Maybe it's time she gave up on pursuing him."

"You and I would have. But this girl seems ultra determined."

Russ leaned to the side a little to look around my shoulder. "At least from what I can tell, she seems to be an attractive woman. Wouldn't you think she'd have been able to find another guy by now?"

"According to her, Evan was the only one she wanted. But if you talk to him, that was never going to happen."

Penelope shouted into her phone, "Hey, listen to me! It just so happens that my dearest, darling pumpkin, Evan, is being railroaded by the sheriff. I have to do something to help him. If you don't help him now, and I mean right now, I'll die. Just die right here on the spot in this crummy restaurant!"

Russ leaned toward me. "She certainly has a flair for the dramatic."

"Yes. Along with dying, just dying on the spot, her shouted words of derision about this restaurant won't do the staff or other patrons any favors."

Penelope huffed out a breath nearly as loud as her words. "I mean it! You will help me, and you'll help me this instant. What? Of course, I can pay you. My daddy is rich!"

A frowning waiter passed us and approached Penelope's table. I didn't want to turn around again and have her recognize me, but it wasn't necessary anyway. I could hear their conversation clearly, from where I sat.

The waiter cleared his throat. "Miss, is there something I can get you?"

Penelope sighed loudly, then said, "Hold on. Some man in boring clothes wants to speak to me." She made a sound like she was shifting on her seat. "Well? What do you want? I actually think you're being rude interrupting me in the middle of a life-or-death call."

The poor guy was just trying to do his job. I could only imagine the expression the waiter wore right then. Irritation? Annoyance? The secret impulse to slap the silly woman in the face? That last one sounded pretty good to me right about now.

The sound of a foot rapidly tapping the floor came from behind me as the waiter replied, "Miss, perhaps you'd be more comfortable speaking to your friend outside or..."

"I am not speaking to a friend," said Penelope. "I am speaking to an attorney. Not that it's any of your business. Whoever you are."

Russ and I glanced at each other. He shook his head as I widened my eyes.

The waiter let out a breath. "I'm afraid your shouting is disrupting other customers' dining experiences," he said. His voice came out tired, as if he'd been chased all over town by a gang of cats while he was covered in catnip.

"How does that concern me?" shouted Penelope. "What do I care if other stupid people's experience isn't what they expect it to be? Do we all always get what we want? Do we? No, we don't. Especially me. My life is in shambles. Nothing is going the way I want it to."

There was a silence before the waiter asked, "Would you perhaps care to order something?" Maybe it was his last-ditch effort to help her get the hint that she needed to be quiet and eat, since she was, after all, sitting in an eating establishment.

A look to my right showed two families angrily leaving the restaurant as they gave backward glances toward Penelope. Not good. And word always spread around town when an incident like this occurred. As a business owner, it hurt my heart to see someone upset enough to leave as a result of another person's incredible rudeness.

"If you'll have some patience and give me a moment," said Penelope, "I'll order something. Even though, after seeing your menu, there didn't seem to be much edible on there. I'll be the bigger person, order food, then leave it on my plate. But right now, can't you see I'm busy doing something more important than you are? And frankly, anything I do or say would always be more important than anything that concerns you."

A huff, which I assumed came from the waiter, was nearly as loud as Penelope's words had been. A few seconds later, the waiter passed by our table, muttering under his breath.

"That was hard to watch," said Russ. "Your poor friend, Evan. To have to have put up with her. Not only in the past, but to have her still sending him messages. I don't even want to imagine what she says in those."

"Yes, I've decided his new name is indeed Poor Evan. Of course, Penelope kept saying that about him, because, in her opinion, him opening a photography studio is a step down from painting and drawing. Like he's failed in life."

"That's ridiculous." Russ waved away the notion with his hand.

"I totally agree. But she has her heart set on him doing what she wants him to do."

"A very controlling girl. They don't even have a relationship anymore and she's trying to direct his future. How awful for Evan to have to deal with her after all this time. How is he taking it?"

"You should have seen the look on Evan's face when she walked into the pastry shop. He went pale and sort of deflated, like he couldn't believe what he was seeing, but knew he couldn't get out of talking to her. Now that I've met her, I can understand why he reacted that way. He just sat there, trying to pretend she wasn't standing nearby."

From behind me, Penelope shouted, "I can't in good conscience allow Evan's fabulous talent to go to waste simply because his teacher in school had caused him to feel inferior. And she made it impossible for him to get into his college of choice without the teacher's recommendation."

"When Evan saw her, did he even say anything to her?" asked Russ. "Or did she simply talk *at* him?"

"Definitely at him. He introduced her to me, then did his best to become invisible."

"And now," continued Penelope, "because of all that horrible teacher put Evan through, I'm having to convince him to carry on, and forge ahead with his true calling. And that doesn't include taking photos of stupid people and their pets."

I bristled at that, having adored all the portraits Evan had taken of my cats and my kitty clients. The man was a genius. And Penelope was a certifiable loon.

The waiter appeared at our table, bringing our food. When he set the plates in front of us, he kept his gaze averted, like a scolded puppy who's been blamed for breaking a treasured family heirloom.

I gave him a warm smile. "Thanks so much. It looks delicious."

His head snapped up and he made eye contact. He let out a relieved sigh, and smiled. "You're quite welcome." He stood up straighter, seeming to have gained back a little dignity from my words. He glanced over his shoulder at Penelope. "I apologize for the disruption. I hope it won't keep you from enjoying your meal. Or from returning again soon."

Russ shook his head. "It won't keep us from anything. It's one of our favorite places. I can guarantee we'll be back, and soon."

I nodded. "Yes, can't wait to dig into this amazing food."

The waiter's shoulders relaxed. "Glad to hear it."

Behind me, Penelope said, "I think we're having a bad connection. I'll try to talk louder so you can hear me!"

My mouth dropped open. She wanted to talk even louder? My ears were ringing as it was.

A screech came from Penelope. "Of course I'm happy that despicable teacher is six feet under! Now Evan might have a chance to get a better job without her coming forward to mess things up. Kind of difficult to cause issues when she'd dead!" She let out a braying laugh, which caused a shiver across the back of my neck.

Since the waiter hadn't left yet, I said, "I'm sorry you have to deal with the disruptions when you're only trying to do your job."

He shrugged. "Goes with it. But this one," he angled his head toward Penelope, "seems especially…" His face reddened as if realizing he'd said too much.

"She seems…rude?" I asked.

Russ nodded in agreement at my word choice.

"That's it exactly," said the waiter. "The bad thing? It's not her first loud visit here."

I sat forward. "Really?"

"No. She was in here yesterday, pulling the same stunt. Talking very loud about some guy. I can only assume it was about the same man who's the focus of her conversation today. We lost several customers when they walked about, some without paying. And one man said he'd never darken our doorstep again. The man insisted I physically throw her out."

Part of me wondered why they hadn't. But having witnessed how volatile someone like Penelope could be, it might be even worse if the waiter had tossed her to the curb. It wouldn't surprise me if she'd have called the authorities, or sicced her lawyer on him. Or worse. Also, even though it was often difficult to do, the mantra that the customer is always right came into play. The hard part was, which customer did a business owner side with, in those situations?

I watched Russ. He shook his head, then lifted his chin toward the waiter. Yeah, I agreed with him. The poor man was having a waiter's worst nightmare.

A loud "Well, goodbye and thanks for nothing!" erupted from behind me. Foot stomps approached. Penelope was coming towards us. I slid down in my seat, grateful to notice that the waiter stood between me and Penelope, so hopefully she couldn't get a good look at me.

"Here's a tip for you, Mr. whoever you are." Penelope shoved something into his hand.

"Why did you give me this?" asked the waiter.

"Because I'm not staying," she said. "But I needed to pay for my time sitting in that booth. I was brought up right, you know. Always pay my way." She stormed to the door and left, to a smattering of applause from other diners.

The waiter glanced down at his palm, then shook his head.

"What's the matter," asked Russ.

"She gave me…one dollar."

The audacity of Penelope Withers continued to amaze me.

"Honestly," said the waiter, "I'd been given instructions to escort her from the premises. She had another two minutes before I had to do it. I'm so glad I didn't have to. I was afraid of what she might do or say when I did."

"I don't blame you," I said. "I'm glad for you that you were spared at least that."

He crossed his arms, apparently relieved to have people to listen to him instead of yelling, screaming, or being rude to him. "Also, If I got it correctly, keep in mind, that customer who just left was yelling, so not always easy to make out her words, something came up about that poor woman who just died."

Russ eyed the waiter. "You mean Agnes Temple?"

He pointed at him. "That's the one."

"What did the customer say?" I asked.

"That Agnes had it coming. That she deserved what she'd gotten. And that it was a shame the timing hadn't worked out so that her death had occurred years ago." He glanced down at our plates. "Hey, sorry to have taken up your time. Allow me to get you some fresh food that's warm."

"No," insisted Russ, "we're fine."

"Well, thank you for listening. It's much appreciated." He stepped away to where Penelope had been seated, tidying up her one-dollar spot for the next patron to occupy.

Thinking about what the waiter had shared about Penelope's conversation yesterday, I stared at Russ. His eyes were wide at all we'd just heard. I thought about Penelope, having been out of the country with her parents for years. Had that kept her from killing Agnes before, but she'd made up for the timing and done it now when she'd just returned?

Chapter Seventeen

Evan had procured four tickets to a fundraiser at our local art gallery to raise money for homeless animals. Hank, Jillian, and I were all too happy to attend. It struck close to home, though, with Betsy taking on Lulu after Agnes's death. While I was relieved that Lulu wasn't left without an owner, the fact that Betsy seemed anything but thrilled to be a cat mom was perplexing.

Hank picked me up and we met Jillian at the gallery after she got off work. Evan was already there, having helped with arranging and setting up the artwork. Plus, he'd volunteered to take photos of the event for added publicity for the animals. He'd already taken adorable pictures of the pets at the local shelter and was arranging them on the walls when we arrived.

Jillian made a beeline for Evan. Hank raised his eyebrows at me, but I smiled. "Young love."

Hank laughed. "Well, good for them. I thought maybe something was brewing there. They're both so nice. They'll be great together."

"Yes, they will."

Hank took my hand and we followed in Jillian's wake. When we reached her, other early arrivals were admiring the pictures Evan had taken of cats, dogs, and rabbits.

"You know," said Hank, "not only will this benefit the animals and the art gallery in terms of publicity, but Evan will come out looking great, too."

I looked over at Evan. He was grinning and nodding as a group of older women gushed over his photos. And they were right. His photography was amazing.

I had a photo he'd done of Percival and Jasper to prove it. Although that had taken some doing at the time, Jasper had just come to live with me, and he and Percival weren't having regular hissy fits and cat spats. But thanks to Evan's patience—and more than a little catnip—the kitties were adorable in the picture, sleeping side by side.

Once Evan's fan club had moved on, he motioned us over. Jillian had stayed beside him the whole time, as if afraid the older ladies might run off with Evan.

At the mental image of them tying him up and stuffing him in their van to drive off with him, I snorted out a laugh. Loudly.

Hank's eyes widened. "Care to share?"

I realized Evan and Jillian were staring at me, too. "Uh, no. Never mind."

Jillian sighed. "My best friend has a, shall we say, colorful imagination." She narrowed her eyes. "Do I want to know?"

I shook my head. "Definitely not."

She waved her hand dismissively. "Fine."

I'd tell her later. But not now, in front of Hank and especially not when Evan was in earshot. I knew Jillian loved me and accepted me for the weird person I was. The other two liked me, a lot. But I didn't want to scare them away.

"So, Evan," said Hank. "Molly told me you took all of these photos. They're great. You've really captured the animals' personalities. Or for the felines, *purrsonalities.*"

Jillian leaned close to me. "Now you've got your boyfriend even sounding like you."

My face heated. Oh great, not again. Why did my fair skin betray me every time someone mentioned Hank and me in the same sentence? I waved my hand in front of my face, which made Jillian giggle.

Thankfully, neither Hank or Evan seemed to have noticed my embarrassment. Good. Because I'd had enough embarrassment for a lifetime showing off my terrible bowling skills.

Evan smiled. "Thank you, Hank. I had a blast doing them. I hope tonight brings in tons of money for the animals at the shelter."

Jillian glanced around the room, where the crowd was growing. "I love that the art gallery hosted this. How did it happen that the two agencies joined up for this benefit?"

"Well," said Evan, "I'm actually on the Art Gallery Board and suggested it after I heard about the high need for funds at the shelter."

She grabbed his arm, causing his eyes to widen. "Evan, that's amazing. Good for you."

He shrugged. "Seemed like the thing to do."

"Don't be so modest," she said. "It was a wonderful idea."

"You're going to spoil me, Jillian Wells."

"Oh, brother," said Hank under his breath. "It's getting deep in here. Time to change the subject?"

I giggled. "Yeah, probably."

"So," said Hank, "why don't you show us around, Evan, since you're familiar with the art gallery."

Taking his gaze off of Jillian, for which he seemed reluctant, Evan nodded. "Sure thing. Let's start over there." He pointed to a far corner, then headed that way. We followed like little ducks in a row, as the venue was now so crowded, there was little space in which to cross the room in any way other than single file.

Once we reached Evan's destination, I stepped closer to the painting, recognizing a couple of familiar names of my pet parents at the bottom of some. "Hey, are all of these paintings done by local artists?"

"Yes, that was another idea I floated to the rest of the board. While the gallery often hosts various artists from around the state and elsewhere, I thought since we were supporting a local shelter, why not do so with local artists' work on display at the same time."

Jillian beamed at Evan, as if he'd invented air.

When Hank gave a muffled laugh behind me, I pretended I hadn't heard. Sure, Jillian and Evan were acting goofy, but it was sweet. I wouldn't have minded a little of that silliness myself, but since Hank had invented the excuse of he and I dating to get me out of having to date a guy I had no interest in, our beginning had been different.

Still, I was happy about Hank and me, and Evan and Jillian, however it all came to be.

At a close by table, a couple of women sat, speaking to guests who were filling out donation cards. I'd be sure to do the same before I left. Even if I hadn't worked with cats and spent my days grooming them, I loved all felines and wanted to financially support their hopes and dreams and finding forever homes.

A man walked up to Evan and wanted to speak to him. With the drone of everyone talking in the room at once, Evan led the man toward a side room. Jillian came closer to stand beside me.

"Look at these amazing paintings," she said. "I could no more do that than climb the Alps."

I crossed my arms. "Yes, they are amazing. And I could no more do that than make a strike at a bowling alley."

Jillian flung her arm around my shoulders. "But you give it your all. That's all anyone can ask. I was impressed with your effort and enthusiasm."

Another muffled laugh from behind me had me wondering if Hank needed a sharp elbow to his rib region. Instead, I grinned at Jillian. "Thank you."

I resumed checking out the paintings, marveling at the number of names I recognized from Whitewater Valley. "There are so many from our town. I had no idea of all the artistic talent." Then I gasped.

"What's wrong?" asked Jillian.

"Look at this one." I pointed to the signature.

Hank leaned closer for a better look. "Does that say Agnes Temple?"

"Wow," I said, "I wouldn't have expected to see her work displayed so soon after what happened to her."

Evan returned from his conversation. "Hey, finding some you like?"

"We were surprised to see one of hers here." Jillian pointed to Agnes's signature.

Evan squinted at the tiny name in the bottom corner and shook his head. "I'd specifically asked them not to display hers. I didn't think it was the right thing to do, considering someone, probably a member of our community, had recently killed her."

Jillian whipped around. "You don't suppose whoever that was is here, do you?"

With a shrug, Evan said, "Who knows? I hate the thought of the killer seeing her artwork and gloating over the fact that she's not here to enjoy it on the gallery wall."

I thought about Evan's words the other day, when he told me Agnes hadn't been a great artist, but thought highly of herself. Yes, she certainly would have expected her work to be here too, among the many beautiful paintings that graced the walls. I looked at hers again. Compared to the one right next to it, I had to admit that Agnes's lacked depth and character. More of a flat scene with nothing to make it stand out.

The one beside it, though, was a lovely view of color, shape, and a certain flair that drew the viewer's eye right to it. I wondered if I knew the artist of this one. Bending lower, I read the name and…

"Evan?"

"Yes?"

"This is yours?"

He averted his gaze. "Um, yes. Since it was my idea for the show, the board insisted mine be included. This is one I did many years ago." He held up his hands. "I hadn't asked for it to be displayed, believe me."

Jillian bumped her shoulder against his. "But why wouldn't you? It's incredible."

Hank and I added our praise.

"Thank you, all," said Evan. "I appreciate it."

Knowing that Evan had gladly traded painting for photography, I wanted to focus on that as well. "While I love this painting, I'm really partial to your pet portraits. They are full of joy and beauty. You know how much I love the one you did of Jasper and Percival."

Jillian nodded. "I've seen one of Molly's cats. I love it as well."

We chatted for a while about the various pictures of pets, each one up for adoption at the local shelter. Along with taking in funds, the shelter was hopeful tonight's event would shine spotlights on the gorgeous pets who were at this moment waiting for someone to snatch them up and take them home.

As I was taking another look at the cat portraits, telling myself that as much as I'd love to give them all homes, two was enough for now, I heard a familiar voice from a few feet away.

When I turned, Ernie was speaking to a well-dressed older woman. I heard him say the word 'unfair.' What was he doing? With Ollie not paying much at the garage these days, maybe Ernie felt the need to seek other employment. Was he here looking for a job and was turned down?

Hank stepped up beside me. "I'm seeing all kinds of people I know tonight. Great, isn't it?"

"Yeah, it really is."

Ernie, still dressed in his oily work clothes from the garage, was pointing to something to his right. And he didn't look happy about it.

"Molly," said Hank. "You okay? You're frowning."

"What?" I glanced at him. "Oh, sorry. No, I'm fine. But Ernie Price is here."

"Okay…"

"He's never struck me as the artistic type."

Hank shrugged. "It takes all kinds of people from all walks of life to truly appreciate art in its various forms."

I stared at him. "That was deep. Have you been spending time with Jillian?"

With a smirk, Hank said, "No, but I did overhear a man say that to his wife a few minutes ago. Sounded good, so I thought I'd try it out."

"You're incorrigible."

"Thank you." He laughed. "You're still frowning, though."

"You're right, of course, that anyone and everyone should appreciate art." I pointed across the room. "But at the moment, Ernie doesn't look appreciative or anything close to happy about being here."

After Ernie waved his arms frantically, he jabbed his finger toward the woman. Her eyes widened, and she took a step back, nearly bumping into a group behind her. Alerted by Ernie's shouts, which were even louder than the chatter from others, the people in the group stared, open-mouthed, as Ernie continued his tirade.

"I'm wondering if Ernie is here looking for a job since things at the garage aren't going well right now," I said.

Hank studied Ernie for a few seconds. "Possibly. I realize not everyone owns dress clothes when it comes time for job hunting. But I'd hope he'd at least have washed the car gunk from his hands."

"Did you just say gunk? Not something you normally use in your job as a veterinarian, is it?"

Hank's eyebrows rose. "With what a startled dog or cat might leave behind on my exam counter? Yeah, gunk pretty much covers it."

I checked out Ernie's hands, and Hank was right about their appearance. It wasn't just a small bit of grease or grime; his hands were covered in it. Like he'd raced out of work to come over here in a hurry, I couldn't imagine what kind of position they might have at the gallery that Ernie would be interested in. But then, what I knew about working at a gallery could fit on the end of a cat's whisker.

It was Hank's turn to frown as he watched Ernie's tirade. "That poor woman. She looks frightened. If Ernie is really asking about a job, it isn't going well. He's a big guy, and she's tiny. I can see why she might feel threatened." He glanced behind us. "Should we intervene?"

The woman's face had gone pale, and her hands shook. She was scared, no doubt. Ernie, though a little daft at times, wasn't normally an angry or violent person. Why was he so upset here tonight?

"We definitely need to do something," I said. Hank nodded. As we began to head closer to Ernie, Jillian and Evan approached us.

"Hey, what's everyone staring at?" asked Evan.

I pointed. "Ernie Price seems to have a major issue with that poor woman."

His eyebrows knit together. "That's Ingrid Ware, the head of the committee for the benefit. I'd better go see what's going on."

Not to be left out, the three of us followed Evan as he made his way through the growing crowd of curious onlookers.

When Ingrid, who was facing our direction, spotted Evan, her body appeared to wilt. "Oh, Evan, thank goodness you're here. Could you please speak to this man? He and I aren't making much headway, I'm afraid."

I had to give Ingrid credit. She'd drastically understated Ernie's wild behavior, even making it sound like it was partly her fault for their dilemma. I'm sure I wouldn't have been even a fraction as patient, or even acting as if I was, if I'd been confronted as she had in a public place.

Beside me, Jillian was practically buzzing, with, I assumed, an immense desire to stand next to Evan as she had before. She slid a glance my way, a question in her eyes.

I shook my head, then patted her arm. I leaned close and whispered, "Let's wait and see what Evan can do with the current debacle."

She sighed, then nodded. "You're right." With her hands clasped together at her waist, she watched them.

Although Jillian had liked Evan for a while now, the quickness with which she latched onto him once it was plain he returned her feelings was startling. With the exception of when Jillian was bowling, her actions were normally quiet and more sedate. Her feelings for Evan must be deeper than she'd had for other guys she'd dated.

I smiled. Evan was one of the good ones. Jillian could do a lot worse.

Evan reached out to touch Ernie's shoulder who at first,stiffened, then seemed to relax. "Listen, Ernie, it seems like there's some sort of disagreement happening here. How can I help?"

With what appeared to be a shy glance at Ingrid, Ernie's face reddened. "I'm so sorry about unloading on you."

Ingrid watched him for a few seconds, then said, "Thank you for saying that. And I'm sorry if I wasn't properly understanding you."

"No," said Ernie. "It was all my problem."

Evan tilted his head. "Is there some way we can help you, Ernie?"

With a quick shake of his head, Ernie said, "No. Not now. What's done is done."

We watched him turn and walk away, his shoulders slumped and head hung low.

Hank's hand grasped mine. "What do you suppose that was all about?"

"No clue," I said. "But I doubt my first thought was right about him wanting a job. There was another reason he was here, and was so upset. I just can't imagine what it could be."

Chapter Eighteen

ord had gotten out about Lorna's unfortunate encounter with Dodge. But worse than that, people were talking again about what Agnes had accused Lorna of shortly before Agnes died. A group of self-righteous do-gooders stood in front of The Sandwich Shack, holding signs. When I got closer, I could make out the scribbles they must have hurriedly written on the signs.

Down with Sandwiches!

Lorna Thompson, A Poisoner!

Save yourselves. Walk on by!

I gritted my teeth together. How dare they do this to Lorna? Intent on storming past them and into the shop, I walked purposefully toward the group. "Excuse me," I said.

"What do you think you're doing?" asked a fifty-something woman with a shag haircut.

"I'm going in that door, right there." I pointed toward the entrance.

"Over my dead body," she said.

A man next to the woman whispered something, then the woman said to him, "Oh. Right." Then to me, "Um, over your dead body, if you go in there and eat or drink something."

"You people are being really ridiculous," I said. "There's nothing wrong with any of Lorna's—"

"I must disagree." said a man with a red bow tie. "It's a proven fact that people have gotten tainted food here."

I placed my hands on my hips. "What proof? What people?"

"Well, at least that Agnes Temple was very nearly poisoned here. I'm quite sure that's why she died."

"Agnes Temple was hit in the head," I replied.

"Maybe Lorna did that too," he said. "If a person is a poisoner, would it be such a stretch to think she'd hit someone over the head as well?"

I huffed out a breath. "I'm going into the shop. Please step aside."

I glanced at the group of protesters. They were an argumentative bunch, but not overly dangerous. Even so, I had no desire to get into a catfight with them right out here on the sidewalk. I glanced behind me. Onlookers had already gathered across the street, taking in the free entertainment.

Still, I needed them to move. I'd come for food, but even more importantly, I wanted to check on Lorna. Right about now, she'd need all the friendly faces she could get.

I stuffed my hand into my purse and pulled out my phone. Waving it like a weapon, I said, "Either you all move, or I'm calling the sheriff."

"You wouldn't," said the man.

I poised my thumb over the keys. I wasn't planning to alert the sheriff, but they didn't have to know that. "Oh, wouldn't I?"

One woman's face paled, and she elbowed the man next to her. "Uh, hey, didn't you and I have that…appointment to get to? I think we should go so we won't be late."

He frowned. "What appointment?"

Her eyes widened, and she angled her head toward my phone.

"Oh, yes. Appointment." He lowered his sign. "I don't know about the rest of you, but my wife and I need to go. Right now. You all can stay if you like."

As the two rushed down the sidewalk, they nearly tripped over the signs they carried. The rest of the protesters filtered out one by one.

Once they were in full retreat, I pulled the door open and stepped inside. There sat Lorna, alone, at an otherwise empty table in an empty shop.

Quickly, I stepped to the table and sat down opposite her. Her eyes were red from recent tears.

I grabbed her hand and gave it a reassuring squeeze. "Oh, Lorna, I'm so sorry those awful people did that."

She pulled a napkin from the dispenser on the table and dabbed at her eyes. "It was awful, Molly. I'd just opened a bit ago, and some customers were outside the door wanting to get in. You know, like there are every morning."

I nodded. There were indeed always people wanting an early drink or snack before heading to work. I'd done it myself many times.

"But those awful people came and stood by the door, saying terrible things about me. And they had signs. Can you believe that?"

"I saw the signs. Those people need a lesson in penmanship."

A faint smile crossed her lips. "I'm so glad you're here, Molly. Thank you."

"You're welcome."

"But wait, how are you here when they…" She glanced past me to the front window. "Where did they go?"

I held out my phone. "I told them that a quick call to the sheriff might be in order."

Her eyes widened.

"I didn't really call. But the threat seemed to do the trick."

"Thank you. I was so upset, I didn't even know what to do to make them go away."

"It's okay. I understand. I would have been in shock, too," I said.

"Yes, definitely shock." She pointed toward the kitchen. "Anna was here, but I had her go home when those people wouldn't let anyone in. I'll still pay her, of course, but she was getting so freaked out by them, I didn't want to upset her further and had her leave by our delivery entrance." She stood. "Now that you're here, let me fix you something."

I tugged on her hand until she sat back down. "Don't worry about that. I think what you need right now is a friend."

Lorna wiped her eyes. "Yes. I do. I'm glad it's you."

"Me too." I smiled. "I'm here to listen."

Her eyebrows lowered in concern. "Don't you have to work?"

"Not yet. I'm good to stay here for a bit. Let me text Veronica." When I'd filled in my assistant about what was happening, she assured me she'd take care of things until I arrived.

Lorna slid down in her chair. "I feel like those people physically ran over me. Why am I suddenly tired?"

"You probably had your adrenaline going with them saying mean things and holding their stupid signs. Once they left, you could relax."

"Yeah, that's probably it." She put her elbows on the table and placed her chin in her hands. "I hate to say it, but their coming here isn't the only bad thing that's happened."

"It isn't?"

"Nope. Unfortunately, I had a visit from the county food inspector."

I shuddered. "Never a good visit when you're a small business owner who serves food."

"So true. It was my first time, and I was totally unprepared. I mean I didn't know what to expect or what to do."

"What happened, if you don't mind my asking?" I handed her another napkin when her others were getting too damp from her tears.

"No, it's okay. After what Agnes said about me, apparently, she sent them a letter about me nearly poisoning her."

"Oh no."

"But I didn't do that," she insisted.

"Of course not. I never thought you did. And other than those nuts who were standing outside just now, I doubt many would believe any of those lies."

Lorna rubbed her temples. "I'll admit I made a mistake by giving her that wrong drink order, but it certainly wasn't poisoned. But they wouldn't believe me and kept hounding me." Her eyes grew wide. "Molly, if they keep after me, and it the health inspector decides to make an example of me, I'll lose my whole business. My livelihood. Then what will I do?"

The door opened, and Sheriff King strutted in.

Lorna gasped and stared at me. "You didn't call him, did you?"

"No, of course not."

"Because if you did, I…" She frowned at me. Did she not believe me?

"Lorna, I promise. I didn't call him."

She relaxed. "Okay. Then who did?"

"I'm guessing we'll find out."

The sheriff hitched up his pants and ambled our way. "Kinda empty in here, isn't it?"

Lorna's hands shook as she pushed herself up from the table. In solidarity, I stood as well.

"Sheriff," I said, "what brings you here?"

"Got a call at the station. Something about an angry mob?"

I faked a frown. "I don't see anyone. Do you, Lorna?"

She shook her head, but wouldn't quite look at the sheriff.

He came closer. "Where are all your customers, Lorna?"

"I…" She shrugged.

I crossed my arms over my chest. "She…ran out of food."

"She what?" He removed his hat, scratched his head, and then replaced the hat. "How does something like that happen? Doesn't seem like very good business practice to me."

Lorna looked at me. Did she want me to continue to speak on her behalf? The nod she gave me was my answer.

"Well," I said to the sheriff. "Just one of those things."

"One of what things?" he asked.

"Um… you know, life?" I raised my hands in the 'I don't know' gesture.

His eyes narrowed. "I can't figure out exactly what's going on there, but I don't like it. Not one bit."

I forced a smile. "Sorry if you wanted something to eat or drink because…"

"Yeah, I know. No food here. That's the darnedest thing." He pointed his finger at Lorna, "Young lady, you better get your act together before you *lose your business* for good."

At hearing his words, Lorna jerked and wrapped her arms around her middle.

I walked toward the sheriff, slowly edging him toward the door. "Nice to see you, Sheriff. Hope to see you again real soon."

He allowed me to gently push him toward the exit, then halted, causing me to nearly stumble. He whipped around. "Hey, what's going on? Are you trying to get rid of me?"

"Why would I do that? Just figured if there wasn't anything to eat, you might want to go elsewhere for food. You know, I think I heard that Paula's Pastries is having a special today. Might want to check that out."

His eyes brightened. "Oh, that does sound good. Thanks for the tip." He stopped again. "But what was all that nonsense about an angry mob here?"

I grinned. "Like you said, nonsense. I'm guessing somebody was playing a trick on you."

He adjusted his hat. "I don't like that. Not at all. Whoever did that better watch their step, or I'll toss them in the slammer."

Slammer? I nearly laughed. But forced my lips closed.

"And by the way, Molly," he said, "don't think I've forgotten about you."

"What about me?"

"You keep your distance from that Agnes Temple investigation. I know Evan Lakes is a friend of yours, but I don't need amateur detectives sticking their big *fat* noses into sheriff department business."

I refrained from reaching up to feel my nose. Mine wasn't a fat as his was. I mentally rolled my eyes at my stupid thought and let it go. Instead, I held up my hand. "Keeping my distance. Scouts' honor." I'd never been a scout, so my words didn't count, right?

He narrowed his eyes. "Well, that's okay, then." He glanced at his watch. "I better hurry to Paula's for the special before they run out of food, too. I hope that's not becoming a trend with food joints around here."

I giggled when he bolted from Lorna's shop and raced down the sidewalk.

A thud came from behind me and whipped me around. Lorna was slumped down in her chair. "Lorna! Are you all right?"

She wiped sweat from her brow. "That was a close call. What if he heard what people were saying about me poisoning Agnes?"

I sat down. "It's okay for now. But don't be surprised if he hears it from someone else. Small-town gossips, you know."

She blew out a long breath. "Yeah, you're probably right. I just don't know how I'll handle it when he does. Then he might consider me a suspect, right?"

"It's possible. But if you're innocent, why are you so worried, Lorna?"

Suddenly, she wouldn't look me in the eye. "There are...things I can't discuss, Molly. Even with you. Things that if the truth came out, I'd be in a load of trouble."

Startled, I sat up straighter. Did Lorna actually have something to do with Agnes's death after all?

The door opened and a large group of people I didn't recognize, entered. I craned my neck to see past them out the front window. Just as I thought. A bus. Lorna was going to be busy for a while.

She jerked as if startled, then turned and seemed to notice the crowd for the first time. "I'd better call Anna to come back in."

I nodded, but wished she'd finished her earlier thought about the truth coming out. That sounded ominous. However, it wouldn't do me any good to try to speak with her more about it now, because the door opened again, and three young couples walked in. Lorna hurried to the kitchen area to stand behind the counter.

As an afterthought, she caught my attention. "I'm sorry, Molly. I never did take your order when you first came in. Can I get you something?"

I shook my head and gave her a wave. What I really needed from her was more information, but I wouldn't be getting that today.

Chapter Nineteen

J illian and I ended up with a lunch break at the same time, and wanted to stop by Evan's photography shop. He'd called to tell us that photos he took at the art gallery were developed, and wanted our opinions.

"I can't wait to see the photos," said Jillian.

"Oh, me too. He's such a talented photographer."

"He's perfect," she said.

I blinked. Perfect? Wow, Jillian was even more smitten than I realized. "So," I said, "when will the two of you start dating?"

Her face paled. "Dating?"

"Yeah, isn't that how it usually works? Two people like each other, find the other person attractive, one asks the other to go out and…"

She grabbed my arm, causing me to halt. "Molly, there is no way I can ask a man out on a date. No way. Why would you even suggest such a thing?"

"Hey, I didn't necessarily mean you'd ask him. Not that there's anything wrong with that. But I figured he'd do the asking."

"Oh." She grinned. "Sorry. I just thought you meant…"

"I think I know you a little better than that, Jillian Wells. You're fearless when it comes to running a library, being my best friend, and bowling."

She rolled her eyes at the last word.

"But asking a guy out? Probably not your strength. Just like it's not mine."

She linked her arm with mine as we continued down the sidewalk. "That's why we're friends."

"Definitely."

We stopped at The Sandwich Shack for sandwiches to go for us and for

Evan. Then, we walked the remaining block to his studio.

Once there we stepped inside the cool, inviting atmosphere Evan had created for his customers. The lighting was soft, light enough to view photos on the walls and at the table where he showed customers the initial prints, but dim enough to be soothing and relaxing. The low, slow jazz music coming from the speakers made me feel like I'd stepped into someplace classy and elegant, even though Evan was as down to earth as they came.

"Hey, you two," he said, stepping out from a back room. "Glad you could make it. I think you're going to love the pictures. Especially since you're both in some of them."

"Uh oh," I said with a laugh. "Maybe they're really bad and he wants us to pay him off to not show them to anyone."

"Or maybe," said Jillian, holding up the sack of food, "we could bribe him with these."

Evan held out his hands to the side. "Please. As if either of you could ever have a bad picture."

I shrugged. "It's been known to happen. At least to me. Probably not Jillian, though."

Jillian smacked my arm lightly. "Stop. You know I have bad ones. Remember the one from that party at Kelly's house?"

I snorted, indeed remembering the slumber party where we giggled, ate junk food, and posed for silly pictures in our pajamas until Kelly's mom stuck her head in and told us to quiet down. Thinking back, I couldn't really blame her. It was four a.m., after all.

"I don't remember that," said Evan.

"It was a girls' night only," said Jillian. "No boys allowed."

"That sounds exclusive." Evan's eyes were wide with interest.

With a grin, I said, "I seriously doubt that you'd have enjoyed watching us laughing at everything and acting like imbeciles."

"Oh, I don't know," he said, looking straight at Jillian. "I bet I would have liked it a lot."

"Well…" Jillian smoothed her hair in a nervous gesture.

"Hey," I said, taking the attention off of Jillian. "We are on a lunch break after all, and I'm sure Evan is busy too. Maybe we should eat lunch and see what Evan's pictures look like?"

Jillian winked at me, seeming glad the focus was off her. "Great idea."

"Sure," said Evan. "The pictures are in the back room. I have them laid out on the table, but I have another small table we could set the sandwiches on. I have drinks in the fridge, too."

We followed him to the back area and set down the sack. I was immediately drawn to the colorful, fun pictures he'd taken and stood in front of the layout.

The first picture I noticed was of Lottie and Florence, who, of course, had their cats with them. In the picture, they were carrying them around, cradled like infants, pointing out to them the pictures of other kitties on what I remembered as a far wall in one corner.

Then, on a wall next some paintings, were several enlarged photos Evan had done of some of my grooming cat clients, along with a sign that told the viewer the images were Evan's work of those who already had a pet.

Next, Evan had captured a picture of Ernie, looking longingly at a painting I didn't remember seeing. In the photo, Ernie's mouth was turned down at the corners, and his hands hanging limply at his sides. Was that before or after his altercation with Ingrid? I hadn't noticed Ernie before his argument with her, so it was possible he'd been there for a while before I saw him.

A group shot was next. It was a picture of Evan with the other board members. Had he set up his camera to take it automatically? In the scene the people were all smiles, giving thumbs up to the camera. The fact that Ingrid looked happy and relaxed made me assume it was before Ernie had caused such a ruckus.

I smiled when I noticed a sweet photo of Jillian and me, our backs to the camera, arms around each other's waists, heads close together as we whispered. Probably something about Evan. Or Hank, Or both.

"Hey," I said, "I didn't know you took this one."

Evan laughed. "That's the beauty of skulking around, getting photos when people are caught unawares."

Jillian mouth curved up into a slow smile. "Skulking? Unawares? Such a wordsmith you are, Evan."

His cheeks reddened. "I…well…"

Seeing that Evan was getting tongue-tied and that we were in a time crunch over lunch, I pointed to another picture. "Look at this one, Jillian."

She watched Evan for a few more seconds, looking every bit like the cat who spied the dish of milk. She might not be comfortable asking a man out, but she didn't seem at all troubled to give him flirtatious looks and comments. Finally, she sighed and glanced down to where I pointed.

"Oh," she said, smiling, "it's Veronica and her husband. What a great shot, Evan."

"Thanks." The color in Evan's cheeks had diminished, but his hands fidgeted at his sides.

Trying to see one at the far of the row of pictures, I leaned closer. The person in the photo was partially turned away, and when I got a closer view, I could tell it was Ollie. "I don't remember seeing Ollie there." I turned to Jillian. "Do you?"

She frowned as she shook her head. "No, I don't think so."

"You know," said Evan, "I took so many shots that night; there were a few that surprised even me when I developed them. In between snapping photos and speaking to people who came up to see me, I was taking pictures willy-nilly."

My eyebrows rose. "Willy nilly?"

He shrugged. "It's just a phrase. Right Jillian?" His eyes widened, hopefully. Was he afraid he'd just uttered something weird?

"Yes, it's an old, well-known phrase. It means without direction or planning."

Impressed, I patted her arm. "I always learn something when I'm with you."

"Same here," said Jillian.

"You do? From me?"

"Of course. The way you work with cats is amazing. They love you, Molly. It's clear on their tiny, whiskered faces. I don't know how, but you seem to emanate a feline vibe that cats run after."

"She's the pied piper of kitties," said Evan.

"Well said, Evan," added Jillian.

I smiled. "Oh, boy, it's getting deep in here."

Evan and Jillian both laughed.

I pointed to the rows of photos on the table. "Evan, these are amazing. I think you included just about everyone who was there. Thanks for letting us have a preview."

"You're welcome. Glad to do it."

Jillian nudged Evan with her elbow. "Molly's right. These are impressive."

"You don't have to gush about them," he said, "I won't make you bribe me with the sandwiches. There's no need. The picture of you two is beautiful. But then, beautiful women are easy to take pictures of," he added.

Jillian smiled. I wasn't sure if Evan had included me in the compliment because I was standing here when he said it to Jillian, but either way, I was pleased.

"Thanks, Evan," I said. "You're good for a girl's ego."

He shrugged. "Just calling it as I see it." With a head tilt toward the food table, he said, "I'm starving. Mind if I dig in?"

"Please," I said, "go ahead. I'll join in a second. But these pictures are so fun. I want to check them out a little more."

"Help yourself." He headed to get something to eat.

Jillian and I pointed, laughed, sighed, and cheered at the various poses, groupings of attendees, and the shots of walls full of pet photos and artwork displays.

The sound of the fridge door behind us and Evan popping open a can of soda made me realize I was ready for lunch, too.

"Listen," I finally said to Jillian. "I'm going to eat, then look some more." I grabbed a small stack of photos and took them with me.

"Sure," she said. "I know we only have so much time before we get back to work. But honestly, Evan, I love every picture you have here."

"Thanks." He took a swig of his drink and chose a wrapped chicken salad sandwich. "Also, thanks for bringing lunch."

"Glad to do it," said Jillian. And I knew she meant that as more than a 'you're welcome.' She also was thrilled for any excuse to see Evan.

We all three pulled chairs to the smaller table so we could eat. My tummy growled, and I gave it a pat. "I'm coming, hold on."

Jillian giggled.

"I can't help it," I said. "You know I have a clock in my stomach."

"I think your alarm just went off." She pointed toward my midsection.

Evan raised one eyebrow. "You guys are fun. I think I need to spend more time with you."

"Spectacular idea," I said, taking a big bite of a ham and Swiss sandwich.

I set down my sandwich, I wiped off my hands, then carefully picked up the picture of Ollie by one tiny corner.

"Which one do you have?" asked Jillian.

"I wanted to take another look at the one of Ernie."

"How come?" asked Evan.

I shrugged. "I couldn't get over him at the gallery. How he acted."

"You're right about that."

"Is your friend Ingrid okay?" asked Jillian.

He nodded. "She's fine. Was a little rattled at the time."

"She handled it well. By the time you went over to help, she seemed more composed."

He grinned. "I think she's used to dealing with complaining board members. Maybe Ernie's outburst didn't affect her as bad as it might have otherwise."

"That's good news," said Jillian.

"And," he added, "because of the success of the event, I've been told that several pets have been adopted as a result."

I smiled. "Even better."

When we were nearly finished eating, the bell on the shop door rang.

Evan wiped his hands and mouth with a napkin. "Let me go see who's here. I don't have anyone scheduled for a session for another two hours, so it's probably just Ricky with the mail." He left by way of a wooden swinging door to reach the front room.

I shook my head. "If it's Ricky, Evan may be detained for a while."

Jillian wrapped up her sandwich wrapper and napkins, then tossed them in a nearby trash can. "Yeah, I know. Unfortunately, I've had to politely shoo Ricky away when he stood at my counter, gabbing, while a long line of irritated patrons waited behind him.

Evan's voice, and that of whoever was with him, grew louder. We abandoned our food and tiptoed toward the door. I pressed my ear to the door. It definitely wasn't Ricky. Or even a man. But I'd heard that voice recently. And I didn't care for the person.

Jillian listened, then frowned. "I can't tell who's out there with him. Can you?"

"Yeah, unfortunately. It's Penelope."

"Evan's ex-girlfriend?" She frowned.

"Yep."

"But why?" Jillian's frown deepened. "Can't she just go away and leave him alone?"

"I wish I knew."

We listened some more, but Evan's response was too low to make out.

Penelope's responses left no room for doubt when she said, "Evan Lakes, you and I have been apart for way too long. Stop this silliness and come back to me. I'm the only one for you, and you know it!"

Evan mumbled something indecipherable.

"There's not another woman alive who cares more about your future than me," she insisted.

I found it interesting that Penelope had mentioned Evan's future, but not anything about him specifically. Or that she loved him. Just where he should go and what he should do.

A sound like a foot stomp came from the other room. I was certain it wasn't mild-mannered Evan, and could easily picture Penelope acting like a three-year-old by throwing a tantrum.

"Pumpkin," said Penelope.

Jillian's mouth dropped open. "Did she just call him...."

"Yep, afraid so," I whispered.

"Penelope, don't call me that," scolded Evan.

"But Pump... Evan, we're not getting any younger. You need to stop your silly hobby of clicking a camera at people's stupid animals and get back to your dream of painting. You're wasting your college degree. You have such talent. You won all those awards! Besides, haven't you missed me? Don't you long to be with me like I do with you?"

Silence greeted us. Jillian pressed so close to the door, I grabbed her arm so she wouldn't go sailing through the swinging piece of wood on hinges. If that happened, and she was lying sprawled, spread eagle on the floor, it would embarrass her to the point she might never look Evan in the eye again.

Either Evan's response to Penelope wasn't audible, or he'd whispered it, because the next voice was Penelope's again. "I'm only trying to do what's in your best interest. Don't you know that?" As her voice rose with each word, it took on a screechy quality to rival any rusty door hinge.

"Penelope, listen. I…uh…appreciate your enthusiasm for what you believe should be my course in life. But believe me when I tell you, I'm very happy where I am. And doing what I do. I'm good at photography. My clients seem to like me and my work."

Jillian nodded vigorously on Evan's behalf.

"I still paint," said Evan.

"You do?" asked Penelope. Then came a light smacking sound. Was she clapping?

Jillian leaned closer to me and whispered, "I didn't know he still painted. Did you?"

I shrugged, not wanting to miss a word of the drama unfolding on the other side of the door.

"But only for my own pleasure," he said. "I love it, sure, but it's not my life's vocation. I don't want that life. To travel, be made over. Plus, the disappointments when things don't go as planned."

"See?" she whined. "That's what I'm talking about. I know how much Agnes Temple hurt you. How she thwarted your plans for the best college and taking the next steps in your true art. Evan, you and I belong together. We need to spend the rest of our lives with each other. I've been so lonely. Won't you please take me in your arms like you used to?"

A gasp came from beside me. My heart ached for Jillian as she was forced to listen to Penelope Withers confess her love for Evan.

Penelope said, "Now that the witch is dead, you can move on to bigger and better things. See? Haven't I already proven how far I will go to make your dreams come true?"

I stared at Jillian. Just how far had Penelope gone?

Chapter Twenty

I was on my way home after my final mobile grooming appointment for the day. Today had been more challenging than usual, with three of my grumpier kitties needing baths in a row. And none of them were particular fans of getting wet. In a normal month, their appointments would have been spread out on different days, but even though Veronica was a whiz with our schedule, some time-space continuum worked against us today.

Percival and Jasper were both collapsed together in my front seat, exhausted from supervising angry cats and their unacceptable behavior. It was almost as if my kitties were embarrassed at the moment to be the same species as those other felines.

I stopped at a red light, one of the few actual traffic lights in Whitewater Valley, and watched a few stragglers walk across the street in front of me. I recognized most, but one in particular caught my attention.

It was Lorna.

She was carrying something in her hand. A bottle. I leaned forward against my steering wheel, squinting in the sun to view it better. The container she held looked an awful lot like...

A bottle of fixer?

Wait. Why would Lorna need something used in professional photography? It was possible she was an amateur photographer, but in my years of knowing her, I'd never heard her mention it, nor had I seen evidence of any photos on her walls. Could she have purchased it for someone else? But who?

My eyes widened. Unless she was using the bottle for another purpose.

Not for developing pictures but as a weapon, like what had killed Agnes. Could the ladies' supposed gossip have had some truth to it, that Lorna, a poisoner, had switched methods and clobbered Agnes over the head?

At the thought, I jerked, accidentally pressing down on my horn. A man right in front of my van jumped, halted, and gave me a glare worthy of a hissing cat.

"Sorry," I said, though with my windows closed, he might not have heard me. Hopefully, he got my apology if he was any good at lip reading.

My horn had not only startled the guy walking past, but me as well. My heart thumped against my chest, taking its sweet time to slow down. A glance toward the cats showed they hadn't appreciated the sudden jarring sound either. Their eyes were still half closed from sleep, but their fur stood out like that of two startled porcupines.

Lorna was already across the street, now turning a corner. I could just make out the pink shirt she wore as she hurried away. Maybe she hadn't heard my horn or, with her back already turned, didn't realize it had come from my van. What was she up to?

Since I had nothing to rush off to at the moment, I clicked on my turn signal, and when the light turned green, followed Lorna at an inconspicuous distance. At least I hoped it wasn't noticeable. It wasn't something I did every day, and relying on recently watched cop shows might not be the best way to gather information on how to tail a suspect.

Jasper must have sensed we were doing something out of the ordinary, because he hopped onto the dash and lashed his tail back and forth as he peered through the windshield. Percival, still a little sleepy, yawned, then watched the scenery pass by out the passenger window as I made the turn.

Lorna was walking at a fast clip. Was it because she normally moved quickly at her job in order to keep her customers happy? I sped the van up a little, not wanting to lose sight of her. However, I was going slow enough that the person in the car behind me crept closer. In my review mirror, I could make out the woman's face. Her pinched expression told me she was anything but happy at my leisurely pace.

I rolled down my window, stuck out my arm, and waved the driver past me.

She didn't waste any time taking my suggestion and added a mean frown, especially for me, as she sped by. But I was on a mission, and I couldn't worry about her negative mood if I happened to be driving a few miles below the speed limit.

When Lorna stopped to speak to someone on the sidewalk, I pulled over to the curb to park, making sure I was still far enough down the block that she might not notice me. My cats' whiskers drooped, as if they were disappointed we'd stopped moving.

"Don't worry, guys, I'm sure we'll be back on the prowl in no time. As quick as Lorna moves, I doubt she'll stay still very long."

Their tails moved back and forth in unison, like furry twin metronomes. I focused again on Lorna and whoever it was she spoke to. When the person turned their head to the side, I saw it was Ricky.

What would those two have in common? I'd never known them to be well acquainted. Maybe Ricky was a regular customer at Lorna's café. And he would, of course, deliver mail there. They'd spoken for a couple of minutes when Ricky pointed at what was in Lorna's hand, then shook his head, causing his ponytail to flip side to side.

My eyes widened when I saw Lorna lift the bottle of fixer above her head, a menacing look on her face. I gasped. Was she going to strike Ricky with it? In daylight, right out on the sidewalk? I reached for my phone from my purse, ready to call the sheriff to report attempted murder, when I realized I'd read the situation wrong.

Instead of causing harm to Ricky, Lorna appeared to pantomime an action, taking the bottle up and down as if hitting a person or an -object. And Ricky didn't seem afraid, just stood there with hands on hips, watching closely. Were they discussing how Agnes had been killed by being struck with a bottle of fixer just like that one?

A minute later, Ricky waved and went on his way, stepping across the street, leaving Lorna standing there, frowning at his retreating back. Then, she continued her way down the sidewalk. I restarted my van, smiling as the cats lifted their tails in interest and twitched their whiskers below their flared nostrils.

I turned the van away from the curb. While my focus had been on Lorna and not the street, I nearly cut off Ollie, who was driving his work truck. I slammed on the brakes and gave him a wave, relieved when he smiled and motioned me to precede him.

With the way he'd been lately, hot and cold, I never knew how he'd react to things.

The cats stared at me after my foot had pumped the brakes. Unfortunately for them, the action had caused them to slide from their perches and onto the floor. I winced at the sound of claws scraping across the dash.

"Sorry, guys. Didn't mean to disrupt your entertainment." Jasper blinked, a sign all was forgiven, but Percival, gave me a definite stink-eye. I'd have to make it up to him later with extra chin scratches and tummy rubs.

I tapped on my accelerator, ready to follow my intended prey. But as I'd been checking on the kitties, Lorna had somehow slipped away. She was as stealthy as a cat.

Where could she have gone so fast? With a check behind me, I didn't see anyone in my lane. Good. Maybe I wouldn't anger anyone else like I had with Miss Pinch Face. I wanted to take my time, carefully searching for Lorna's whereabouts.

I headed to the end of the block and turned left, choosing left because to my right, it dead-ended in an alley, and there was no sign of anybody hanging around there. I swiveled my head back and forth, checking out the sidewalk and peering through store windows, but no luck. Where had she gone? It didn't seem logical that she'd prance around town carrying that bottle of fixer.

I remembered Evan showing me the one picture of the ladies and their cats, and how in the background was a grainy shot of a couple of people talking, one holding what looked like the same object Lorna now carried.

Were they connected?

I turned left again, planning to check out this entire block before heading to the next one. The more I thought about Lorna carrying a possible weapon around, the more skittish I felt. Did anyone else who saw her with that think it was strange? Or was I on edge because I'd witnessed Agnes's crumpled body lying next to a bottle just like that one?

When I'd nearly completed my trek around the block, I spotted the pink of Lorna's shirt again. Once again, I slowed my van and parked along the other side of the street, halfway down the block from her. She was now directly in front of Evan's studio.

Lorna stood on the sidewalk and glanced around. Was it my imagination, or did her expression appear to be guilty? Or even angry? The cats and I kept our gazes on her as she stepped to the door, then gave it a tug.

Nothing happened. She tried again, but the door remained closed. Next, Lorna leaned away from the entrance to get a better view of Evan's front window, which happened to sport a sign I recognized, one that said, *Out for a while, please come by later.* Either Evan was out on an errand, or he was in his dark room and didn't want to be disturbed.

Lorna shook her head, then spun around and gave a glare to anyone in the vicinity who might be close enough to see it. I ducked down in my vehicle seat, then realized that wouldn't do me much good since I was driving my mobile van, which she would recognize. But that wouldn't make any difference since I often parked in this area to come and see Evan, or stop by other shops. Me parking here wouldn't be out of the ordinary. Even so, since I'd rather she didn't spot me or the cats, I quickly grabbed them, held them on my lap, and slid down until I could barely see over the steering wheel.

Jasper whacked Percival as if it was the other cat's fault that he was now missing the free show through the windshield. Percival hissed in return.

"Listen, you guys," I said as I stroked their fur. "Just stay like this for a minute, okay? I need to see what Lorna is up to."

Neither cat relaxed, but they did stop pawing and hissing. I counted that as a win.

I was a pretty good lip reader and caught what Lorna was saying. Nothing for polite company. Why would she be so upset that Evan wasn't there? And why would she take a bottle of fixer to his studio? Or had she hoped he hadn't answered, but that the door would have been unlocked?

Was Evan in danger? Would she try to harm him with the same type of weapon that had killed Agnes? Or had Lorna taken an extra bottle of fixer from his studio in hopes of doing someone else in, then changed her mind and wanted to slip it back inside without anyone knowing?

The cats had finally settled down and were now half asleep, right at the time Lorna stomped off the other way down the block. I blew out a long breath, glad she hadn't noticed my van, or if she had, didn't think anything of it.

With a screech, Jasper leaped up from my lap and hopped to the passenger seat. Percival's ears tilted forward, and his eyes widened.

I frowned, "What's going on, kitties? Did you hear something that—"

Footsteps sounded from the other side of my van. I jumped six inches above my seat when a knock sounded at the passenger window.

Trying to control my breathing, I hit the button to lower the window.

Oh perfect. It was Sheriff King. In stalking, um, watching Lorna, I hadn't even heard him skulk up to my van.

He leaned closer to the window, then spotted my furry security guards who were hunched down, side by side on the seat, looking ready to pounce. The sheriff sputtered something unintelligible, not uncommon for him, and took two steps back.

If I could have given Percival and Jasper high fives—or in their case would it be high-fours? —I would have. Instead, I gave them silent thanks and waited for the sheriff to dole out his usual warning, scolding or general dressing down that I was unfortunately used to.

Wanting to get it over with, I said, "How can I help you today, Sheriff?"

He waved his hands in the cats' general direction. "You can start by getting these… creatures… away from me."

"They aren't doing anything wrong. They belong in this van. You don't."

He sputtered nonsense again.

"Was there a particular reason you wanted to see me?" I asked. I crossed my arms over my chest, hoping for a somewhat menacing appearance. It might not have mattered to the sheriff, but it made me feel better just the same.

Perhaps simply to vex me, he mirrored my body language. "And just what are you doing sitting here in your van?"

"I'm parked here. Is that a crime?"

He glanced left and right. Had he been hoping to see a fire hydrant or a No Parking sign? "Well, uh…I just don't like it, is all."

I shrugged. "If that's all you wanted to say, then I really can't help you today." I knew I was being rude, but I needed him to go away, and quick. The longer he stood here, the more likely Lorna might walk away, and I wouldn't be able to locate her again. And if he spoke too loud, it might put her on high alert if she was indeed doing something out of line.

The sheriff pointed his finger at me, but kept his distance. Jasper stared at the finger a couple of feet away, and his haunches wiggled.

My cat wanted to pounce through the open window!

I grabbed him right as he leaped, stopping him from biting the official's digit. My concern wasn't that my cat would put tooth indents in the sheriff, but more that the man might somehow take a swat at my cat. Or worse, have him carted off to a shelter somewhere for causing harm to a human.

Nope, wasn't going to happen. I'd saved Jasper once already from the sheriff doing just that, a few months back when Jasper's owner had been killed, and I'd taken over being his mom. I wouldn't allow it to go that way again.

Sheriff King's eyes were rounded as he stared at Jasper, but since no contact was made, I hoped he'd let it go.

In silence, I waited for him to say something. Finally, with his hands safely stuffed in his pants pockets, the sheriff narrowed his eyes and said, "Molly, I'm warning you. Don't let me find out that you've been immersing yourself in a murder investigation again."

I continued to watch him, but said nothing.

He pointed at me, glanced at my cats, then pulled his hand back to his side. "And keep those disgusting wild animals away from me, or there'll be trouble."

Knowing anything I said at that point would indeed get me in hot water because the only words forming on my tongue were snarky or angry, I clenched my jaws shut.

However, the hisses that came from both of my cats aimed in the retreating sheriff's direction assured me they had no such qualms about speaking their minds.

As he finally drove away, I let out a breath. Now to see if Lorna was still...

Shoot, I didn't see her. She must have moved on. I'd have to let Evan know that she'd been carrying around a possible murder weapon and that she'd tried to enter his shop.

I petted Jasper and Percival until they calmed down enough to settle together in a ball of fur on the passenger seat, then I raised the van window. As I pulled away from the curb, I tried to focus on the street so I wouldn't pull in front of anybody again. But I couldn't shake the thought that Lorna was up to something. And that it wasn't totally innocent on her part.

Chapter Twenty-One

"I hate to put my cat through this," said my client, Gerald Jennings, "but my sister, Gertrude, is coming for a visit, and she hates dirt. I mean, she actually has a vendetta against it. I thought it would be gentler and kinder for you to give my cat a bath than for her to do so. She tends to be a bit…rough when it comes to cleaning anything. Even something that breathes."

"It's not a problem," I said, "I had time today. Glad to fit you in."

"I really appreciate it," he said as he laid his hand on his cat's head.

The cat, Herbie, glanced up at me with big, sad eyes, let out a mournful meow, and aimed a mud-covered paw in my direction.

I rubbed his face, at least the part of him that wasn't as sticky, and said, "It'll be okay, buddy. We'll get this over with, and you'll be your old handsome self again."

Herbie meowed again. It probably was uncomfortable to have dried; caked mud stuck in his very long, thick fur. I didn't blame him for being upset.

"I know," I said. "You don't want a bath today, but you're now wearing a mud coat. But if your aunt is coming to visit, don't you want to look your best?"

The cat blinked up at me, then his shoulders sagged, as if he'd do it, but wouldn't have to like it.

After testing the water pressure for the bath, I placed him in the sink—not an easy task since Maine Coon cats can get up to twenty-five pounds—and began spraying off the mud.

"Gosh, sorry," said Gerald, pointing toward my sink. "That mud's gonna clog up your pipes."

"Don't worry. With all the cat hair that goes down there, the mud won't be any worse." I had a regular pipe checkup with my friendly neighborhood plumber. He loved me. As long as I was in business, he'd stay busy too.

Gerald nodded. "That's good, anyway. I'd hate to cause you any more inconvenience than Herbie and I already have."

I smiled. "Honestly. I'm glad I could help. I had a cancellation, and you and Herbie fit right in. How did Herbie happen to get in a mud puddle anyway? He's an indoor-only guy, isn't he?" I really hoped that situation hadn't changed since most cats fared better and remained healthier if they lived indoors.

"Yes, I still keep him indoors, but I discovered there's a rip in my back door screen, and he got through it."

I eyed the huge cat, taking in his length and girth. "That must be a big rip."

"Well, it is now." He glanced down at his cat. "I knew there was a small one, and I'd been meaning to get it fixed. But honestly, it was only an inch long, and I figured it could wait a bit. You know, with my sister coming and all." He placed his hand next to the side of his face and whispered, "I've been spending my time cleaning everything in my house, from the rafters to the basement floor." Was he afraid his sister might hear him if he talked in a regular voice? She wasn't even here.

I was sure my house could be tidier than it was, but I didn't have the time to do that thorough of a cleaning just to please a visiting relative. "Wow, your sister really must hate dirt."

"With a passion," he said.

I could think of lots of situations to be passionate about that would be more worthwhile, like perhaps a cute veterinarian.

Pushing away thoughts of Hank, I refocused on my work and let the muddy water drain completely, then gave Herbie a quick second rinse. When I was satisfied that the majority of the mud was down the drain, I reached for the bottle of shampoo and poured a healthy quantity into my palm. Since Herbie was larger and fluffier than most of my clients, he needed more shampoo than other cats. Especially after frolicking in sloppy brown mud.

"Anyway, today I couldn't find him in the house," said Gerald. "I searched everywhere. I called his name. I whistled. I shook his treat container." He shrugged.

"Yeah, that last one usually works for mine." If I even glanced toward the drawer where I kept my cats' treats, they magically woke from their deep sleep and ran to the drawer, arriving there before I did.

"Same here," he agreed. "But today? No such luck. Then I noticed that there were claw marks on the screen." He pointed toward the door. "And the hole was big. Big enough for an extra-large cat to wiggle through."

Herbie was facing his dad and let out a howl.

Gerald stepped closer and rubbed his cat beneath the chin. "I know. It's okay. You were just having fun. I'm not mad."

The cat rubbed the side of his face against his dad's hand and purred, the sound as loud as an outboard motor.

"Awww," I said, smiling. "That's what I like to hear."

"Me too," said Gerald. "When I hear that, I know he's okay."

I massaged the shampoo all over Herbie's body, from his skin out to the ends of his long strands of fur. The cat closed his eyes, seeming to enjoy the sensation. It probably helped that the products I used were infused with a little catnip that helped calm my clients during their appointments. "How did you figure out where he was outside?" I asked. "You have a big yard," I angled my chin in the direction of his property.

Gerald spread his hands. "A murderous bunch let out a tribal scream and—"

I gasped at the word murderous. "What?"

"Oh, sorry." He chuckled. "I love birds. I meant a murder of crows, you know, a group of them? Well, apparently, they didn't take kindly to a feline interloper being right below their favorite tree. And boy, did they yell at him."

"I guess a large cat at the foot of their usual perch might get a bird's attention." I had indeed heard birds yelling at cats. In my case, the local starlings squawked at my kitties through the window screens in my house. Jasper in particular, took great delight in hissing right back at them, leaving a disgusting spray of hiss for me to clean up.

"You've got that right. Anyway, I hightailed it out to the back of my yard, near the woods, and there sat Herbie. Covered from cheeks to tail in dark brown goo. He even had some dripping from his whiskers."

I rinsed the cat again, watching as the last of the mud swirled around the drain along with the shampoo and disappear. "Yes, there was quite a bit of, um, goo."

Gerald waved his hands. "So, I ran toward the birds who were circling and diving, and they scattered. I probably looked like a maniac, yelling and clapping my hands at them. But I didn't care. I had to get them away from my little guy."

I held in a smile at his description of his cat as little.

"When I reached Herbie," he continued, "all I could see was his huge green eyes and the white fluffy fur in his ears. He was so scared of the birds, he didn't even run from the base of the tree once I'd chased them off. He was pretty meek when he allowed me to pick him up, mewing like a baby."

I grabbed one of Herbie's front paws and massaged an extra bit of shampoo around the fur tufts in between his toes, then did the same with his tail. I rinsed again, until I no longer saw or felt anything sudsy on the cat. "Well, Herbie, I'm guessing you might not try that mud puddle trick again, huh?"

His meow was more of a wail this time, loud and long.

With a chuckle, Gerald said, "As frightened as he was when I rescued him, I think he learned his lesson."

I scratched beneath Herbie's chin and said, "You're going to be a good boy from now on, aren't you?"

His meow came out as meek as a kitten's.

"Yep," said Gerald, "lesson learned."

Grabbing a nearby towel, an extra-large one, I wrapped it around Herbie, then snuggled him against me as I dried him off.

Gerald crossed his arms and frowned, as he glanced out the open back of my van toward his house.

"Are you okay?" I asked.

He scratched his head. "You know, in all the excitement of finding my cat encased in sticky mud, I just now remembered something else."

"Oh, What's that? Something about the crows?" I was relieved his mention of murder had been about the name of a group of birds, not another person found dead in Whitewater Valley.

Once Herbie's fur was partly dry, I retrieved my blow dryer and finished the job. When I was done, the kitty's fur looked like that of a gorgeous runway model's hair: clean, long, and flowing. He really was handsome.

"No," said Gerald. "Not about the crows. Once they scattered, they cawed for a while, but didn't come back. But it was while I was still outside with Herbie that I heard another cat screeching."

My pulse quickened, hating to hear anything bad happening to any feline. "Was it a neighbor's cat, do you think? Was it hurt?"

"I think it was a cat who lived a couple houses away." His eyebrows lowered and he tilted his head. "No, I don't think it was hurt. There was a dog barking and the cat seemed annoyed, that's all. But what I remember when I looked up to see where the other cat might be, was that I spotted someone I'd never seen in my neighborhood for a very long time. And it surprised me."

Herbie sat still, eyes closed, as I ran my brush over his back. His purr grew louder, causing Herbie and I both to grin.

"Who was the person you spotted?" I asked.

"Ollie Smith."

"Why was it surprising?" I ran the bristles of the brush across the cat's tummy, then his tail, causing his hind end to raise, which was a common reaction of cats when they enjoyed the sensation of something smoothing down their fur by their tails.

"Because a long time ago, when we were young and stupid," said Gerald, "Ollie used to get into regular bar fights."

"Really?" I asked. I finished the brushing stage by carefully fluffing up the fur between Herbie's ears and above his eyes. The cat blinked, then rubbed his face against my fingers.

Now that the cat was clean, dry, and brushed, I tied a bright blue ribbon loosely around his neck. He batted at the ends for a few seconds, but didn't try to dislodge it. He'd been to visit me enough times that he knew the drill and was comfortable with whatever I did. I had to admit, not only did the cat look better, he smelled better, too. That had been some stinky mud.

"Yep," said Gerald. "Ollie had a terrible temper back then. I had no use for the guy." He gave a dismissive wave of his hand. "When he'd act like that, I tried to keep my distance. Of course, like any young guy, I got rowdy sometimes, but not violent. Not like Ollie."

Even though Ollie had shown a different side lately, a more negative side, I couldn't reconcile him being a fighter to the man I knew now. However, I hadn't known him nearly as long as Gerald had. Being young together would give a person a whole other set of memories to reflect on.

"Okay," I said, "But why was it surprising to see him in your neighborhood? It seems like he's always all over town, picking up vehicles to tow into his garage."

"Because in all the years following an especially bad bar fight, he'd seemed to purposefully stay away from this part of town."

I frowned. What could be a reason for avoiding part of town? With a few exceptions, the citizens were nice and welcoming.

"Ollie avoided this area because he'd been thrown in jail for really messing a guy up during that bad fight, black eyes, knocked out teeth, and if I remember right, a broken collar bone. The other man had gotten a restraining order. After that, we didn't see Ollie in any of our regular hangouts anymore. And he definitely didn't come to our neighborhood to see anyone."

I couldn't imagine having to legally stay away from places because I'd harmed another person. Ollie really must have had a violent streak. Had that tendency returned? His behavior lately had been puzzling and disturbing, at least to me.

I picked up the cat and gave him a kiss on the top of his head. "Good job, today, Herbie. Well, the bath part, anyway." I wasn't going to compliment him on encasing his entire furry body in thick, brown mud.

The cat's meow this time wasn't mournful, just his normal loud howl. He must have felt better following his spa treatment today.

"Was Ollie remorseful for hurting the other guy?" I asked Gerald.

"Who could tell back then? He was always mad about something. Was upset with the world in general, always wanting to argue and fight, even if there didn't seem to be a reason for it. Like he had all this negative energy that needed to come out, no matter who got in his way, or who he hurt in the process."

Shaking my head, I said, "I've taken my van to him for years now, and for the most part, he's calm and seems nice." I wouldn't bring up my current suspicions about Ollie having possibly killed Agnes until I knew more. No use stirring something up when Gerald didn't have the best opinion of Ollie. Besides, Gerald might not know much about the murder of Agnes anyway.

"Yep, he is now. I think that restraining order finally did the trick once he saw how people who'd once wanted to hang out with him started to avoid him."

He smiled when I handed him Herbie, gave his cat a hug then, holding his cat close, tucked him beneath his own chin.

"Still," said Gerald, "I have to think that if you're born with a tendency toward violence, deep down, it would still be there."

Maybe he was right, even though I hated to admit it. I really liked Ollie and hoped all of this evidence against him was circumstantial. "Like maybe if provoked hard enough, he might resort to hitting someone again?" I asked.

"Yep, that's it exactly."

And would Ollie have been so angry with Agnes about her trying to keep Ollie out of his uncles will, he hit her on the head with Evan's bottle of fixer?

Chapter Twenty-Two

A product I ordered in the mail wasn't off by a little, but by a mile. It was a pet harness and was big enough to fit a dalmatian. Since none of my clients were anywhere near that size, I opted to return it. And since I didn't have confidence in giving it to Ricky to take back to the post office for me, I opted to take it myself.

The walk to the post office was pleasant, but that had a lot to do with Jasper and Percival going along as my tour guides. It was a good thing I had some extra time, because the attention they gave each blade of grass and tiny stone along the way, was intense.

All three of us blinked when we stepped into the darker interior of the post office from the bright sunshine.

"Hello there," called Edna Garing, the postal assistant.

I waved, but may not have been quite facing the voice. Finally, my vision cleared, and I herded my cats toward Edna.

"Good to see you and your menagerie," she said.

"Thanks. Nice to see you, too."

She eyed the box beneath my arm. "What'cha got for me today?"

"Something I ordered for a cat, but if I ever run into a feline that's this big, I'll run and hide."

Her eyebrows shot up when I tugged the harness out of its box to show her.

"I see what you mean," she said. She held out her hands and took the box. "It might fit my neighbor's pony. Let's see if we can get this processed so your kitties can finish their walk."

"Thanks. They do like to take their time, that's for sure."

She grinned. "That's what makes cats fun. You never know what they'll do next."

"Edna, you are a wise woman."

She laughed. "Let's get this ready to go." As she prepared a label for my return, she said, "Hey, since you're checking into what's going on with Agnes Temple's murder…"

Did everyone know what I was up to?

"…I have something that might just float your boat."

I stepped closer, always ready for new information. "Great. I'm all about the boat. What do you have?"

"Well, two things. First, it's about Ricky Notts."

His name sure did seem to be popping up a lot lately.

"Really? What happened with him?" I realized I was asking about her co-worker, but since she broached the subject, I didn't feel as bad. Any information leading to the identification of the murderer was fair game.

Edna printed out the label and affixed it to the box. "See, Ricky is basically harmless. That was, at least until recently."

I thought about the conversations I'd had with him in the past few days. There did seem to be more drama than usual. "What happened recently?"

As she set the box aside, then gave me a receipt for the package, she said, "A woman came into the post office, and Ricky happened to be here, loading his bag for his daily route. The lady lit into him."

"What about?"

"She claimed Ricky continually got her mail mixed up with others on her block and she was tired of having to deal with it, going to her neighbors' houses and fixing the problem herself."

I shook my head. That sounded like most days in my neighborhood, too. "Essentially doing Ricky's job for him?"

"Exactly." Edna crossed her arms over her chest. "I hate to say that about somebody I work with, I mean Ricky, is a nice guy, after all. But there are days I feel like I'm doing part of his job myself. At least I get paid by the post office. Our customers shouldn't have to fool around with getting their mail right."

Jasper tugged on his leash until I gave him some slack. Percival did the same. What were they doing?

Edna peered over the counter. "Looks like the kitties want to check out the new display." She pointed behind me. When I checked over my shoulder, I saw a display of boxes stacked in a pyramid shape.

Boxes, of course. An amusement park for felines.

"They can climb on the boxes if they want," she said.

I frowned. "Are you sure? They're likely to either climb inside, knock them all over, or, if they have their preference, both."

With a smile, she said, "Nah, don't worry. The boxes are filled with reams of paper, so they won't move much, and I taped the lids temporarily for just that purpose."

For the purpose of me bringing my cats in here?

"You never know what customers might come in here or what pets or toddlers they might have in tow. I thought the display might be cute and sort of whimsical."

"It definitely is. Well, okay, if you don't mind, I'll let the guys explore."

"Please do," said Edna. "It might be the only fun thing that happens around here today," she chuckled.

"I can't promise fun, but I doubt it will be boring."

"Then it's all good." She laughed.

I unlatched each cat's leash, leaving them wearing only their harnesses. It took them only three seconds to approach the boxes, crouched down as if investigating some foreign land, then edge close enough to sniff the handmade cardboard building.

Jasper pawed at the corner of a box, sniffed again, then hopped onto the lowest box. Percival sat and watched Jasper, seeming not interested as he washed his paw. But I knew better, that was my cat's way of saying, *I know you want me to check this out. And I will, but only in my time.*

I glanced at my watch, counting down the seconds—forty-nine, as it turned out— until Percival stopped licking his paw, stood up on his hind legs, and thoroughly sniffed several square inches, as if three inches to the left would smell that much different than what was right in front of his nose.

Seeing the cats were well-behaved, at least for the moment, I turned back to Edna, ready to hear the rest of what she'd been telling me. "So, What did Ricky do when the woman made her complaints?"

"He verbally attacked her."

I blinked. "Ricky?"

"That's right. I stood right here and witnessed it. I was shocked. You could have knocked me over with an empty envelope. He yelled and stomped around, telling in her no uncertain terms that she was mean, evil, and I might have even heard the word witch."

My eyes widened. Witch? Holy cow. "Wow." I'd seen Ricky upset and irritated, but to verbally attack somebody? He must have been wound way too tight that day. Besides, it couldn't have been the first time a customer complained about his ineptitude at doing his job properly.

"When the lady had said her piece, she stormed out," said Edna. "Ricky waved his arms around, ranting about the unfairness of how he was being treated."

At Edna's description of Ricky, I flashed back to him waving his arms at Dodge in the library. Had he snapped? Just couldn't take people's criticism any longer? The fact that he'd mentioned Agnes causing problems for him was amplified when coupled with his actions at the library, and now this.

I'd definitely be keeping my eye on Ricky.

"There's more," she added.

I watched the cats, making sure they hadn't torn the cardboard village to shreds. So far, it appeared to be intact. "What else?" I said.

"It's about that crazy lady. You know the one."

I shrugged. I could think of several right off hand, some of them being my pet parents. Or possibly me on a bad day. "Sorry, not sure who you mean."

Edna peered up toward the ceiling as if deciding how to explain it. "Let's see. She's new in town? Or, I guess she used to live here a long time ago. Went to school here or something. Close to your age, I'd guess. A friend of that photographer in town, Evan Lakes."

The light went on in my head. "Oh, Penelope Withers?"

She snapped her fingers. "That's the one."

"What happened with the crazy, er, Penelope?"

"She marched in here, and I do mean marched…"

I nodded, remembering how she'd entered Paula's Pastries. I could also imagine she'd done the very same when she'd confronted Evan in his studio, even though I was listening shamelessly on the other side of the door.

"Penelope came in yesterday carrying a large mailer envelope and two bundles of papers," said Edna.

Normally, that wouldn't sound like a strange thing to do at a post office, but having met Penelope and witnessing her toddler-like behavior, I didn't trust her motives. "Did she say what the papers were for?"

"She was only too happy to tell me."

I waited a few seconds to hear the rest. Wasn't Edna going to say it?

Seeming bored with the cardboard boxes, Percival moved closer, then stood on his hind legs, pawing at the side of the counter as if he desperately wanted the information too. Jasper, who'd already abandoned the boxes and had been dozing off while sitting next to me, startled awake at Percival's pawing. He joined his cat brother, running his paws down the wood in a rhythmic fashion.

Did my silly cat even know why he was copying Jasper?

Ignoring my cats, I placed my hand on my hip. "Okay, so what were those papers Penelope had with her?"

Edna scrunched her eyebrows together. "What?"

"The…papers?" I realized I was tapping my toe in impatience, and forced my foot to stay still.

"Yes, what about them?" She blinked several times, like she was trying to figure me out.

"You were going to tell me what they were…" I lifted my shoulder up, then down.

Edna frowned. "I didn't already do that?"

I shook my head.

"Oh," she waved her hand. "Sorry. Just daydreaming about the sandwich I'm going to get at The Sandwich Shack when I get off work. Have you tried their new Reuben? It's to die for."

Even though I was starting to get annoyed that she wasn't paying attention to our conversation, at the mention of a sandwich, my stomach growled. And it was loud. Jasper's eyes grew large, then he growled up at me.

I chuckled. "Sorry, Jasper, I wasn't growling at you." I refocused on Edna. "Yes, I have tried the Reuben. And you're right. It's amazing." Although using the term "to die for" right after Agnes had kicked the bucket was a little disconcerting. "Anyway, you were saying?"

She smiled. "Yes, well, that Penelope person had sheaves of paper. And you know what they were?"

I sighed. *You were supposed to tell me.* "No, I don't know…yet."

"Artsy-fartsy." She rolled her eyes.

My head jerked. "Excuse me?"

"You know, frou-frou stuff. Art."

Now, it was starting to make sense. "Oh, the papers had something to do with art? Like paintings?"

She pointed at me. "Exactly. Apparently, Penelope was sending off some sort of applications to a place called Amix School of Art and Design."

I gasped. Amix was a highly rated education facility for artists. And it was located in Europe. Was Penelope hoping to gain admittance there? Or was it for Evan? Or maybe both of them?

"Did she say anything else?" I asked.

"Oh yes. She said she couldn't wait, and at that, she took a little hop—actually hopped—into the air."

"Why couldn't she wait?" But I had a sneaking suspicion I knew what was coming.

"She was over the top excited to go there with her boyfriend."

I rubbed the side of my face. "Her boyfriend, of course, being…"

"Evan Lakes."

"Poor Evan." I cringed, realizing I'd labeled him as that before. But for having to deal with Penelope, who was indeed crazy, I did feel sorry for the guy.

I glanced down at my cats, who, I was glad to see, had settled down and were no longer mauling postal property. Would damage to a government counter qualify as something to be jailed for? I tried to imagine my kitties in tiny orange jumpsuits. I shook my head. *Must focus on my task.*

"Okay," I said to Edna, "after Penelope talked about those papers, and Amix, and Evan, did she add anything else?"

Whatever Penelope might have told Edna, I wanted to know. Because it sounded like Evan's ex had an agenda. And after having met her, I could tell she wasn't going to back down if there was something she wanted.

"She did say something disturbing," said Edna.

That didn't sound promising, not at all. "Which was?"

"That she'd wasted enough time being a nice person, waiting around for Evan to come to his senses and be with her, and go back to his life's calling of being an artist. And that she'd do whatever it took—she held her fist in front of her like she'd like to hit someone—the get what she rightfully deserved."

As I took a minute to digest that information, I knelt down and refastened the cats' leashes to their harnesses. Once they were ready to go, I stood. "Thank you for the information. And for letting the cats have some play time."

"My pleasure. Good to see you again."

As the cats and I navigated our way to the door, I decided that If Penelope had considered herself a nice person before and had acted like such a brat with Evan years ago, what in the world was she going to be like now? I wasn't sure I wanted to find out.

Chapter Twenty-Three

I'd agreed to do Evan a favor by dropping off pictures he had of Lulu to Betsy. Since Betsy worked at the sheriff's station and Evan was doing his best to keep out of Sheriff King's sights, for the most part, I volunteered to go in his place.

As I stepped into the station, the whirring of an overhead fan was nearly hypnotic, the blades going round and round at a certain point in the cycle, emitting a tiny squeak. Did the sheriff keep the noisy fan on purpose? Maybe he hypnotized his suspects, hoping they'd spill all their secrets so he wouldn't have to do the work himself. I knew my imagination was having sport with me, but if anyone was mean enough to do that, it would be him.

Betsy was sitting at her desk, working on an ancient typewriter. I knew they had computers, so why would she need to use that?

"Hi, Betsy."

She jumped when she heard my voice. "Oh. Molly."

Betsy had been so ambivalent about Lulu, not acting interested when I'd done Lulu's grooming, that I decided to let the continued conversation about whether or not she really wanted a cat go for now.

I reached into my purse and brought out an envelope. Handing it out to her, I said, "Evan thought you might like these."

Her brow creased. "What is it?" At first, she didn't even reach toward me for the envelope, just frowned at it, but when I held it closer to her, she reluctantly grasped it.

"They're photos of Lulu. He thought you might like to have them."

"Oh." She didn't appear to be at all excited about them, or even particularly interested. She set the envelope on the side of her desk, not bothering to check them out.

I shrugged. "I realize you didn't own Lulu when he took them, but wouldn't it be fun to have some professional shots of your new pet now?"

Betsy stared at me, but remained silent. If she was going to act like a mime and not speak, this would be a very short visit.

I pointed to the envelope. "Evan took them a couple weeks ago, so they're recent ones of the cat. The photos were actually done at Agnes's request."

Betsy jerked at Agnes's name just like she had the last time I spoke to her. When she still hadn't opened the envelope, I reached over, picked the envelope up, and removed the photos.

I flipped through them, searching for my favorite, the one where Lulu was lying on her back, all four paws in the air, winking one eye at the camera. She was a beautiful cat, even though she was moody, just like Agnes had often been. But cats often did pick up on their owner's vibes. And Agnes's vibes would have been negative to say the least.

I held the photo toward Betsy. "How about this one? I thought Evan did a fantastic job of capturing Lulu's personality."

"What are you talking about?" asked Betsy.

"Uh... Lulu? Doesn't she look cute in this picture?" I jiggled the picture a little, then felt silly. It was a move I used when trying to get a cat's attention, either mine or a grooming client's. But it might not get the same reaction from a woman.

Barely glancing at it, Betsy shrugged. "I guess."

Even though I hadn't wanted to get into her reasons for taking ownership of a cat she didn't seem to care about, even a little, as a cat lover, I couldn't stand not knowing why. And frankly, if a person took a cat and didn't love him or her, what sort of life would that poor kitty have? I placed the pictures on her desk.

I glanced behind me to make sure we wouldn't be overheard and was glad to see no one nearby. Especially the sheriff. "Betsy, I'm very concerned about something."

Her eyebrows drew together, nearly touching. "About what? Do you need to see the sheriff about something?"

"No." That was the last thing I wanted. "This is about you."

She let out a sigh so long it seemed to wear her out. "What are you talking about, Molly?"

"I think you know, "I said.

She crossed her arms over her chest and wouldn't meet my eyes. "No. I have no clue. Now if you don't mind, I have work to do and…"

"Betsy, I'm saying this as a friend, all right?"

That got her attention. She looked at me, and her eyes softened.

"We've always gotten along really well, right?"

She nodded slowly. "Yes, we have."

"I only want to help you. I'm on your side for whatever is going on." She opened her mouth to reply, but I held up my hand. "And don't say there isn't anything going on. Because it's obvious you're stressed about something. I'd like to help if I can. I'm a very good listener."

A faint smile lifted her lips at the corner. "Yes, you are a good listener. You always have been."

"Thank you." I returned her smile and waited for more.

Betsy leaned to the side to peer out her office door, then shook her head. Was she afraid somebody was listening outside the open doorway? She stood and walked around her desk to close the door. When she returned to her seat, her appearance was that of a deflated balloon, spent, out of air, and no remaining energy to do anything about it.

I pointed to a nearby chair. "Mind if I sit down?"

She shook her head. "No, please." She sighed, and her body arched forward, as if she'd crumpled right there in her chair. "Molly, I've been avoiding telling anyone this, but…I think I should. No, actually, I have to. Keeping it inside is tearing me up."

I sat and placed my purse on the floor. Apparently, whatever Betsy had going on sounded deeper than I'd imagined. Now that she was willing to talk to me, I didn't want to rush her. I crossed my legs, placed my hands in my lap, and waited.

She looked at the pictures of Lulu on the desk, but didn't touch them.

What was it about the cat that made her act afraid?

Finally, she gave a quick nod. Was she confirming to herself that it was time to get whatever was bothering her off her chest?

"Listen," she said. "What I'm going to tell you might sound sort of crazy."

I shrugged. "That's not a problem. There's lots of crazy in my life. I'm all about it."

She gave a quick chuckle. "Good, then maybe I'm telling the right person. All right, here's what happened. The origin of this goes way back to when I was in high school."

"Okay." Betsy had been a few years ahead of me, but we didn't get better acquainted until after we had graduation.

"It's about Agnes Temple," she said.

I sat up straight in my chair. "Agnes?"

"Yep."

"Then, you taking Lulu wasn't just so you could have a cat?" I asked.

"Definitely not. I've never had a cat. Never even liked them. And as you heard from my big-mouth boss in your shop, I am indeed allergic to them."

"Then why…"

She held up her hand. "It's a weird story, but I'll get to that part."

"Sure, please go on."

"Well, when I was in school, Agnes did something awful to me. It… It's something I never really got over. In fact, I can easily say I loathed the woman."

Leaning forward, I said, "Whatever she did must have been terrible."

"It really was. Especially to do it to an awkward teenage girl, it was devastating."

I nodded in sympathy. My teenage years were hard and uncomfortable, at best.

"So, I had her for art class. Did you have her when you were there?" she asked.

"No, I had another teacher. But from what I'm hearing from others, I was fortunate to have someone different."

"You were. Believe me. I'm not sure I've met anyone who liked having her for a teacher, unfortunately. Well, one day in class, a boy had drawn a very lifelike caricature of Agnes. He had her baring sharp teeth and wearing a witch's hat. I'd laughed when I saw it but didn't think much else about it."

"I hate to say it, but her personality might make a person think that about her," I said. "She could come across as scary and mean."

"Yeah, I agree." Her shoulders relaxed. Was she relieved to be telling someone her story? "Even though I didn't return his feelings, the boy had a crush on me. He was always drawing funny things to show me. The next day, when I came to class, I found that same drawing stuffed in my art room cubby. I didn't know what it was until I tugged out the piece of paper, but when I turned it over and saw what it was, that was the exact moment Agnes walked up behind me."

My mouth dropped open. "Wow. Did she go ballistic?"

"Surprisingly, no. Not at first, anyway. She stared at it but didn't say a thing. So I thought, good, maybe she'll just take it in stride. You know, kids doing dumb stuff. But then she sort of snapped, lit into me about it. Like how could I be such a terrible person to draw a picture like that of a teacher."

"But you hadn't done it," I pointed out.

"Exactly. I made sure to tell her that I hadn't been the one to draw it, but she didn't believe me. I tried to tell her it was one of the boys in class. I didn't name him because that would have only gotten him in trouble, too. But she said I was making it up to cover for myself."

I frowned. "You must have been so scared."

"I was. But no matter how many times I tried to explain, she refused to believe me. The boy even heard us talking and admitted that he'd drawn it and put it in my cubby, but she had her sights set on me and wouldn't budge. She said he was only saying that because he liked me, and I shouldn't allow another person to take the blame for the thoughtless thing I'd done."

I swallowed hard, imagining being a teenager again and at the mercy of a cruel teacher.

"I'm so sorry, Betsy, that must have been awful."

She huffed out a breath. "That's not even the bad part."

My eyes widened as I waited for what was next.

"About a week later, we had a school assembly. Remember those? The ones where the teachers would give us an update of what cool projects they were doing with their students?"

"Sure, I remember. I always thought those were boring. It seemed all about the teachers wanting to outdo each other."

"Well, Agnes decided to use her five minutes of fame that day to embarrass me." Betsy pointed her thumb at her chest.

My heart sank on her behalf. "Oh, no…"

"I had no idea what was coming. At first, I thought it would be okay when she brought out a painting that was turned away from the audience. That was nothing new since she liked to show off some of her own work during those times."

"You know," I said, "now that you mention it, I do remember her having her own paintings at those assemblies. I thought it was weird for a teacher to do that instead of giving the spotlight to her students."

Betsy nodded. "You're right. It was weird. I overheard a couple of teachers talking one day about how inappropriate it was for her to do that, but since she was such a force to be reckoned with, nobody was brave enough to call her on it. Maybe they were afraid she'd do something to make them look bad, and they didn't want to risk their positions at the school just to say something about her."

"Let me guess, it wasn't one of her paintings that time?"

"No." Her gaze dropped down to her lap. "It was mine."

"And…what happened?"

She held up her hand. "I fully admit that I have very little artistic ability. It's just not my thing."

"But you have lots of other talents, Betsy."

She smiled. "Thank you. Yes, I do. But art was never my gift."

"That's okay, though."

"I know that now. But back then? Especially that day at the assembly, it was terrible."

"What did Agnes do?" I asked.

Betsy's eyes narrowed, her expression growing hard. "It meant everything to me to be good at something. I really wanted to be good at it. I tried so hard. My grandmother had been an accomplished artist and I'd always wanted to be just like her. Hoping I'd start to show signs or having inherited her amazing gift. But it never happened. Now matter what I did."

I was so glad to be past those awkward, painful teenage years. Even small things back then seemed harsher, more dramatic, and life-altering than they did now.

"When she turned the picture around," said Betsy, "I think every single person in the room gasped. Then, the laughter began. It grew so loud, I finally ran from the room and hid in the girls' restroom. I stayed there until the final bell for school rang, and the halls were quiet. I slunk out of the building and back home."

Unable to hold in my question, I blurted, "What was the painting of?"

"It was of me. I'd done a self-portrait. It had been one of our class assignments. We were supposed to either look in the mirror or use a recent photo of ourselves to create the picture. Actually, for me, it had been one of my best works. That was until Agnes added her own special changes to it." Tears filled Betsy's eyes.

I handed her a tissue from a nearby box, waiting until she was ready to continue.

"See, when Agnes turned the photo around and I recognized the outfit in the picture of the one in my recent class photo, I thought it might be okay, since it was my best work."

"So what happened?"

Betsy dabbed at her eyes with a tissue. "Agnes had changed the face and head of the girl in the photo to a big, pink, grinning pig. And proudly announced that it was my self-portrait."

Teenage girls had it the worst, worrying about their appearance and if anyone, especially boys, would like them and think they were pretty. How crushed Betsy must have been. "That is terrible. You poor girl."

"It took its toll on me. I stayed at home for a few days, telling my mom I was sick. But she finally figured out I wasn't and made me return to school."

"How was it when you went back?"

"That first day was the worst, but I never fully lived down what everybody believed was my artwork."

"Something like that could change your whole experience at school, having people laugh at you," I said.

"Unfortunately, that's what happened. Kids I only knew in passing stopped making eye contact, instead laughing behind my back after they'd walked past. Even my friends stopped hanging around me, saying they were embarrassed to be associated with me."

"How shallow of them."

"Yes, but you know that's how kids can be. Especially teenage girls."

"True," I said. "But still wrong."

"Yes."

I let out a long sigh, in commiseration with the girl Betsy had been, and what she'd had to endure from a cruel teacher. "But I still don't understand why you took Lulu. You could have found someone else to take her, maybe. A person who didn't have those allergies. Did you try that?"

She shook her head. "I couldn't. Even after what Agnes had done to me, what I did in retaliation was worse."

"What was that?"

She dabbed at her eyes again, then tossed the used tissues in a nearby trash basket. "I...sent an anonymous complaint so she wouldn't get the principal's job. I listed some very strong reasons why, including her cruelty to me as a student and that I didn't want any kids in the future to be subject to the authority she'd have if she was made principal."

I watched her for a few seconds. "But that doesn't mean you'd have to take on a pet you didn't want."

"Maybe not, but I knew that being principal was what she wanted more than anything in the world. As soon as I did it, I regretted it. But it was too late. I couldn't very well tell them it was me. That sort of blows the anonymous part. By then, the damage was done, and Dodge Zaminski kept his job. And when she was murdered, my guilt increased even more." Her eyes filled with unshed tears again.

"I think I understand. Taking on Agnes's cat was something you could do."

"In atonement, I suppose." She shrugged. "It's not much, but at least Lulu won't have to go to a shelter."

It all made sense now, why Betsy had been acting so strangely. I stood and rounded her desk, wrapping my arms around her shoulders. "You're a good person."

She sagged against me. "I sure don't feel like one."

"We all make mistakes, Betsy. But taking on Agnes cat? That's a wonderful thing."

When I pulled away from the hug, Betsy looked up at me and said, "I know I haven't been receptive to your suggestions about Lulu and me getting treatments for my allergy. But to make this work, I'll need your help, Molly."

"You've got it."

Chapter Twenty-Four

Veronica and I each had our own rooms where we groomed cats, but we liked to leave the doors open so we could chat. I wanted to get Veronica's take on the suspects so far in Agnes's murder, about Betsy's reason for taking on Lulu, and about Edna's comments at the post office about Ricky.

As Veronica finished bathing her client, she said, "I'm glad to finally know why Betsy had taken Lulu, but wow, what a story that went with it."

"I know. How awful to have gone through what Betsy did with that terrible painting Agnes had shown to the whole school."

"True," said Veronica, "but I meant more that Betsy had sent that anonymous message about Agnes to the school board. That took guts. She could have been in a lot of trouble if she'd gotten caught at the time."

"It did, but her guilt over doing that was why she wanted to adopt a cat when she's allergic."

"I'll give her big points for that. And I hope she can get some relief from her symptoms. I can't imagine not being able to be around cats all the time."

"Same here," I said. "It would be terrible, wouldn't it?"

My kitty client, Angelo, turned, looked at me, and meowed.

Veronica snorted a laugh. "Obviously, the kitty agrees."

I gave Angelo a kiss on the head and gave his long fur a final brushing. I finished up by tying a bright yellow bow around his neck and placed him in his carrier. Immediately, he gave himself a tongue bath to remove the offending effects of the bath. Not every one of my clients did that, but Angelo did every single grooming visit. I laughed, watching him contort his body in all kinds of painful-looking positions to get every last speck of water cleaned away.

Veronica was still blow-drying her client, Philly, so I took Angelo out front to wait for his mom to pick him up, and I stepped behind the counter.

When the door opened, it wasn't one of my pet parents, but was instead Dodge. He'd never come in before. What in the world would he want?

I waved. "Hi. Welcome to Fabulous Felines. How can I help you today?"

He halted mid-step, then studied me. "I know you, don't I?"

I nodded. "If you can remember back a few years, yes."

"You went to Whitewater Valley High."

"That's right."

He glanced around the room for the first time. "Is this your shop?"

"Yes, it is." I stood up a little taller, always glad when someone new seemed interested in my Fabulous Felines.

"I'm pleased to see one of my former students doing so well for herself, um..." His shoulders lifted in a shrug.

"Molly Stewart."

"Right." He nodded. "I would have gotten there eventually."

"You had so many students come through the school. I'm sure it's difficult for you sometimes."

"Yes, that's right."

I clasped my hands together on the counter. "How can I help you today?" I glanced at his hands again, but I didn't see a cat carrier or leash in his grip.

He met me at the counter. "I have a young cat I got at the shelter. And I'd like to teach him to walk outside with a leash and halter. I was hoping you could recommend something for me."

With a smile, I said, "Absolutely. And first of all, congratulations on your new pet."

He shrugged. "Thanks. I went to the shelter thinking I might find a pet for my friend's son, but ended up finding one for myself instead."

"Or," I said, "the cat found you."

His eyes widened. "Does that actually happen?"

"All the time." I chuckled. "Cats know when they've met their special human. They're very smart creatures." I pointed to my left. "Let me show you what we have in stock." I led him to some shelves at one end of the room, where I carried any kind of apparatus or supplies for a feline. "Also, I have some suggestions for where to find really good instructive videos for training." I reached to a higher shelf and pulled down a box where I kept information and pamphlets for pet parents.

I handed him three fliers. "Any of these will be helpful, but you might want to watch all three to see if any of their various techniques are better than the others for your needs."

"Perfect," he said, as he accepted the fliers, then moved closer to the shelf to study the leashes and harnesses.

"How big is your cat?" I asked.

"He's...." Dodge held out his hands to indicate the cat's size.

"Probably needs a small size, but if he's young, you'll need to upgrade in a few months."

"All right." Dodge put the fliers into his shirt pocket.

Veronica stepped out of her room, carrying Philly in one arm and the carrier in the other. She gave a nod and smile to Dodge, then said, "Molly, could you give me a hand? You know how temperamental some cats can be," She pointed her chin down at Philly.

"Yes, sure. Mr. Zaminski, would you excuse me?"

"Of course. And my former students have permission to call me Dodge."

I nodded, but wasn't sure I could do that. Even though I thought of him in those terms, it might be different to actually call him that to his face. But he did request it, so I'd at least try.

After three attempts, Veronica and I finally had Philly settled inside her carrier. The cat promptly hissed and turned, giving us a view of her back, a cat's way of saying, 'go away, I don't like you anymore.'

When I returned to see if Dodge had found a leash set up he thought his cat could use, he handed me one and said, "I'll take that one."

"Great. Let me get this sacked up for you."

As he followed me back to the counter, he said, "Since your business is grooming cats"—he waved his hand in the direction of the main room—

"maybe I'll set up an appointment for Luther to be groomed. Would that be something you think would be a good idea?"

Veronica giggled. "I think I can speak for Molly when I give a wholehearted yes."

I grinned. "Veronica is right. I'd love to meet your cat and groom him." I tilted my head toward Veronica. "Do you have time to check the schedule for Mr., er, for Dodge and his cat?"

Her eyebrows rose at my use of his first name, since she knew he'd been my principal, but to her credit, she didn't comment. "Of course. Let's see what we have available."

Dodge followed her to the other end of the counter and waited as she tapped the keys on her computer.

The door opened, and I expected Angelo's mom. I was wrong. It was Ricky.

I let out a groan I hoped nobody noticed. Now was not the best time for Ricky to show up. Would he and the formal principal have a repeat of their apparent altercation like at the library? Dodge had appeared so irritated that day. Angry, even. I couldn't stop thinking about his former profession of hitting people.

When Dodge turned to view the new arrival, his shoulders slumped. And I was pretty sure I'd heard him groan, too.

Ricky's eyes lit up, and he flung his mailbag to the floor. "Mr. Zaminski! Imagine running into you again so soon."

"Yes, just imagine," he muttered.

Since Ricky hadn't called him Dodge, I surmised Ricky hadn't been invited to do so. Had Dodge not been fond of him even when he'd been a kid?

Hoping today's interlude wouldn't result in anything negative, but not wanting to be directly in the line of fire if it did, I quickly slipped back behind the counter to stand beside Veronica.

Since I'd already told my assistant about the scene in the library, her widened eyes didn't come as a surprise.

Dodge sighed, then said, "Hello, Ricky. Again."

Ricky practically hopped across the room until he reached Dodge. He grabbed his hand and shook it so hard I half expected fingernails to fly off.

I watched, spellbound, as Ricky began to reenact his bizarre behavior from the library. Veronica leaned over. "Is that like what you told me about?" she whispered. "How he acted at the…"

"Yep. Weird, right?"

"He looks like a deranged chicken."

"Yes!" I whispered. "You nailed it."

As Ricky waved his arms and stomped his feet, Dodge crossed his arms and gave an eye- roll. "Um, Ricky, while I'm, uh, pleased you enjoyed that trip, don't you think it's time we moved on?"

"Trip?" I blurted out, then covered my mouth. Why couldn't I keep my thoughts inside my head where they belonged?

Ricky halted his gyrations and stared, open mouthed at Dodge. "But… Mr. Zaminski, how can you say that?" He turned toward me and Veronica. "Ladies, this man is a bonafide hero. You won't believe it when I tell you what happened."

Dodge shook his head, "I don't think we should continue to—"

"No," insisted Ricky. "I must. This story should be preserved for the ages. Passed down from generation to generation."

"This is getting ridiculous," said Dodge. "It happened so long ago. Why must we rehash the past?"

Ricky blinked. "But it's something I've always remembered fondly. I don't understand why you wouldn't want to shout it from the rooftops."

Even though I was dying to hear the rest of whatever Ricky was so excited about, I kept silent.

Veronica, however, had no such willpower. "Hey," she said, "you're killing us here. What the heck happened that was so exciting?"

Dodge tried to wave Veronica away. "Honestly, it's nothing."

"Nothing?" said Ricky. "I'm appalled and, frankly, deeply hurt that the experience meant so little to you."

This was getting more bizarre by the second. I nudged Veronica, hoping she'd keep badgering them so I wouldn't have to.

Veronica didn't disappoint. "All right, you two. Somebody's going to tell us what happened." She glanced at her watch. "And we have more furry clients due any time, so get cracking, will ya?"

Ricky's eyes widened. But Dodge looked resigned.

As if in class, Ricky waved his hand in the air. "Oh, pick me!"

Veronica gave him a solemn nod. "You may continue."

Ricky grinned. "Thanks. Okay, so anyway, we were camping and..."

"Camping," said Veronica. "What kind of story is this, anyway?"

Ricky's eyebrows lowered. "It's a camping story. Pay attention."

I had to admit, it wasn't anything like what I'd imagined. But I waited, knowing that when Ricky wanted to discuss something, the other person was pretty much stuck there until Ricky temporarily ran out of words.

"Well," said Ricky, as you probably know, "Mr. Zaminski was my boy scout leader and—"

Veronica and I shrugged. How would we have possibly known that?

"—we were on a camping trip. It was dark out, nighttime, of course."

"Of course," she said.

"When this huge beastie..."

"Beastie?" asked Veronica.

"It was a rabid raccoon," said Ricky. "Rabid, I tell you." He bared his teeth and formed his fingers into claws.

Dodge held up his hand. "Let's be clear here. It was a baby raccoon. And pretty timid, actually. Not rabid."

Ricky's eyes widened. "But where there's a baby, there's a mom. You taught us that, Scout Master Zaminski."

Dodge opened his mouth, must have reconsidered, and snapped it closed. But I could tell by the redness around his collar he was getting miffed. As I watched him, his hands closed into fists. I elbowed Veronica and tilted my chin toward him. When she spotted his fists, she let out a gasp.

"Right?" Ricky said to Veronica. I knew you'd find it as exciting as I did." He clapped his hands in apparent glee.

Suddenly wanting to get the conversation to end, and hoping it would be in time for Dodge to be able to leave before he decided his boxing career wasn't over, I waved to get Ricky's attention. "So what happened with the, um, baby beastie?"

"It was magical, let me tell you, Molly. Scoutmaster Zaminski was a ferocious guardian. Protector of all the boys in our troop. He was so brave, he fought with the raccoon, who was a very large one, even though young. It was like watching hand to hand, or should I say hand to claw, combat. And he chased the wild thing out of our camp so we would no longer be in harm's way."

Knowing Ricky's severe tendency to exaggerate, I switched my focus to Dodge. Again, I wanted to hear his version but didn't want to make matters worse since his expression was that of an angry badger. Or maybe, in this case, a very large, annoyed raccoon.

Veronica, however, couldn't hold it in and pointed at Dodge. "Is that how you remember it?"

His eyes narrowed at Ricky. "I told you we didn't need to talk about this."

Ricky's mouth dropped open. Then he uttered, "But..."

"I'm only going to say this once, then we're never going to speak of this again." In full principal-scout master mode now, Dodge had Ricky's attention.

With a slow nod and blinking away tears, Ricky said, "Yes, sir."

Standing to his full height, crossing his arms over his chest, Dodge said, "Ladies, what happened was this. A raccoon, very small and... um, fluffy, like a kitten you two might groom, wandered into our camp. I didn't feel like messing with it, so I took some leftovers we had from supper and tossed them down the side of a nearby hill. The raccoon chased them and seemed to enjoy the leftover hotdogs. End of story."

Veronica huffed out a breath. "That wasn't a very exciting story."

Ricky was actually pouting. While I felt a little sorry for him, with his huge tale diminished so quickly by someone he looked up to, it took everything in me not to laugh.

Knowing Veronica as I did, I grabbed her arm, gave it a warning squeeze, and shook my head.

She frowned at me, but shrugged. In a whisper, she said, "So Ricky, in deranged chicken mode, was acting out the way he perceived the raccoon attack when you witnessed him with Dodge in the library."

"That's my take."

Dodge, still red-faced, approached the counter. Veronica grabbed my hand. Did she think I'd protect her if Dodge was still in anger-I-want-to-hit-something mode?

I squeezed her hand, then released it. Focusing on Dodge, I said, "It was nice to see you again. Did you get everything you came in for today? A schedule for a grooming appointment and your cat harness and leash?"

"Yes. Thank you." He held up the bag. "I got everything I needed..." He glanced over his shoulder at Ricky, who was staring out the front window, giving us a view of his back, like a chastised cat might do. "...and a few things I hadn't asked for. Or wanted."

Dodge gave us a nod, then purposely made his way across the floor. When he reached the door, he gave a consolation to Ricky: "Good to, uh, see you again." And left.

Ricky, his expression morose, watched his old scoutmaster walk out the door, turn to the left, and head up the sidewalk. He turned back toward us, still pouting. "Gosh, he sure remembers what happened differently than I do." Then his face brightened. "But it makes sense, doesn't it?"

Almost afraid to know the answer, I said, "What makes sense?"

"That he's well, old. Those kinds of people forget stuff, right?"

Veronica tensed beside me. "Those kinds of people?"

I tapped her hand to get her attention. "I'm sure Ricky didn't mean you, Veronica. Right Ricky?"

His eyebrows lowered as he studied her. "Gee, no. Mr. Zaminski is super old. Veronica is only sort of old."

Veronica's mouth dropped open. Before we could say something she and I both might regret, I waved to Ricky. "Well, nice to see you again. Have a great day."

"Same to you. By the way, Molly, congratulations again on your wedded bliss. I sincerely hope you and Hank Chenoweth will be the happiest of couples."

Oh no, now Ricky's special news about me was out. How many people had he already told today that I was not only married, but married to the town's veterinarian?

Veronica's feet scuffed against the floor. I could feel her stare before I turned to see it.

With one hand on her hip, she eyed me. "Well, would you like to explain that one, Miss Molly? Or should I say Mrs.?"

Chapter Twenty-Five

Even though I'd just had my vehicle serviced, my window washing fluid had run out. Didn't Ollie usually check that as part of his checklist? I'd have to go back over there to buy some fluid. Sighing, I pulled up the schedule on Fabulous Felines' computer screen. I had forty-five minutes until my next client. Hopefully, that would be enough time to get there, get what I needed, and back.

"Don't worry," said Veronica as she stepped up next to me. "I'll be here. If Greta comes in early, I'll stall her."

"And just how will you do that? You know how persnickety she is."

Veronica gave me a cheesy grin. "I'll sing her show tunes, of course. Maybe add in a little tap dance and top it off with some razzle-dazzle."

I rolled my eyes, but laughed. "Yeah. You do that. I can't wait to hear how that all turns out."

Percival and Jasper followed me to the door.

I bent down and gave each cat a chin scratch. "Sorry guys, I need to hurry. I won't be gone long though."

Sad faces stared up at me. Some days, it was tough being a cat mom.

As I edged out the door, hoping to contain them inside the building, I smiled when I heard Veronica shaking the treat jar to get their attention away from trying to follow me.

I drove the short distance to Ollie's repair shop, and parked on the street. Stepping inside the shop by way of the smaller of the two doors, I was shocked to hear yelling when I entered. What was going on?

Walking on my tiptoes, hoping not to make too much noise, I edged farther inside. The area where I stood was in a shadow.

Ollie was standing toe to toe with Jed Martin, the owner of a local secondhand book shop. Jed brought his cat, Regis, into my shop every so often for a grooming. My mouth dropped open as I watched the scene unfold. Ollie, yelling so loud right in Jed's face, it had to hurt the other man's ears. Ollie waved his arms, his face darkening to a dangerous-looking shade of purple.

He looked like he might explode.

So far, both of them were so engaged in their interaction, they didn't seem to notice me. Should I leave and come back later? Or call the sheriff to report a...

A what? A disagreement? And argument? Seeing no blood or bruised skin, it didn't appear that any punches had been thrown. And having an argument might be upsetting and traumatic, but it wasn't a crime. Would it be right to call the sheriff, if no one had actually been harmed?

I decided to wait. Maybe if things got blown way out of proportion and did escalate to physical violence, I might have to notify Sheriff King, even though I'd rather not. Doing so would be a last resort. Plus, the way Ollie was acting reaffirmed my hunch that he might have killed Agnes. I wanted to stand here and listen for anything else that might be useful to help Evan get out from beneath the sheriff's very large thumb.

Jed's brow creased as he stared back at Ollie. "Now listen here. I don't have the money to pay my bill right now. You know I'm good for it, though."

"That's not going to cut it. Not this time." Ollie tapped his shoe on the concrete floor, the sound echoing in an otherwise silent room.

"But you've let me do it in the past," said Jed. "You were always so decent to let me pay if off later, in installments, if I needed to. What's so different now?"

Ollie crossed his arms over his chest. Speaking through clenched teeth, he said, "It's different now because my situation has changed."

With lowered eyebrows, Jed said, "What's that supposed to mean?"

"I'm out of money." Ollie's expression was a mix of anger and desperation.

Jed shrugged. "So work on more cars. Then you'll make more money. See?

Problem solved."

A harsh laugh came from Ollie. "Oh, and if everyone is like you and doesn't pay their bill, how will that help me?"

"Sorry to cause you trouble, Ollie, honest." Jed's face reddened in embarrassment. "We've always been friends, haven't we? But I just can't pay you right now. I just can't. But I will, I promise. When I can." He reached out to touch Ollie's shoulder, but Ollie smacked his hand away.

With his eyes wide and mouth dropped open, Jed took a step away. "Hey, what gives?"

"You're not getting away that easily," said Ollie as he grabbed Jed by the shirt collar, backing him into the side of Ollie's desk, then releasing him.

I gasped. Even though Ollie had been moody and even angry at times lately, I'd never seen him physically threaten somebody. The look in his eyes had a murderous glint. He'd turned into someone I didn't even know anymore.

I took a step closer. Would Ollie actually try to kill Jed? This had escalated quickly. I reached for my phone, ready to call the sheriff. It was time for my last resort. Before I could dial, however, Ollie's words stopped me.

"You're just like all the rest of them, aren't you?" His words came out sounding like a hiss.

Jed's head jerked back. "What's that supposed to mean?"

"Take away my money, my livelihood. Try to ruin me."

"I'm not doing any such thing," said Jed. "I'll pay you. Just not today."

"That's not good enough anymore." Ollie waved his arms. "How am I supposed to live, to pay people what I owe if my so-called customers don't pay me first?"

"Listen, Ollie, why don't we just cool down and—"

"No! Don't you see? It started with *her,* and now you're doing it too."

Jed frowned. "Started with who?"

"Agnes Temple."

"You mean that lady who died?" asked Jed.

"That's right. Thank goodness she stopped breathing before she could do any more damage to me. She deserved what she got." Ollie grabbed Jed by the upper arms.

I sucked in a breath. I thought back to overhearing Ollie on the phone with someone, talking about Agnes's attempt to talk Ollie's uncle into leaving him out of his will. Had Ollie's words just now been an admission of guilt for killing Agnes?

Jed stiffened beneath Ollie's grasp. Had he taken Ollie's words the same way I had? "Hey, Ollie, wait… what are you going to do?"

"I have a good mind to squeeze the life out of you. Right this second." His hands moved from Jed's arms to his neck.

Jed's eyes budged out from fright as his face paled.

There wasn't time to call the sheriff and have him here to intervene before Ollie seriously hurt Jed or worse. Maybe I could cause enough distraction to allow Jed to get away.

I moved forward, out of the shadows. "Hey!" I waved my arm. "What's going on with you two?"

"Molly!" Ollie dropped his hands from Jed's neck as if the other man's skin had burned his palms.

Walking closer, I put my phone in my front pocket, knowing I could grab it quickly if need be. I clasped my hands together in front of my waist, hoping to appear non-threatening. "Sorry if I interrupted something here. Just needed to get some windshield wiper fluid."

Ollie's eye were glazed. Was he even seeing me at all? He didn't even blink, as if he was in a trance.

I pointed toward a display where Ollie kept bottles of oil, windshield wiper fluid, and car decals. "I can help myself. Should I go get what I need, then pay you?"

Ollie jerked, seeming to come out of whatever state he'd been in. He shook his head, stared first at me, then refocused on Jed. How was I going to not only get these two away from each other but try to calm Ollie down so he didn't kill someone? Or…kill for a second time.

Jed glanced at me, then at Ollie. When it appeared that Ollie was watching me, Jed took one step back. Then another.

"Listen," Jed said, "I…I really need to go." He took another step toward the entrance.

Ollie let out a sound like Percival's growl when Jasper got fed before he did. "Where do you think you're going?"

"I have to leave. I'll…I'll l talk to you later, all right?" He turned and fled out the door, leaving me alone with Ollie.

Wanting to bring some sort of normalcy to the situation, which was nearly asking the impossible, but I'd try anyway, I pointed again to the display. Maybe if I brought up the mundane reason I was here, he'd snap out of his mood. It was worth a try. "So, about the wiper fluid," I said. "Should I just…"

Ollie moved closer to me. His face was still red, and something dark burned in his eyes. "Molly… You don't need to go anywhere right now."

I swallowed hard, then squeaked out, "What?"

He glanced toward the door and back. "What you just saw, between him and me…"

"I, uh…" I held up my hands. "Nothing that happened here concerns me. None of my business. All I want is to buy the stuff for my van, and I'll be on my way."

"I don't think so." Ollie crossed his arms over his chest. Was it my imagination, or was he standing taller than he previously had? Was he trying to intimidate me? It worked.

I checked over my shoulder, hoping someone, anyone, would come into the shop right that second, but the only ones in the building were Ollie, me, and the thousands of nervous butterflies tumbling against each other in my stomach. "But, um, I need to leave and—"

"You've seen something you shouldn't have."

I shook my head. "No, I don't think so. It's all good. What happens between two people is their business. "

"You're right about that. You won't tell anyone what you saw."

"Um, no. I… won't." I held up my hand like I was testifying in court. Except in this case, I promised not to speak.

Ollie leaned closer. "I know you won't. Because if you do, you won't like that outcome. Trust me." His hand clenched into a fist. He hadn't hit Jed, but if I hadn't walked in when I had, would he have done it? Would he try to hurt me now?

Ollie's hand relaxed and dropped to his side. He glanced around the room as if just realizing where he was; then he shook his head. "Oh no."

"What?"

"I did it again," he said.

"Did… what?" I asked. What in the world was going on with him?

As he reached into his pocket, I pressed my lips together to hold in a scream. Did he have a gun? A knife?

Instead, he tugged out a large pillbox. He flipped it open with a worn down fingernail, snagged a capsule, and popped it into his mouth. With his eyes closed, he said, "You'd better go Molly. Right now."

He didn't need to tell me twice.

I swallowed hard and backed up, thankful that Ollie hadn't manhandled me the way he had Jed. I pointed to the door. "Never mind about the wiper fluid. I'll…" I took another step. "I'll get it some other time."

Spinning on my heel, I rushed to the door. When I reached the sidewalk, I ran to the driver's side of my van, jumped in, and drove away.

My hands shook as I clutched the steering wheel. A hard thump came from my chest as my heart pounded a fast beat. When I reached Fabulous Felines, I sat in the van for a minute, as

I calmed down.

Veronica's face appeared from the other side of the front window. She lifted her hands in a what's up gesture. I got out of the van and walked inside.

"What's going on, Molly? You don't look so great."

I glanced around. "Is my client here yet?"

"No, she called a couple of minutes ago to cancel. Something about a sore toe."

"The cat's toe?"

"No, hers. She said she'd call back next week to reschedule."

"Okay. Probably just as well." I rubbed my face with my hands, trying to erase the fear.

Veronica studied me closely. "Your face is pale, and your hands are trembling. What happened while you were gone?"

Seeing no one else in the shop, I motioned her to sit with me in a couple of chairs beside the window.

"Molly, you're scaring me." She grabbed my hand and cradled it in hers.

"Join the club," I said.

"What does that mean?" she asked.

I realized how cold my hands were now that her warm one held one of mine. "I'm scared too. I can't believe what just happened. Or I should say, what nearly happened. It could have turned out even worse."

She grabbed my other hand. "Tell me."

I recounted what I'd walked into. And how Ollie was yelling and had grabbed Jed's shirt collar, then had his hands around his neck. Also, what Ollie said about Agnes. And what he'd said to me.

"He threatened you?" she asked.

I nodded. "I can't believe it. I know he's been unpredictable lately, but come on, it's likable, friendly Ollie."

"Yes," she said, "it is hard to take in. He's normally so even-tempered."

I slipped my hands from hers and rubbed my upper arms, which had gone cold. "He seemed like a totally different person. Angry, violent, then talking about having done it again."

Her eyebrows lowered. "Did *what* again?"

"I don't know. He reached into his pocket and took some kind of pill."

"Do you think he's on something? Like drugs? Maybe that's why he's been acting so weird lately."

I shrugged. "It's possible. Maybe the loss of income and the threat of losing his business sent him over the edge."

"Maybe." She watched me for a few seconds, then said, "And I don't discount what you've said, not for one minute."

"But…"

"But like you said, it's Ollie. There must be something going on that's driving this. Whatever is happening to him has caused him to act out in this terrible way. I'm really thinking about that pill he took. It might have been something that's messing with his personality, making him act out so badly. Heck, I feel angry when I even have to take steroids for those hives I get sometimes."

I smiled. "Maybe you were just irritated because you were itchy."

She smiled back. "That doesn't help it any, does it?" She gave me a hug. "I'm so glad you weren't hurt."

"Thank you. And I agree with you. There's something going on with Ollie, that's made him turn into somebody we don't recognize."

"Even with that, do you think he might have killed Agnes?" she asked.

"I think it's a distinct possibility. I don't want to believe it, though."

"Neither do I."

The patter of tiny paws came from the back side of the counter. Jasper and Percival came running toward me. Both cats had their eyes half closed.

"Let me guess," I said. "They had a nap while I was gone."

"You hadn't been out the door five minutes when they curled up together on the blanket you keep in the corner of your grooming station."

I reached out with both hands to give each cat a head rub. The purr level was so loud, I couldn't help but laugh.

Veronica smiled. "It's going to be okay. We'll get this figured out."

"Yeah, I know. I just hate that the killer might be Ollie."

Chapter Twenty-Six

The next morning in the shop, I was still upset over yesterday's altercation with Ollie. I picked up my phone when it indicated I had a text. When I noticed it was from Ollie, I nearly dropped it.

Veronica rushed over. "Are you all right?"

"It's Ollie," I said. "He sent a text."

"What did it say?" She put her hands on her hips and waited.

"I don't know."

Her eyebrows lowered. "Why don't you know? You've got your phone right in front of you."

With a shrug, I said, "Um, scared to look?"

Even though Veronica wasn't my mother, the look she gave me could be classified as one from a parent. "Molly," she said, "give me the phone."

"Why?"

"I'll read your text since it appears you're reluctant to." She held out her hand, palm up.

I handed her the phone. "Of course, I'm reluctant after yesterday. Do you blame me?"

"No, I don't, but you still need to see what he has to say. Maybe it's not bad." Leave it to Veronica to find sunshine everywhere she looked. But wasn't that one of the many things I loved about her? Even so, I didn't share her positive outlook when it came to this.

Still, once she set her mind on something, I had a hard time saying no to her. I sighed. "Go ahead and check. But I'm telling you, it won't be good."

She swiped my screen with her thumb, then tapped on my message icon.

She silently read the message, then her eyebrows rose.

"What?" I asked, grabbing her arm. "Is it bad? It's bad, isn't it?" What if Ollie wanted to finish what he'd seemed to start yesterday? That he was so concerned I might tell another person about what I'd witnessed, that he couldn't trust me, and wanted me to disappear, for good. My heart skittered around in my chest, thumping hard.

"It's not bad. I promise, Take a look." Veronica returned my phone to me.

My eyebrows shot up. "Really? It's not bad?" I read the message, then said, "Well, what do you know?"

"See?" She poked my shoulder. "Not as bad as you thought."

I reread the text, wanting to convince myself that my fears were unfounded.

Molly, I owe you a big apology for what I said yesterday. I've had lots of things going on lately, but that was no reason to take it out on you. I'm actually going to start anger management therapy because of my temper. I'm taking medication to help with it, but can't seem to remember it all the time. Please stop by tonight if you can so I can explain more what's been going on in person. It would mean a lot to me. Hope to see you.

Ollie.

Relief coursed through me. "Wow," I said. "I'm so glad to be wrong about Ollie being the murderer. It just never made sense, did it, that he could become so violent?"

"I'm glad too. I knew there had to be some reason he was acting that way. And if he was skipping his meds, doesn't that make sense?"

I nodded. "Yes, that explains quite a bit. I hope he can get everything in order so he can get back to being his old amiable self again."

"Will you go and meet him this evening?" she asked.

"I guess I really should. It might be uncomfortable after the things he said yesterday, but…"

Veronica tapped my hand. "I think you should go too. I'll even volunteer to close up the shop so you can get out of here. His apology sounded sincere in the text. He must really feel bad about what he said to you for him to send you that. Poor guy, probably embarrassed at his words and actions, and at having neglected medication that might have helped his anger issues."

"You don't need to stay later tonight," I said. "It's my turn to lock up and make sure all the kitties have been picked up by their parents. We do have a trade-off schedule, you know." I gave her a light bump with my shoulder to hers.

"I don't mind, honest. Please. I insist." She fluttered her eyelashes, which meant she wanted something.

"Oh, I get it. If you stay, you'll want something in return, like…oh, I don't know, blueberry croissants?"

Her mouth dropped open in mock surprise. "What a great idea. Thank you for thinking of it."

"Yeah, right. I know how this all works." I laughed, so grateful to have Veronica as my trusted assistant and even more as my good friend.

"That's because you're a smart girl. And because you love me."

I grinned. "Yes, I do. Okay, it's a deal."

Our day at Fabulous Felines kept us hopping. A couple of pet parents came early. And they weren't the type of people to what to wait around, even though they'd come at the wrong time. Luckily, one client was mine and one was Veronica, so neither one of us got double-slammed. I was able to catch up, but Veronica ended up with yet another person who insisted their kitty needed to be seen today, even though their actual appointment wasn't for two more days.

"Veronica," I said, "why don't I cancel going to see Ollie? You'll need help here by the time you're through. I don't want to leave closing up with you since you'll be working on kitties until the last minute."

She shook her head. "No, you go. I've got this. I want you to hear what Ollie has to say. I know you thought he was likely the murderer, but his text sounded so apologetic. Maybe he'll be able to shed some more light on why he's been so off lately."

I sighed. "You're right. I should go. I've been thinking the same thing, actually. His text sounded more like the old Ollie. I would like to see why he's been so erratic lately." I shrugged. "Maybe I was way off thinking he's the killer."

"Even though I think he might not be guilty either, there's still that nagging thought in the back of my head…"

"Yeah, I know. But I need to find out for sure. The sheriff isn't going to do it, and I want to help clear Evan's name. If Ollie is innocent, I really think I'll get a good feel for that tonight. I so want him to be innocent."

"And if he's guilty after all?" asked Veronica.

"Then I doubt he'll want to harm me. I mean, if he's truly going to apologize and wants to do it in person, that tells me he's got other things going on and feels bad that he erupted at me yesterday. I really like Ollie. I just want to see what's up with him."

"I think you're on the right track, Molly. I like him too. Now get going." She motioned me away with her hands. "I'll want all the details of what he said when you're through. Be sure to call me as soon as you're finished, okay?"

"I will. I promise. As soon as I'm done." I gave her a wave, then got Jasper and Percival fitted in their harnesses and leashes. I'd take them with me, as I planned to go home as soon as I was done speaking to Ollie. Once in the van, I sent a quick text to Hank about seeing Ollie. I was sure he'd want the latest info too, when I was finished later tonight.

When I arrived at the garage, the main door was closed. I was used to seeing it open so I could drive inside with my van. However, it was past closing time, so it made sense it wouldn't be accessible right now.

I parked on the street, then assisted Percival and Jasper to the sidewalk.

"Okay, you two," I said, "I doubt this will take long. Ollie just wants to apologize. Then we can head home and get you guys some supper."

At the mention of mealtime, both cats clamored at my feet, pawing and purring.

"Yeah, I know. I'm hungry, too. Hang with me for a bit, then we'll head out."

When I pushed open the second entrance used by those who were there to pay a bill or make a purchase of something for their vehicle, the first thing I noticed was the quiet. No machinery, engines, or people talking. Normally, every time I was in here, it was often so loud people had to shout to speak to each other.

But not lately. And definitely not today.

The cats stayed close to my legs, as if sensing the difference as well. Or maybe they picked up on my surprise at the absence of noise. I took a few steps inside.

"Hello?" I called. "Ollie?"

No answer. Maybe he'd stepped out and his assistant, Ernie, was keeping an eye on things for a bit.

"Ernie? Are you here?"

Again, nobody moved, stirred, or spoke.

"Anybody?" I asked.

Jasper meowed at my feet, the sudden noise jarring in the silence. I bent down and petted his head, then Percival's. "It's okay, kitties. I'm sure Ollie, or someone, will surface soon."

At least, I hoped so. My stomach growled, reminding me that I hadn't had time for much to eat since this morning. At the sound of my loud intestinal gurgle, both cats jerked and stared at me.

"I'm sorry," I said. "I can't help it."

Percival licked his paw to console himself after being startled. Jasper bumped his head against my ankle in the understanding of my difficult situation. A cat always understood empty tummy issues.

A crash came from the direction of a back room off of the main work area. I slapped my hand over my chest, hoping my heartbeat would slow. Glancing down, the wide-eyed expressions my cats wore probably mirrored mine. But at least I knew somebody was in the building besides us.

"Ollie?" I called. "Is that you? It's Molly. I got your text."

Nothing happened for a few seconds. Then, footsteps.

But it wasn't Ollie.

Ernie now stood a few feet away, something in his hand. I squinted, as he was standing partially in the shadows. When he moved, I could see it was a bottle of whiskey. He stumbled a couple of feet closer, and I saw his face. Eyes, half shut, face reddened.

Was he drunk? And where was Ollie?

"Uh, hi," I said. "I was actually looking for Ollie. Is he here?"

Ernie shook his head, then took a swig from his bottle; when he finished, he let out a long breath, the fumes from the alcohol causing my eyes to water. What was going on?

He studied me, then glanced down. When he saw Percival and Jasper, he frowned. "Should have known you'd bring your mongrels along."

"Mongrels? What are you talking about, Ernie? I can see you're drunk."

"You bet I am," he said, grinning.

I frowned. "But I'm not here to see you, anyway Ollie texted me this morning and—"

"No. He didn't."

"Didn't what?" I asked.

"Ollie didn't text you."

"Yes, he did. He wants to talk to me. Apologize for—"

"That was me."

"Ernie," I said, exasperated that in his inebriated state, he was mixing things up and wasting my time. "Why don't you go get Ollie for me so I can speak to him and then get out of here?" I eyed the bottle still in his hand. "Does your boss know you've been drinking on the job?"

"My boss isn't smart enough to see what's right in front of him."

"What's that supposed to mean?" I tugged the cats' leashes so they'd stay close to me. Ernie was acting extra weird and it was creeping me out.

"Molly, you don't know what you've walked into."

"Yes, I do. Like I said, he asked me to meet him here tonight."

He tipped the bottle to his lips for another long drink, then shook his head. "You don't understand."

"I know you said he hadn't been paying you much lately. Could it be because he's unhappy with you for"—I pointed to the liquor bottle—"*that* happening in his auto shop?"

"Nope, that has nothing to do with anything." Ernie took a step closer. Too close. What was he doing? Had he lost his sense of personal space as a result of his over-imbibing? Next to me, Jasper arched his back and hissed. Not to be outdone, Percival did the same.

"So, Molly," said Ernie. "Glad you could make it. Wasn't sure you'd come after Ollie land blasted you yesterday."

I frowned. "Wait, you were here? You heard that?"

"Sure." He grinned. "I was in the back room the whole time."

"Why? Were you hiding?"

"I wanted to see how it played out. How I could use it." He waved his free hand, the motion causing him to nearby stumble.

I huffed out a breath. "You're not making any sense. Use it? For what?"

"For this. For today."

"Listen, Ernie. It's obvious this isn't the best time for you. Not sure what's going on and why Ollie isn't here but…"

"Like I said, I texted you, not my tightwad boss."

This was getting more bizarre by the second. I gently tugged the cats' leashes again, wanting them as close to me as possible. I didn't like where this bizarre scene seemed to be headed and wanted to get out here soon. However, the nosy cat part of me wanted to find out what was going on with Ernie. And why I was really here.

Maybe I should play along with Ernie, see why he kept saying he was the one who invited me here tonight. "Okay, Ernie, why did you text me? And why did it come from Ollie's number?" That might jar some sense into him once he realized he'd said something that made no sense.

"Because I used his phone when he went to the men's room. I wanted you to come here. Some things I needed to say." He shrugged, causing his bottle to tilt just enough that a few drops of whiskey landed on the floor in front of us.

I took a step back for one reason: wanting to distance myself from Ernie, but also to keep my nosy cats from sniffing or licking Ernie's drink of choice from the floor. If the three of us needed to skedaddle out of here and quick, I didn't want my cats to be tipsy in the process.

"I can't imagine what you would have to say to me," I said. "It's not like we know each other all that well, since I normally deal with Ollie." I glanced around, hoping Ollie would show up. "Where is he, anyway?"

"He had to take his dog to the vet to have something done. Not sure what."

"You mean to Hank Chenoweth?"

"That's right. I guess the animal doc has later hours one night a week?" His eyes widened. "Oh hey, you two are a thing, right? I'd nearly forgotten. Guess I've had a little too much to drink." He hiccupped loudly, causing Percival to whip his head upward and stare at Ernie.

A little to drink? "So Ollie's not coming?"

"Nope. Don't expect to see him until tomorrow morning."

I let out a sigh. "All right. This is getting me nowhere. You're drunk and not making much sense at all. So I'm going to go since I'm hungry and need to feed the cats. I'll just have to speak to Ollie later."

Jasper gave a mew worthy of a tiny kitten, but Percival howled.

Ernie grimaced. "Can't you control those furry rats?"

I frowned. "Rats? Now you listen here—"

He leaned closer, now putting his face close, way too close to mine. "You're not going anywhere. You're going to stay. And you're going to listen."

"And why would I do that?" I put on a brave front, hoping he wouldn't see that I was getting very nervous around him. Trying to reason with a large drunken man wasn't on my list of fun things to do tonight. Or ever.

"Because I'm not going to let you leave." He tossed his bottle to his left, causing what was left in it to leave a puddle on the floor. I jumped at the sound of the bottle hitting the hard surface. And since my attention was diverted by the ever-growing wet stain, I wasn't watching Ernie.

Big mistake.

I gasped when his long fingers clamped onto my wrist. "Hey!" I shouted. "What do you think you're doing? Let go of me!" My heart hammered hard in my chest.

"Not until you listen to what I have to say."

Knowing it wasn't smart to get in a fight with someone who was drunk, I decided to let him have his say. Maybe then he'd let me and the cats be on our way.

"Fine," I said through gritted teeth. "Say what you need to. Then I'll go."

He pushed me backward until the backs of my legs came in contact with the dreaded sticky plastic chair. He gave one final push, and I was seated against my will. Thankfully, I still had hold of the leashes, so the cats hadn't run off to who knew where. After the tire fiasco here the other day, I didn't need a repeat of that. Especially not today.

Trying not to grimace at having to sit in my least favorite spot, I forced myself to look up at Ernie. How had I not noticed how tall he was? With me sitting, he towered over me. Not a great position to be in when he was drunk, had yelled at me, manhandled me, and forced me into a seated position. And I still had no idea why he'd impersonated his boss to get me to show up here. There had to be a reason. But part of me was afraid to hear what it was.

I glanced at the kitties. They were both staring up at Ernie as well. Their tails lashed in unison, side to side, with Jasper's being extra puffy. I loved their show of solidarity not only to each other but to me. But I wasn't sure that would help me much right now. Sure, they'd been instrumental in rescuing me from the clutches of a murderer a few months ago, but could they help me get out of this jam with Ernie?

Chapter Twenty-Seven

Ernie paced back and forth in front of us, swaying slightly every time he turned. How long was this going to take? I needed to figure out a way to get out of here, but he was too big, strong, and let's face it, sometimes people were even angrier when inebriated. What chance did I have from where I now sat?

"Ernie," I said.

He halted and lowered his eyebrows, looking puzzled as he tried to focus on me. Had he forgotten I was here?

I tried again. "Listen, it's obvious something weird is going on here, but I need to leave. Okay?" I pointed toward the door in case he was so toasted he forgot where the exit was.

"No."

"What?"

"Like I told you, you're going to listen to what I have to say."

Along with being frightened, I was also ticked off. "But you haven't said anything!"

"Well, then, Miss Molly, I'll start right now."

I let out a sigh, wishing I hadn't left my cell phone charging in my van. It had been nearly out of power, and I took advantage of what I assumed would be a short visit here to give it a boost. How could I let somebody know what was going on?

Veronica knew I'd be here, but other than me calling her when my supposed meeting was over to give her the scoop, would she even expect me to contact her? If this went on too long, would she come down here to find me? She might panic if she tried to call and I didn't answer my phone. Hank had probably read my text by now, but I hadn't told him I'd call him afterwards. Although I would have, as I was sure he'd be interested in what happened.

I eyed Ernie, who stood with his hand on his hips, glaring at me. Why was he so mad? And why at me? But this wasn't getting me out of here.

"Hey!" I yelled. Percival and Jasper skittered their claws on the floor, running in place to escape the noise.

My loud voice also startled Ernie in the otherwise quiet room. His eyes widened. "What?"

"This is taking a really long time. You want to tell me something. Can we get on with it?"

He shook his head as if trying to clear it. I could imagine his brain striving to make connections, his thoughts sluggish. Finally, he stood up straighter and crossed his arms over his chest. "Sure, okay. So here it is. See, I needed to see you to make you understand what you've done. People who do wrong things need to be punished."

I jerked. "What have I done?"

"You nearly ruined everything for me."

"I have no idea what you're talking about. Maybe you confused me with someone else?" If he'd also been drunk when he texted me, was it possible he'd intended the message for a different person?

Ernie bristled. "I may have had a drink or two—"

Or seven or eight...

"But I definitely meant you, Molly Stewart."

A chill ran across my shoulders at the way he spoke my name. "Fine. You say I ruined things. What things?"

"For starters, you meddled where you shouldn't have. With the way things played out. Or should have played out."

"You're not making any sense."

"All right, I'll be direct. You stirred up trouble by being a nosy busybody, you messed up my plans for Agnes Temple. Her death. And I'm the one who caused it."

My loud gasp had the cats scrambling to run away again, but I still held onto their leashes. Even though shocked at Ernie's confession, I had the wherewithal to reach down and comfort my babies in the current mayhem. But my heart raced like a cat with the zoomies after a long eighteen-hour nap.

"I see I have your attention now, Molly."

Oh, he had it all right. But I still didn't understand. "Why don't you just tell me how you think I did that, Ernie? Because it's still unclear to me how I could have ruined anything for you."

Ernie spread his hands. "I had it all arranged. I broke into Evan's studio and waited for Agnes."

"Why would you do that? Do you even know her very well?"

"That woman took so much from me. My dreams for the future. My sense of self, and well-being."

I shook my head. "I'm sorry you feel that Agnes had done this to you, but..."

He pointed his finger close to my face, making me want to back away, but there was no place to go. "You can't possibly understand what it's like to feel this way. Lost. Confused."

"Of course I can. Things don't always go the way I want them to."

"You have everything. A great business. A guy who likes you. And friends."

He had me there. I was so fortunate to have all of that. "But surely you have some good things in his life as well? I know things aren't going great here," I waved my hand around the room. "But there are other jobs out there. And I'm guessing you have people you care about, right? Who could maybe help you figure out what your next move should be?"

He ran his hand through his hair, causing it to stick out in sweaty spikes. "I have no one. And the only thing I cared about, that I got me through one day and into the next, was taken from me by none other than Agnes Temple. If it hadn't been for her, I'd still be doing what I was great at and making money from it. I was finally on my way to creating a better life for myself. But she ruined every hope I'd ever have of that. I hated her so much, I..." His hands clenched into fists, and his face reddened.

I held my breath as I watched him. If what he said was true, and he'd murdered Agnes, what would stop him from doing the same thing to me right now? And my babies. I looked down at the cats, who were pressed so tight against me, I'd have indentations of their bodies into my legs.

I needed to get Ernie to talk some more. If he did that long enough, maybe the liquor would finally overtake him and he'd pass out. Or better yet, someone would realize I'd been missing for too long and come to look for me.

I thought of his fake text to me and decided to start there. "So Ernie…how did you get her to show up, anyway?"

"He blinked slowly as he tried to focus on my face. He swayed a little, but then stood up straight. With his hands on his hips, he said, "The old hag wasn't much for technology, so I couldn't text her. I had to leave a note, an actual typed paper, under her apartment door, telling her I had something special to show her."

"But why would you think she'd meet you there?"

"I signed the note, Evan Lakes." He gave a slow smile, obviously pleased with himself.

"So, what…" I lifted my shoulders in a shrug. "…he expected Evan to show her something?" Since I knew Agnes had hated Evan, it would've taken something special to entice her beyond her negative feelings toward the photographer.

"That's right," said Ernie. "In the note, I mentioned pictures of her cat. I hoped her imagination would take it from there, and she'd rush right over to see them."

I thought of the ones I took to show Betsy of Lulu. Poor Agnes. She would have loved those photos of her cat.

I leaned forward on the chair. "But why? Why did you kill her?"

"Because she took something from me that I'll never get back. You know how I'd told you Ollie barely had enough money to pay me?"

I waited for him to say more. Where was this going?

He swayed a little, but shook his head, then continued. "Well, I needed a way to support myself. There was no way I was getting a second job. I have my pride, after all. The one here"—he waved his hand, indicating the large room—"allowed me to barely scrape by."

"Then what did you do, if not get another job?" I asked.

"I painted."

My eyebrows shot up. All I'd ever known about Ernie was that he was a mechanic. He didn't strike me as an artist. But what did I know? I wasn't one, either. "What did you paint?"

"Whatever the latest sought-after picture happened to be. See, I'm what you might call a closet painter."

"I've never heard of it," I said.

"Just that I like to paint, but don't make a big deal of talking about it. Plus I happen to be really, really good." He gave a crooked grin.

"Okay, so…you make extra money by painting. How does that work?" I asked.

"Art dealers, let's say, ones who aren't on the up and up, contact people like me to help them out."

I narrowed my eyes. "Wait a second. Do you mean you paint pictures illegally?"

"If you have to give it a label, then I guess, yeah. I excel at doing reproductions of famous paintings." Even in his inebriated state, he had apparent pride in his work, even if he was committing a crime by doing it.

I remembered seeing him at the art gallery and wondering what he'd been doing there. At the time, I'd assumed he was looking for a job. Now, there seemed to be a different reason. "I saw you at the gallery the night of the fundraiser for the animal shelter."

His face fell. "Yeah, apparently, a lot of people did." I'd had a few drinks beforehand. Don't remember everything real clearly."

"Why were you there?"

He crossed his arms. "I'd submitted one of my paintings, one of my originals, to be hung on the gallery wall for the benefit. I never heard back. So I went to see if maybe they'd displayed it and not told me. It wasn't anywhere in the gallery. But do you know, someone had the gall to hang one by that hack, Agnes?"

"Yeah, I saw hers there. Even though yours wasn't shown, I guess it's good you didn't try to show one of your, um, recreations."

"I'm not that stupid." He tried to brush his bangs away from his face, but ended up poking himself in the eye instead.

I let his comment hang in the air for a bit, then said, "Let me guess. The copies you painted sold as originals. And then the dealers, and you, get the profits?"

"You're a fast learner, Molly."

I frowned. "Not much of a compliment coming from a thief."

"I never said I stole paintings. Just created them. Or redid them."

"Same thing." I shrugged. "You took money for something that wasn't yours. The money should have gone to the original artist for their own paintings. Not to you."

He pointed his finger very close to my face. "Probably not a good idea to make me mad."

"The way I figure it, you already are, Ernie. You must be to hold me here against my will after having sent me a misleading message. I get that you were angry at Agnes, but why did you have to go so far as to kill her?" I tried to keep my voice steady, even though it was becoming very clear there wouldn't be an easy way out of my current situation.

"Because Agnes discovered what I was up to with the recreations," he said. "She was going to turn me into the authorities. And she wouldn't listen to reason. I'd even offered to cut her into the deal if she'd keep her mouth shut. But the old hag said she had standards, if you can imagine that, and wouldn't listen. And since I didn't particularly want to go to jail for trying to support myself, Agnes had to go."

As much as Agnes had been an unpleasant person, and most who knew her hadn't cared for her, I was still appalled at what Ernie had done. "She didn't deserve that."

"Not your call, Molly. She was going to ruin my life. It was the only way I could come up with to stay out of prison and still get to do what I love by painting."

I wanted to point out again that his own actions had been illegal, and that's the reason he might have gone to jail, but the intimidating look he gave me stopped me cold. He leaned over me menacingly, making me press back against the back of the seat.

Percival took a swat at Ernie's shoe, but it didn't seem to faze the large man. Ernie never took his gaze from me. Jasper went a step further, raking his claws on Ernie's pant leg, but the denim of Ernie's work pants must have been too thick for the cat's claws for penetrate.

Ernie reached out his hands—how had I never noticed how large they were? —and aimed them for my neck. I tried to push back farther against the chair, but it couldn't press back any further.

When his fingers clamped around my throat, my hands grabbed at his fingers, clawing at them to release me.

And when that happened, the cats' leashes dropped from my hands.

As I struggled against Ernie, a brief thought floated through my mind. At least now Jasper and Percival might have a chance to run and hide somewhere. And that they'd be safe. Hopefully one of my dear friends would take care of them.

Darkness played at the edge of my vision. Was this it? Would Ernie get his way, and I'd be gone?

I gasped in a breath and grabbed my throat, which was empty of hands besides mine. What happened to—

I forced my eyes open, and my jaw dropped.

Because a few feet away, with rope would around his feet and lower legs, was Ernie, lying on the floor, reaching out with his long arms for something. What was it?

My eyes were completely focused, and I let out a louder gasp. "Get away from them!"

Ernie attempted to grab Jasper and Percival. The murderous look in his eyes said he'd like to do to them what he'd tried to do to me. I couldn't let that happen!

I stood, woozy at first, then caught finally my breath and took one step. Then another. My legs seemed sluggish, but I had to save my babies! I reached them, staying just far enough out of Ernie's reach to stay safe. When the cats saw me, they dropped the ends of the rope, which they'd clasped between their teeth. They'd tied up Ernie's feet. My furry heroes.

But Ernie had given up trying to grab the cats and was unwinding the rope. He'd soon be on his feet and—

Before I could step away, Ernie grabbed me and held me. Iron chains couldn't have been any tighter around my body.

Percival tried again to claw and bite at Ernie's legs. Jasper followed his brother's lead. But it was no use. Ernie was stronger than all of us.

We were doomed.

A loud metallic squeak made me jump as the large garage door came to life, rumbling as it opened. Had Ernie done it with a remote? But how? He was too busy restraining me to have anything else in his hands.

"Molly!"

I wilted in Ernie's arms at the sound of Hank's voice. Thank goodness! How did Hank open the garage door?

But another set of hurried footsteps came from behind him. It was Ollie.

Ollie stepped close to us, hands held out toward his assistant. "All right, Ernie, let the girl go."

"No! Stand back, Ollie. This doesn't concern you."

"It won't end well for you, Ernie. You don't really want to harm her," said Ollie.

"Watch me," said Ernie, tightening his grip.

Hank let out something like a cat's feral growl and threw himself at Ernie, trying to wrench his arms from me. He tugged and pulled, but Ernie, so much taller and heavier, didn't budge, which meant I didn't get to budge either.

Ollie tried to help but even with the two of them, they couldn't get me free. Would Ernie get his way after all, making sure today would be my last one?

A vehicle door slammed right outside the open garage door. Who else was here? I struggled against Ernie's grip, but had no way to see around him for a possible rescue by another person.

Sheriff King stormed across the floor, his gun in his hand. "Let her go, Ernie! Now!"

Ernie let out a resigned sigh, then dropped his arms. My shoulders tingled as life flowed back into them.

"Molly, are you okay?" Hank pulled me a safe distance away from Ernie and held me close. But this time, I felt safe and protected. I allowed myself to totally relax, knowing that with Hank holding me, everything would be all right.

When my cats ran to us, Sheriff King hopped out of their way, as if they were a couple of stampeding buffaloes that might run him over.

Hank released me, but only so he could stoop down and pick up the cats. He handed Percival—who purred loudly—to me, and he held Jasper, who reached over to pat my face with his paw.

Hank angled his head toward a far corner. "Let's get out of the way of the sheriff doing his job."

As we walked, me leaning heavily against Hank for support, I said, "How did the sheriff even know I'd be here? How did you know? How did Ollie—"

Hank laughed. "One thing at a time. Ollie had brought his dog into my office to have me treat a cut on the dog's foot. Since you'd sent me a message saying you wanted to speak to Ollie and hear his apology, which I wasn't a fan of, by the way, considering how he'd been acting lately..."

I grimaced, knowing I'd caused Hank to worry.

"I'd planned to head over to the garage about the time that you were supposed to meet Ollie. When he showed up at my office, I was surprised since he was supposed to be meeting you. He and I both figured out something was wrong, so we came here."

"And the sheriff? How did he know?" I asked.

Ollie walked toward us. "That was my doing, Molly. I wasn't sure if it was Ernie behind it, but I had a suspicion. He'd been acting strange lately, drinking at work, and a couple of times, I saw him trying to open my safe where I keep the cash. When I heard you were supposed to meet me, I wanted to see what was up since he'd been acting weird."

My eyebrows lowered. Ernie hadn't been the only one acting weird.

Ollie held up his hand. "I know. You must have thought the same about me."

Although I was relieved Ollie hadn't killed Agnes, I was nevertheless still concerned about Ollie's anger issues. "Honestly, yes. I…thought…"

Ollie tilted his head, then said, "Ah…because of my temper and that you'd overheard me talking about someone on the phone the day you were here, you thought maybe I'd done Agnes in?"

I gasped. "How did you know I'd overheard you ?"

"Pretty hard to miss seeing you through the window, crawling around after your cats."

My face heated. "I'm sorry I suspected you, Ollie."

He shook his head slowly. "Given the circumstances, I can't really blame you. It's like this. I take medicine to help with my moods, but I'm terrible at remembering to take it regularly. When I take it, I'm fine. When I don't…well, you saw the result of that. I can't believe some of the things I have said and done lately. I'm so sorry about that." He hung his head.

I reached out and touched his shoulder. "I'm just glad things are better for you."

"Thank you, Molly. And I'm just sorry it was Ernie who killed Agnes."

I nodded. "Me too."

"Well," said Ollie, "the sheriff is waving us over. Guess he'll want to question all of us."

"Okay," I said. "Be there in a second."

Hank looked down at me. "Are you really all right?" He rubbed my arm with his free hand. "I mean, did Ernie hurt you?"

I shook my head. "I'm okay. I'll be a little sore for a bit, but nothing serious."

"I'm so relieved. You have no idea how scared I was when I walked in and saw that scene." He kissed me on the cheek. When he pulled away, I saw that he was fighting off tears.

My heart warmed. "Thank you for caring. And for coming here to check on me. You saved my life." I smiled. "And these two," I jiggled Percival in my arms. "They came to my rescue too."

"What did they do?" He eyed Jasper, who gave Hank a nose kiss.

"See that rope lying on the floor?" I pointed across the room.

"Yeah."

"While I was being choked—"

His eyes widened. "Wait, what? You didn't tell me that." He eyed my throat. "You do have bruises starting to form. Do you need to go to the hospital, or—"

"I'm fine. Honest. If I really thought I needed medical care, I'd go, I promise." But just remembering Ernie's strong hands compressing my throat made me shudder. It could have ended so differently if my rescuers hadn't shown up.

"All right. Go on," he said as he eyed my neck again.

"When Ernie temporarily let me go I looked down to see his feet and legs were bound up in ropes." Percival moved around in my arms until he could see my face. He gave a little trill, and then purred.

"And these two…" said Hank.

"Yes, they each had an end of the rope in their teeth. With them doing that, they gave me just enough time to catch my breath. And then you came in."

Hank hugged me with both cats held in between us. There was a lot of purring. And some of it was from me.

Chapter Twenty-Eight

The next morning at Fabulous Felines, it was difficult to get much work done. Veronica and I had each done two groomings while trying to speak to Jillian at the same time. The kitties, so used to being bathed and brushed, didn't seem to mind the chatter going on around them, so I figured I might as well get my job accomplished while trying to satisfy my friend's questions.

For a while, I conversed with Jillian as she stood in my grooming area doorway, but as soon as I was finished with my current kitty, I brought the cat out and placed her in her carrier for her mom to pick her up.

"Do you have another cat grooming right now?" asked Jillian.

I checked the clock behind her on the wall. "No. Not for thirty minutes."

"Great," she said, "then you'll be able to talk to me better, and we won't be busy working, and we won't be interrupted or—"

The door opened, and Hank entered. He'd been here earlier, but had to slip back to his office to give yearly shots to a dalmatian. "Hey, I'm back. What did I miss?"

Jillian smiled at Hank, but I knew she would have liked to have had a little time with me alone.

The door opened again, and Evan rushed in. In spite of Jillian's disappointment at not having me to herself for a bit, her smile grew wide when she spotted Evan.

Evan grinned back at her, then said to me, "Sorry, had to do a portrait for three poodles who don't like each other. I got it done, but it was a struggle." He met my gaze. "Too bad dogs don't like catnip, right, Molly? It sure helped when we did the pictures of Jasper and Percival before."

"You're right," I said. "Without it, my photo of them might be a blur of slashing tails, flattened ears, and smacking paws."

Veronica came out, carrying her kitty client. "This girl is ready to go." She walked across the room to the area by the entrance and placed the cat in her carrier. The kitty immediately began licking her fur, attempting to remove all of Veronica's efforts. With a shrug at the cat, Veronica came back to the counter.

"Okay," she said, "I hope you guys didn't say anything important while I was in there. Because I want to hear every detail."

I shook my head. "You haven't missed anything. I think we're just now getting ready to—"

When the door opened again, I grinned. It was Russ. I rounded the end of the counter, met him in the middle of the room, and gladly received one of his warm hugs.

He pulled away and studied my face. "You're really all right? I know you called last night to tell me, but I wanted to check you out for myself."

"I really am okay. Promise."

He gave me a final hug, then turned toward the others. "I don't know about you guys, but I need more information."

Everyone agreed.

With the support of my family and friends, my tiredness from the ordeal of yesterday lessened. Instead, I felt buoyed by the love I felt in the room. I went to the counter and stood behind it, wanting to be able to make eye contact with each person. Plus, I only wanted to say it once, since some of it I'd rather forget.

A thump came from the other end of the counter. Jasper had jumped up, and now stood in front of Hank. When my cat spotted me, he trotted closer, then flopped down in front of me for a tummy rub. Percival jumped up after him, making a beeline for me. Not wanting to be left out, he plopped down next to his brother, lay on his side, and meowed loudly.

"Okay, you guys," I said to the kitties, "I can do double duty as I talk." When I reached out a hand to each cat, the symphony of purring began.

I glanced at the others. "Well, as you all know by now, Ernie, unfortunately, was the one who killed Agnes Temple."

"I still can't believe it," said Evan. "One, that he was guilty, and two, that you, Molly, Jasper, and Percival, were so diligent in trying to free me from having to go to jail. Thank you so very much."

"You're more than welcome, Evan. I'm just so glad the real killer was caught."

Jillian, who stood at the end of the counter, fidgeted in place. I knew she was about ready to burst, wanting to say something.

"Molly," she said, "did Ernie really try to strangle you?" Her hand rose to touch her own throat.

"Unfortunately. But Percival and Jasper bought me some time by grabbing ends of a rope and running around Ernie's ankles until he was tied up."

"What smart kitties," said Veronica in admiration.

Jasper meowed at Veronica.

"You're welcome, Jasper," she answered.

Russ held out his hand to get my attention. "But why did Ernie do it? What was his reason?"

"Believe it or not," I said, "Ernie was a closet artist. He loved to paint, and, according to him, at least, he's good."

Evan nodded. "I actually saw some of his work when the sheriff hauled something he'd found in Ernie's house back to the art gallery. Ernie really is good. Too bad he didn't do something legal with his talent."

"Unlike you," said Jillian to Evan. "Your amazing talent with photography is awesome."

Evan's face reddened, but I could tell with the way he looked back at Jillian, he was pleased at her comment.

Russ leaned forward against the counter. "What did Ernie do that wasn't legal?"

"Actually," I said, running my fingers through Percival's fur again when he'd given me the stink-eye for stopping, "Ernie did recreations of famous works, then a shady art dealer sold them as originals."

"I bet that was lucrative," said Hank, shaking his head in disapproval.

"Yep," I said. "It was. Well, it would have been if Agnes hadn't found out and threatened to turn him in."

"Ah," said Russ, "that explains his motive then. She could have ruined his on-the-side livelihood."

I nodded. "Exactly. Ernie told me he'd tried to entice Agnes by offering to cut her in on his deal, but she refused. He said he felt he had no choice but to end her life." Noticing Percival had drifted off to sleep, I was ready to give my hands a rest when Jasper eyed me and meowed. "Okay, kitty, sorry. Didn't mean to neglect you."

Veronica harrumphed. "Leave it to a cat to pick the moment you're doing something else to demand attention."

I laughed. "But if not for the cats, what would you and I do all day?"

"Good point." She smiled.

"So," said Jillian, "now we all know about Ernie's motive. But what about the other people you suspected of murdering Agnes?"

"Right," I said, "I told you about seeing Lorna carting around that bottle of fixer?"

She crossed her arms over her chest. "Yes, what was that about?"

"I can answer that," said Evan. "Apparently, Lorna had received the bottle in the mail by mistake and had tried to return it to my studio, but I was out. I'm guessing, from Molly's description of Lorna seeming angry, she was upset at having to bring me something herself that I'd ordered."

Hank snorted. "So Ricky delivered the fixer to the wrong address?"

"Yep," said Evan.

I was pretty sure every person, and possibly even my sleepy cats, rolled their eyes at Ricky's squirrelly behavior.

"But wait," I said, "at one point, Lorna told me she was in trouble about something but couldn't talk about it. Anyone have any idea what that might be about?"

Evan continued, "Now that the real murderer has been caught, Lorna admitted something to me when I was in there for lunch yesterday. She was so relieved that Agnes's murder had been solved, I think she just wanted to spill everything to the next person who came in. That happened to be me."

"What did she admit to doing?" I asked.

"Remember when she delivered the wrong drink to Agnes?"

I nodded.

Evan glanced around at all of us, then said, "Lorna now admits she did that on purpose, just to get a rise out of Agnes for all the trouble Agnes has caused her by badmouthing The Sandwich Shack. Not poison, like people were saying."

"No," I said, "I never thought she'd poison anyone. But wow, that's way different from what she told me, how the drink was meant for another table and was given to Agnes by mistake."

"Yeah," said Evan, "I think she was worried at the time, that if Sheriff King found out she'd given it to her on purpose, amidst talk of Lorna being a poisoner, she might have been hauled off for questioning. And that possibility scared her to death. Also, those people in the background of the picture I showed you of Lottie and Florence?"

I nodded.

"Just last night, I had time to fiddle around with the photo and was able to zoom in to get a better look. It turned out to be Lorna and Ricky."

"What were they doing with fixer?" asked Jillian.

"Apparently, Ricky delivering my orders to Lorna wasn't a one-time thing. She was trying to get him to do his job and deliver it to my studio and was waving the bottle of fixer at him, but he wouldn't take it. Said he was off-duty, and it wasn't his job to carry around a delivery on his off hours."

Veronica shook her head. "Our government worker at his finest."

Jillian tapped the counter to get our attention. "Okay, I know Betsy took on Agnes's cat, Lulu, after feeling guilty for something she'd done to Agnes way back in school. Does she still have the cat?"

"Thankfully, yes," said Hank. "Betsy does indeed have Lulu. She brought the cat in to see me for a checkup. When I asked her how things were going, Betsy smiled and said she'd gotten allergy shots, has been spending as much time as possible with Lulu, and that they are bonding."

Veronica gave a happy sigh. "That's wonderful. I'm so happy for both of them."

CHAPTER TWENTY-EIGHT

"So am I," said Hank. "Always love a happy ending for a pet and their owner."

Jillian tapped her chin for a few seconds as she gazed up at the ceiling. "All right, then, how about Penelope?" She looked directly at Evan, who squirmed.

"Yes, Molly, as well as I, suspected Penelope after things she did and said," he said.

Russ nodded. "Oh, yeah. The way she spouted off on the phone in Leaning Tower of Pizza made her seem terrible, didn't it, Molly?"

"You're right. And the way she treated that waiter was despicable. I felt so sorry for the guy."

Jillian hadn't yet looked away from Evan. "Is the witch, er, I mean Penelope, still in town?"

He closed his eyes for a second, then said. "Thank goodness, no. I think I finally got through to her that I wanted nothing to do with her, her plans for my supposed career, and definitely not anything romantic with her."

"Good to know." A slow smile formed on Jillian's lips. "Very, very good."

Russ shifted against the counter, then said, "And as for Dodge, he had indeed had a vendetta against Agnes when she tried to take his position as principal away from him. I think, with his temper and being a boxer, he might have been capable of killing her, but as we know, it was Ernie."

"Wait," said Veronica, "I'd heard that Ollie said there'd been a terrible bar fight between Dodge and some guy a long time ago. What had the guy done to make Dodge go crazy and beat him up?"

Russ shrugged. "Apparently, the guy said something derogatory about Dodge's mother."

"But I still wondered about something with Ollie," said Evan. "Molly and Jillian had spotted him taking an envelope stuffed with money from a customer when he was working behind the counter at the bowling alley. They said it seemed suspicious at the time. What was that about?"

Hank nodded. "Yeah, thanks to my receptionist's ability to wrench information out of anyone, she got Ollie to talk about what had been going on there. It turns out that the other guy was an old friend of Ollie's who was lending him some cash to get him through for a while."

"Nothing nefarious in that," said Veronica. "But I bet it looked that way at the time."

"Yeah," I said, "it did. With the way Ollie had been acting, everything he did led me to believe he'd been guilty of thumping Agnes on the head with the fixer bottle."

"How's Ollie getting along now?" asked Russ. "Is he doing any better with things?"

Evan nodded. "I actually ran into him just before coming here. He said he's going to meetings to help with his gambling addiction and seeing a therapist for his anger issues. And, he's bought himself one of those little medical alarms to remind him to take his meds."

"That's good," said Veronica. "If he hadn't gotten organized, I was prepared to go help him get himself in order. I just can't stand disorganization."

I winked at Veronica. "One of the reasons we love you."

"Thank you," she laughed. "It's my one superpower."

"And as for Ricky," I added, "he'd been furious with Agnes for the way she'd treated him about his job performance."

"And his hair," added Veronica.

I nodded, "That's right. And for splitting him up with his one true love." I placed my hands together over my chest and gave an exaggerated sigh.

"From when he was ten." Veronica shook her head. *"Ten!"*

"But," I said, holding up one finger. "Even though I suspected him, looking back, I can't see him going so far as to actually kill someone. I mean, come on… It's Ricky."

The door opened, and we all turned.

"Speaking of inept postal workers…" whispered Veronica.

I lightly smacked her arm. "Uh, hey, Ricky. How are you today?"

Ricky's eyes lit up at the group, and he gave a goofy smile. "Hey, did you guys hear the news?"

"What now?" asked Veronica, tapping her foot.

I held in a sigh. With some of the crazy things Ricky came up with, I could only imagine what it might be this time. Hopefully, he wouldn't starting talking about the girl of his dreams, Hildegard, again. I wasn't sure Veronica could stand it.

Ricky set his mailbag on the floor and clapped his hands together twice. "You may or may not have heard this, but Molly and Hank are experiencing wedding bliss! Isn't that awesome? I hope I didn't miss the party." His face fell as he took in the people standing around the counter. "Oh, is this the party? Was I invited?" He frowned as he eyed the counter. "But where's the cake?"

Everyone's gaze turned to me. Jillian and Veronica, already having heard Ricky's false declarations, both smirked. Evan and Russ stared at me.

Then, Hank's eyebrows rose. "Uh, Molly, anything you'd like to tell me?"

About the Author

Ruth J. Hartman spends her days herding cats and her nights spinning mysterious tales. She, her husband, and their cats love to spend time curled up in their recliners watching old Cary Grant movies. Well, the cats sit in the people's recliners. Not that the cats couldn't get their own furniture. They just choose to shed on someone else's.

Ruth, a left-handed, cat-herding, farmhouse-dwelling writer uses her sense of humor as she writes tales of lovable, klutzy women who seem to find trouble without even trying.

Ruth's husband and best friend, Garry, reads her manuscripts, rolls his eyes at her weird story ideas, and loves her despite her insistence all of her books have at least one cat in them. See updates about her cozy mysteries at Ruthjhartman.com.

SOCIAL MEDIA HANDLES:
https://www.facebook.com/ruth.j.hartman
https://www.facebook.com/profile.php?id=100063631596817
https://twitter.com/RuthJhartman
https://www.bookbub.com/authors/ruth-j-hartman

AUTHOR WEBSITE:

www.ruthjhartman.com

Also by Ruth J. Hartman

Brushed Up on Murder (Book 1 in the Mobile Cat Groomer Mysteries)

Butterfly Betrayal (Book 1 in the Seneca James Mysteries)

Dial M for Meow (Book 1 in the Kitties Bookshop Mysteries)

Murder She Meowed (Book 2 in the Kitties Bookshop Mysteries)

Hairballs and Homicide (Book 1 in the Kitty Beret Café Mysteries)

Felines and Fatalities (Book 2 in the Kitty Beret Café Mysteries)

Meows and Mayhem (Book 3 in the Kitty Beret Café Mysteries)

Ring of Death (A Dorey Cameron Mystery)